Djinn

Sang Kromah

Dedication

For Mommy, Daddy, Moh, and Grandma Magdalene.

Thank you for giving me wings.

Watch me soar.

Djinn

CHAPTER 1—SCHOOL HARD

Imagine not being able to tell whether it's you or the person beside you who's schizophrenic. That's the story of my life.

Most mental illnesses have thousands of web pages devoted to them online, but whenever I insert my symptoms into a search engine, I get pages upon pages of fanfiction.

The only word that describes my appearance is "peculiar." Almond shaped eyes might be considered beautiful on some people, but my almond shaped eyes can't decide whether they're green, amber, or gray, so "frightening" becomes a more accurate description. The changing colors of irises may not sound scary, but my eyes are the size and shape of a little green man's. Maybe I'm exaggerating a bit, but this is what I see when I look in a mirror. Peculiar.

I'm not white. But I'm not black. Well, at least I don't think I am. I'm somewhere in between. Maybe. I've asked these same questions about my background, but the topic of race has always been off-limits with my grandmother Gigi. So, on an EEO survey, I have to choose *other*.

Gigi has always made excuses for people's confusion. Words like "exotic," "unique," and "special" are thrown around, but never "pretty," "cute," or "beautiful." People tend to stare, but when I look back and attempt to make eye contact, they look away in fear. How do I know it's fear? Because I can feel what they feel. It doesn't happen with everyone, just with typical people. While most people see race or ethnicity when they first meet, it isn't that simple for me. Through my eyes, there are two types of people in this world, and the color of their skin has no part to play in the matter. With the Typicals, their emotions rub off on me when they're in close proximity. It's even worse if they happen to make eye contact; I see things— sometimes truly horrible things. It's like being in a room full of babies who are screaming at the top of their lungs for attention. Luckily for me, eye contact is as rare as my interactions with Typicals. When I do have to be around people, I have to keep my hands busy or I'll go into shock.

And then you have the Others. They're a little harder to explain. I can't feel what they feel and, when I see them, I know exactly what they are. They're ethereal. Some are beautiful, but there's always a haunting element about their appearance and presence that makes people want to avoid them. You would think I'd prefer their company since I can't read them, but they scare me.

When I was a kid, my grandmother would tell me I was imagining these things, that I had an overactive imagination, so I just stopped talking about them. Claims like those would land me in a psychiatric ward, so, to block out emotions, I began carrying a deck of playing cards with me everywhere I go. Now I constantly shuffle, distracting myself from all the emotions that are vying for my attention.

"Bijou Fitzroy!" My grandmother's voice startles me out of my closet. "You harass me about going to school, and, now that I've agreed, you're going to be late on your first day. *Allez! Dépêche-toi!*"

She always becomes more French when she's yelling.

"Webster's defines a door as a moveable piece of wood that people use to enter or leave a room, but if Miss Manners were here, she'd insist on you knocking on said door before entering my bedroom."

My grandmother, Gigi, is not amused as she addresses me with a cold blue glare. The chilly look, combined with her crown made of a tightly wound blonde bun, brings the term "Ice Queen" to mind.

"If you can memorize the entire dictionary, you have no business going to high school in Hicksville, USA." She comes toward me in that intimidating way of hers, the way the Victoria's Secret angels fly down a runway. "We could scrap the whole high school idea, go back to homeschooling, and spend the day exploring Eldersburg."

"We live in Sykesville, Gigi, and I'm going to school. You know, like normal kids do?" Since moving to Maryland, Gigi and I have been in a constant argument about this. Sykesville and Eldersburg are neighboring towns with smudged borders. They're so smudged, in fact, that you can live in Sykesville while your next-door neighbor lives in Eldersburg. It really doesn't matter because the towns share one zip code. "My problem is that I can't find anything to wear."

Sang Kromah

Gigi rushes into my closet and, five seconds later, emerges with skinny jeans, a cute top, a cardigan with elbow patches, and tan Oxfords to match.

"How did you do that? I've been in there for the last half hour and nothing."

"It's a gift," she says, leaning against the wall, her impatience apparent. "Magic, really."

Gigi isn't like other grandmothers. Yes, she's the mother of my mother, but other than that, she looks as regal and young as Grace Kelly in *High Society*, and dresses like her too. She hardly looks like anyone's grandmother, which is why calling her grandma is forbidden, and hence the name Gigi. Hell, we don't even look related. She's pale and tall with bone-straight, long, blonde hair. I'm of a darker hue, about five foot seven, and although my hair is long, it's so black and wild that I break combs and brushes on a weekly basis. So she's Tracy Samantha Lord and I'm Holly Golightly's ethnically ambiguous half sister with the crazy curls. We look nothing alike.

"I really don't understand the need to go to high school here," she says as she follows me to my mirror with the only brush in the house that hasn't lost the battle with my hair yet. "Jou Jou, you're in the eleventh grade, and it's the middle of the school year. And besides, with your marks, you could get your degree now." She's right. I've been homeschooled my entire life. With a photographic memory, retention of information makes schoolwork simple, but I'm sixteen years old and I've never set foot in a school building, never had a friend.

I know why I'm supposed to respect her opinion about my education. She's been a mother to me since my mom died during childbirth, and my father is an unknown entity. Parents should be respected, but our relationship is a strange one. To me, she's Lilith Fitzroy, my vain grandmother who looks too young to be a grandmother. To the world, Gigi is the international bestselling paranormal romance author, Anastasia Powers. She writes under a pen name to conceal her identity from the world, and whenever some nosey journalist starts to get close to discovering who she really is, we pack up and move. This is why I've been homeschooled my entire life. This is why she's not very comfortable with me making friends with random strangers, but all that changed last month when she bought a house in Maryland and decided to move us here. It's a huge change from the big cities we're used to. Imagine leaving Park Avenue for a home at the end of a cul de sac in a development where most of the houses look the same, the grass is measured, and people smile when they really want to spit at you. Sykesville may be a little too normal, but it's home now, and I'm glad we're here.

After Gigi gives up the fight of taming my curls, we leave for school.

On the way, she continues trying to convince me to go shopping instead of going to Liberty High School. "Last chance to change your mind." Her tone is less than enthusiastic as she glares at my new peers with disgust. "Didn't you say once that you wanted to write a book? I could talk to my agent, and we can make it happen."

Just as I'm about to retort, a figure wearing a black hoodie and black jeans comes into view. He's standing completely still, staring at me, as the crowd maneuvers around him. I close my eyes tight in disappointment, knowing that he's found me once again.

"You're not here. You're not here. You're not here," I whisper to myself. When I reopen my eyes, he's no longer there.

Maybe I'm imagining him, but this hooded figure has been following me since we lived in New York, always appearing in the middle of a crowd but never this early in a move.

"No! No! No!" Gigi interrupts. "You're not doing this again. If you're going to attend school with these people, no weirdness and no talking to yourself. The last thing we need is these people running us out of town or attempting to burn you at the stake because you start doing or saying things they don't understand."

She can be such a snob. She fails to realize how much I need this. I could get into any top-tier university, but when it comes down to the test of relating to my peers, I fail miserably. I have zero social skills, and I am sure I will be a laughingstock once I open my mouth. The girls will probably snicker and point, while the boys won't bother looking at me at all. But I'm not too concerned about the boys.

There is one boy though, a boy I've always thought about. The disappointing part is that he only exists in my dreams, faceless like so many characters in dreams. Though I don't know what he looks like, I think about him entirely too much. I know this makes me certifiable, but he's the only friend I've ever had. He was my playmate as a kid and grew to be my protector, keeping me safe in my dream world.

I'm sure other homeschooled kids have friends and some semblance of a social life, but not me. Gigi is an overprotective hawk, watching my every move, keeping me busy with one activity or another. I have been taking martial arts, gymnastics and piano lessons for as long as I can remember, but none of these activities involves an outside individual. She's always taught me, so it's always just been us.

"I love you Gigi," I say as I exit her red Jaguar F-type, "but I'll write a book after I get some real-world experience."

"You're so special, Jou Jou, and my fear is you may be too special for small-town folks," she murmurs. I'm sure her words are supposed to be comforting, but they put me on edge even more. I smile weakly as she pulls off.

Cursed is a more fitting description.

Cutting through the schoolyard chatter, a flood of emotions hits me like a bloodcurdling scream at the beginning of an Anastasia Powers novel.. It's sometimes hard to separate my own feelings from the influx of emotions that come from others. I pull out my cards and begin shuffling. It must look like I'm about to do some magic trick. I shuffle so fast I have no need to look at the cards as I survey the school from the entrance to the yard. It looks large for a small-town high school. I glance around as I try not to run through the crowd to the entrance. They all look so comfortable with each other. They've probably known each other since kindergarten and won't welcome the arrival of a weirdo who will unbalance things.

I definitely don't fit in.

"Check out the cards," a blonde girl says as I walk by. She isn't exactly one of the Others, but something's not right about her. "Don't *we* belong in a freak show!" The sarcasm in her voice is venomous.

Something about her makes me stop walking and shuffling completely.

"Tell me she doesn't have a perm," another girl says as they continue toward the school.

My heart beats wildly, but the moment she leaves, everything returns to normal. Or as close to normal as it gets for me.

I am becoming more agitated by the second, so I resume shuffling my cards and walk away. I'm relieved to enter the front office. It's not as intimidating as the entrance of the school. The walls are a pale shade of blue and in dire need of a paint job.

Breathe, I tell myself as I walk toward the front desk, clearing my throat.

"Hello, I'm Bij—"

I am interrupted mid-sentence by a dirty look from a frail, spray-tanned receptionist with salt-and-pepper hair. She looks up from her romance novel as if I have disrupted the juiciest part, and she points in the direction of a tall boy I hadn't noticed until now.

"Hi, I'm-"

"Bijou Fitzroy. I'm aware."

Normally, I would've been irritated about being interrupted for a second time, but I am distracted.

He's perfect.

His lips are so full that I can only pray he has horrid teeth to make me feel better about my own appearance. He's slender, muscular, and tall. A veil of dark lashes almost hides the intensity of his eyes. He looks as though he's swallowed a piece of the sun, and its golden rays glow within his flawless skin. Though we don't know each other, there is something familiar about him.

"Well, that's kind of rude," I say. "You know who I am, and I have no idea who you are." His silence and unblinking stare make me nervous, so I keep yammering. "Okay, you have about five seconds to say something before I start believing you've been stalking me."

He just stands there staring at me with deep-set, gray eyes—never blinking. I can't help but stare as well. It takes me a moment to notice he's making direct eye contact with me. No one ever does.

He tilts his head to the side like a dog ogling a shiny new object when a sudden look of mystification etches his dark brows, and he contorts as if something ghastly has appeared before him.

He looks sideways.

Have I somehow offended him?

He turns back. "My apologies. G'day, I'm Sebastian."

G'day? Is this how high school students talk? It's nothing like *Pretty Little Liars*.

He reaches out to shake my hand, not giving me more than a glance. I stop shuffling, stuffing my cards into my leather satchel to take his hand.

The touch of his hand sends a jolt of electricity through my body, and flashes of a familiar scene of someone drowning surges through my mind until he retracts his hand, putting an end to the vision.

It's obvious he feels something as well.

The look of concern returns to his face, and then he quickly looks away.

"Just consider me your personal tour guide, eh? They want you to follow me 'cause we have identical schedules, so where I lead, you'll follow. No sooking and no whinging."

The more he speaks, the more evident his accent becomes.

I nod, intimidated by his assertiveness, but I am intrigued.

"Right-o, let's be on then." He starts toward the door, expecting me to follow. "Hooroo, Mrs. Reaper," he salutes the unfriendly receptionist, who actually smiles at him, exposing teeth smudged with red lipstick.

The halls are quiet as we make our way to first period.

"Liberty High," he says. Not a ripper. Small town, so lots of bogans, but it's fair dinkum."

"I don't mean to be rude, but I didn't understand half of what you said."

He doesn't stop walking. He doesn't even look my way. He smiles as if my comment is right on time.

"It's Aussie-speak."

"Why don't you just talk like everyone else?" The stupid question escapes before I have time to censor it.

"Why would I want to be like everyone else when I can be myself?" He holds the door open for me. "Being normal is highly overrated, ta."

He looks at me point blank and winks.

Is it possible he knows there is something *off* about me? My curiosity vanishes once I step into the classroom.

You know that feeling you get when you walk into a room and think everyone's staring and talking about you? Well, imagine being able to *feel* what they are feeling about you as well. Not good. I grab my cards and begin to shuffle as if my life depends on it.

There are two empty seats in the front and another two in the back. The safest bet would be to sit in the front—shorter walk—but Sebastian steers me to the back instead, his hand gently touching my elbow. At least I'm not electrocuted or seeing visions this time.

Walking to my seat, I feel myself appraised by curious eyes, but when I look back, they all look away.

They're afraid, and I can feel it.

"What a coincidence," a familiar voice spits. I look up to see the pushy blonde from earlier, sitting with her disciples. My heart sinks as I plop down into the seat indicated by Sebastian.

The instructor, a nimble-looking man with skin the color of brass, enters.

"Good morning, class. I hear we have a new student in our midst, so why don't we do things differently today?" There are sighs and a few grunts throughout the room.

"Even though we're more than halfway through the semester, let's all introduce ourselves. Welcome to

Mythology & Folklore!" He makes a sweeping, dramatic gesture pointing to the whole room, then himself. "I'm Mr. Jennings, and I have the pleasure of teaching you what very well may be the most interesting course of your high school career. What I have to teach can't be found in any book that Carroll County Public Schools can provide. You will not only be studying myths, legends, and creatures, but also creating a few stories of your own. Outside of the classroom, I want you all to find myths and legends that intrigue you and bring them to class for discussion." His enthusiasm is contagious. His excitement makes me reconsider my doubts about enrolling.

Gigi never taught me anything like this, which is odd since her career involves writing about the paranormal. She never told me fairy tales when I was younger, fearing my perception of reality would be tainted. The closest she ever came to telling me a fairy tale was when she read *A Clockwork Orange* to me because I wouldn't shut up one night, which, if you ask me, has tainted my perception more than *Cinderella* ever could. I observe that my classmates seem as intrigued by Mr. Jennings as I am. I gather that Mr. Jennings is very likeable. He is well-dressed and has an obvious charm. But wonder if he is new as well; there is something else about him that doesn't sit right with me. Behind the cover of fake confidence, his eyes hint that he is as lost as I am.I try looking into his eyes, but he avoids eye contact. It doesn't take long for me to realize I get the same strange feeling from him that I got from the blonde.

"Let's start off with introductions." Before he can utter another word, the tall, pushy blonde mean girl from earlier stands, reciting the extended Lifetime Movie Network version of her life story. I would have preferred the CliffsNotes version. She speaks so fast and says so much that the only things I gather from the monologue are that her name is Amanda DeVoe but everyone calls her Mandy, she is a cheerleader (I suspect she's a big skank, too), and she loves pink.

Why am I getting such a strange feeling from her?

The class is huge. By the time Mr. Jennings gets to the back of the room, I am more exhausted than nervous. I am interrupted just as I am about to stand to recite my autobiography.

"Right-o, I'm Sebastian Sinjin. As you can probably tell, I'm not from around here." There's some polite laughter, but Mandy overdoes it. "My parents uprooted my twin sister, Amina, and me from Oz and moved us here a couple months ago."

His dark hair is full, wild, slightly long and curly. His dimpled cheeks rest below high cheekbones. As he speaks, he sweeps up his hair, putting it into a ponytail in one swift movement. There are pathetic sighs from girls swooning over him in every corner of the classroom.

No wonder he carries on the way he does. He has groupies. I roll my eyes.

And yet, there is something more to him than meets the eye. Something that sets him apart from anyone I've ever seen. Something that is hidden well behind a mask of buoyancy. If there was any doubt in my mind before, this moment confirms that there is nothing typical about Sebastian Sinjin. He is one of the *Others*.

Oh no. What am I doing? It's my first day of school, and I'm crushing on the first boy I saw, one who looks at me with pure and utter disgust, not to mention that whole electric-shock-and-vision thing. I'm not even ready to process that level of weirdness.

He flashes a sardonic smile at the class and continues. "I played footy at my old school, and I'm just an average bloke. If you have trouble understanding what I'm saying, just ask. Cheers."

He takes his seat and begins sketching in a sketchbook that he's covering, so no one else sees.

The classroom is quiet. As I stand carefully, trying not to do anything embarrassing, my hair begins falling in my face. It's too long. I should have worn it up. I didn't blow-dry it this morning, so my curls are wild.

"I'm Bijou Fitzroy. I've never had to introduce myself to a room of strangers before." I give a hint of a smile, nervously shuffling my cards. "But I'm happy to be here." I sit down quickly, still shuffling.

Some smile, some mumble, while others just stare.

"Now, would you do us the pleasure of continuing with your introduction, like telling us where you're from and how you're able to shuffle those cards so swiftly without ever looking at them?" Mr. Jennings says.

Once again, I stand—still shuffling.

"Let's see, I'm a transfer student. In fact, I'm a new student all around. I've never even been in a classroom before. I've always been homeschooled by my grandmother because we move around so much." I

freeze. *Stupid. Why am I telling them all of this?* It's
like I have diarrhea of the mouth. "And I just moved
here from New York City."

I take my seat, thinking I've fulfilled this
requirement, and then the questions begin.

"Why did your grandmother teach you and not your
parents?" a nosey boy from the front row asks.

"They're dead," I answer, which is true of my
mother, but I hate explaining anything about my
phantom father.

"I am so sorry. Do you miss them?" Mandy asks,
sneering.

"You can't really miss something you've never
known." This isn't true. I have no memory of my
parents, not even a picture, but even so, they come to
mind quite often.

Seeing how uncomfortable I have become, Mr.
Jennings changes the subject. "That's a unique name,
Bijou. Do you know the origin?"

"It's French for jewel. I was actually born in
France."

"Parlez-vous français?"

"Un peu, un peu," I answer bashfully, taking my
seat. I am lying again. I'm fluent. Gigi, on the other
hand, speaks multiple languages.

"I spent a few years all over France
doing...research," he says with a look of intrigue.
"Where in France were you born?"

*What is this—twenty questions? Why am I being
interrogated?*

"Paris," I answer, irritated.

"Tell us about the cards," a curly-haired, blonde boy with a baby face shouts.

I stop shuffling and look at Mr. Jennings who looks just as anxious as my peers.

"Go on, Ms. Fitzroy," he urges.

"Well you see, I'm a psychic," I joke. "My best friend, Willow bought them for me to use for divination." I laugh as I say it, but no one else does.

Sebastian shakes his head and looks away as if embarrassed on my behalf.

I'm not just joking. I'm lying. I have no friends. All of my high school experiences come courtesy of *Buffy the Vampire Slayer*, so I grasped for a name and came up with the character Willow on the fly. According to TV, friendships are easy to come by, no matter what your quirks may be. Your vibe attracts your tribe. My tribe comes in the form of fictional characters, particularly in the form of Buffy's best friend, Willow Rosenberg.

"So, why don't you just use tarot cards?" Mandy asks.

"It was a joke."

"So why the cards?"

"It calms me when I'm nervous. And there used to be 52, but I leave one with my name and a clue to my destination at each place I leave behind." I shrug, I feel like I have already said too much. "It's kind of like people do with signing yearbooks, so someone knows I was there."

"Sounds like the calling card of a serial killer," Mandy says with a smirk.

As the questions come, I shuffle faster. I know I should stop, but their staring will be the least of my worries if I do. I don't even want to know what they are feeling, so I shuffle under my desk.

"Interesting," Mr. Jennings says as he walks toward his desk. Then he moves on. "Class, this is a new quarter and we're changing things up. I'm no longer going to be the only one telling stories. You'll each get a turn. The schedule goes up tomorrow, so start writing those stories."

Various conversations erupt around the room.

"This is your chance to use your imagination, express yourself, and take a break from SnapChat," he concludes, and the bell rings. "I'll explain more about the assignment tomorrow," he says, and then he looks at me. I bolt out of the room because Mr. Jennings looks like he's inspired to go for another round of questions.

Sebastian isn't much of a guide. After first period, it's apparently sink or swim. I don't actually expect him to hold my hand and deliver me to each class, but he could at least speak to me occasionally or point me in the right direction.

By midday, everyone has already heard my life story and learned about the cards. Everyone seems to know who I am now; at least I don't have to explain anymore.

"What class do you have next?" Mandy appears out of nowhere, almost giving me a heart attack.

"Lunch." I look at her with apprehension.

She smiles warmly and says, "You can eat with me, and I'll fill you in on the gossip."

Why is she being nice to me?

There is still something off about her. I can't seem to categorize her as Typical or one of the Others.

In the short time it takes us to get to the cafeteria, I have already been filled in on most of the school's gossip. She knows something about everyone we pass in the hallways. Her commentary is priceless, but I still wonder why she's being friendly all of a sudden.

Our lunch table is pretty full, or so I think until I look over to see Sebastian's table. It doesn't seem as if he's only been here a few months since the beginning of the school year. His table is full with people adding chairs just to sit there. He stands out in the crowd that surrounds him—effortlessly at ease.

He really has the tortured, bad boy act down—the perfectly messy hair and a fashion sense that says, *I do what I want. Deal with it.* I roll my eyes and hiss through my teeth, unjustifiably bothered.

Everyone at my table is in my first period class. Mandy tells me their names again, though I doubt I'll remember them all; there's Kim Tanaka, Aften Noble, and Christa Stein. Kim is quiet, but Aften can't seem to stop giving me side glances and whispering to her short, busty, red-headed friend, Christa. There are three boys here as well—Roland Richardson, Brian Freedman, and Jason Bellingham.

Roland keeps staring at me as he discusses some disgusting theory about boobs with Brian and Jason. I shuffle my cards consistently beneath the table, blocking out the swarm of emotions that surround me. I'm beginning to wonder if I'm capable of handling this social experiment.

Calm and steady emotions don't affect me as much as the stronger, vibrant moods. In fact, I wish calm emotions would have the most effect on me because maybe then I wouldn't constantly be on the brink of a nervous breakdown.

The person whose energy seems to be bothering me the most though, is Mandy's. Her emotions are all over the place. When she stares at Sebastian, I can feel lust but also some sort of resentment. As if that isn't bad enough, she has a deranged animosity toward someone sitting at our table that would make me pass out if it weren't for my cards. But Mandy hides it well beneath a composed mask of foundation paired with a pink smile.

Everything seems to stop as a new girl flutters into the cafeteria. She's petite, wearing a fitted, black sweater dress, walking toward the popular table. She is beautiful, with glowing skin that looks like honey, a heart-shaped face, and dimples deeper than Sebastian's. Her hair caresses her shoulders in a cascade of golden curls.

She smiles, exuding a childlike innocence that dances around her—like smoke emanating from an ember that could start wildfire.

"Who is she?" I ask, still staring. As if she hears me, the girl stands in place and returns the stare, looking me dead in the eyes.

There is something enchanting about her eyes. They are a brilliant shade of blue, like the ocean. She looks at me as if she knows me, and I can't shake the feeling that I know her, too. We both look away after a time. She is like Sebastian, but somehow different.

"I don't know her name, but I think she and Sebastian are a *thing*. She's pretty new as well, and I see them together a lot," Kim replies.

Our eyes follow the golden-haired beauty as she takes the seat next to Sebastian.

A hint of jealousy flickers within me.

"I guess Mandy's going to have to find someone else to fixate on," Aften mumbles to Christa, who seems to agree with everything Aften has to say.

"Mandy, don't you think it's a little too soon for you to date, since…" Christa doesn't get the opportunity to finish her statement before Mandy kicks her beneath the table. Even my cards can't block the shock and pain the redhead feels from Mandy's reaction.

Aften jumps to Christa's defense and an argument ensues.

"I don't know what's up with you guys and this new frenemy crap, but I'm over it." Kim, exasperated, stands. "See you later, Bij," she says, leaving the table.

Even though the table is no longer full, the lingering emotions are overwhelming. Whatever it is that Mandy doesn't want said, it has everyone on edge. It's obviously something big. I can already tell this year will be interesting.

CHAPTER 2—GO FISH

After lunch, we all part ways, and I walk to my fourth period Survey of Literature class.

The classroom is the smallest I have been in all day. By the time the rotund instructor walks in and calls attendance, it is clear the only person missing from the tiny classroom is Sebastian. He's probably with *her*.

Ten minutes after class begins, Sebastian comes strolling in, nonchalant, as if he is right on time. The instructor, Ms. Shayne, looks less than impressed as Sebastian slides into the seat behind me.

"Tardiness will not be tolerated in my classroom, Mr. Sinjin!"

"I'm sorry for any inconvenience I may have caused. Shall I remove myself so that you may tend to the students who arrived in a timely manner?" he asks. It doesn't even sound like him, especially without his colorful slang.

She smiles, charmed by the accent and the false sincerity. "It's no problem at all. After all, everyone's entitled to one tardy." She continues her lesson as if she was never interrupted.

There are many short stories and one novel we're required to read throughout the quarter. I have read a majority of the stories and the book as well.

Today's story is one I've always related to, "The Ones Who Walk Away from Omelas" by Ursula K. Le Guin. The story is simple, actually. It tells the story of a utopian city that seems perfect on the outside but hides a dirty secret. In order for the city to remain beautiful, peaceful and prosperous, an ill-fated child has to be kept in misery and darkness, hidden from the world.

"Are there any volunteers, class?"

I'm not paying attention. I'm not even sure what Ms. Shayne is talking about.

"I'm sorry, volunteers for what?" I ask.

"That's very kind of you to volunteer to read the story aloud, Ms. Fitzroy."

"But I didn't..."

"You can skip the commentary."

She knows I wasn't volunteering. Evil troll.

"'With a clamor of bells...'" I begin. I look at the book as I read out of habit, but I already know the story by heart. My photographic memory allowed me to breeze through homeschool. It's not something I want publicized, so I prefer keeping up the pretense that I am actually reading from the book. Gigi has no idea either.

The first time I read this story, I automatically thought of myself as the forgotten child.

Gigi has done her best to take care of me, and I appreciate it, but I do feel forgotten. Her materialistic need to buy clothes, buy jewelry, or buy anything with an exorbitant price tag is sickening. She fails to realize that money can't solve every problem or fill every void.

I want more than that. I want to know about my family, or to at least know what kinds of people came before me. Don't I have any other relatives? I have never been ill-treated like the child in Le Guin's story, but it feels like I have been punished for the death of my mother.

* * *

By the time the bell rings again, I am overwhelmed by the constant switching of classes. Just when you get used to being in one place, the freaking bell insists you have to move on. I should be a pro. The bell is like a metaphor for Gigi.

I slowly collect my belongings. Not excited about P.E., but at least it is my last class.

On my way out, I notice Sebastian staring at me curiously.

"What are you looking at?" I ask him, fearing I have food stuck in my teeth.

"No need to be sus," he responds calmly with a voice that makes me want to melt. "What's with the tattoo on the back of your neck?"

"What do you mean, *sus*?" Instantly, I touch my neck.

"*Suspicious,* genius. I'm not that difficult to understand. Try to keep up." He shakes his head as if I'm slow. "So, what's up with the weird tattoo? It's so detailed. It's kind of..."

"Kinda what? Creepy? It's not a tattoo, *your highness*. It's a birthmark." I tend to forget about the dreadful thing because I never see it. "I know it's weird. It looks like an eye."

"Wait, you mean to tell me you were born with an eye in the back of your head?"

"Correction, it's on the back of my neck, and you're not funny." I feel the juvenile urge to stick my tongue out at him, but I resist. "Anyway, how did you see it?"

"Um, I was sitting behind you last period while you were fiddling with your hair and pretending to read."

His accusation catches me off guard.

"I don't know how things work in Australia, but I've been reading since I was five. And call it a hunch, but if your reading is anything like your English, then I'd be more concerned with that than a stranger's neck."

Why the sudden interest in me?

He stares at me for a moment. "We're going to be late if we don't start walking now."

I follow, still surprised he is talking to me.

"Wait a minute," I say as reality kicks in. "Won't you get in trouble with your girlfriend if she sees you walking with me?"

He looks genuinely baffled. "What girlfriend?"

"The girl you were with at lunch. You know, curly, blonde hair and really blue eyes?"I try to look like I don't care because I don't.

It doesn't work. Amusement suddenly dances on his face, giving him a devilish edge. A chill works its way up my spine.

"What's with the aggro?" A look of realization comes across his face, accompanied by a subtle smirk. "Do I detect jealousy in your voice, Jewels?"

"Aggro? Talk normal. And what exactly am I supposed to be jealous of?" How dare he. Even if I am a little jealous, he has no right to point it out. "Wait, what did you just call me?"

"Aggravation, Jewels. Isn't Bijou French for jewel?"

"Well yes, but..."

"Well, I guess you've answered your own question," he answers cockily. "So lighten up, lass. Everyone needs a nickname."

"And the blonde girl with the curly hair is my twin sister, Amina."

"But you don't really look alike."

He only shrugs.

"Blimey. I almost forgot." he stops, shaking his head. "We've gotta stop at the school store."

I follow him down a narrow flight of stairs, tired from the constant change of locations, but silently grateful that he's being friendly to me.

When we arrive at the makeshift store that looks like it had once been a closet, he hands a note to the tall, balding man, standing in the doorway. He then, looks me up and down as if he's appraising me.

"Can I help you?" I ask, tempted to punch him for looking at me like that.

"I reckon you're a small, but Reaper thinks you wear a medium."

The balding man returns, handing me a plastic-wrapped uniform

"Why this for?" I say, giving it back to him.

Sebastian takes it instead, handing him a gold voucher that read, $20.

"You need it for P.E., ya buffhead," Sebastian says, laughing at me.

I don't say anything as I follow him to our individual changing rooms and we part ways. Upon entering the girl's locker room, I find all the girls wearing swimsuits. Fear and panic rush through me.

"But my schedule says P.E," I say, hearing my own voice tremble.

"Yes, and today starts our swim unit," Mandy says with a smirk. "You're such an android."

I bolt out of the locker room, bumping into Sebastian.

"Oy! Shouldn't you be running *into* the locker room?" he asks, holding my arms to stop me from running away.

"Let me go!"

He obliges.

"What's wrong, Jewels? You look petrified." His voice and eyes are sincere.

"I'm not good with water."

"I'm hoping you mean bodies of water and not water in terms of hygiene?" He poses it as a question, but his half smile tells me it's a poor attempt at humor.

"I almost drowned once. My friend, Willow, saved my life," I lie once again.

The truth is, when I was younger, I used to have a recurring dream. In it, I was on a beach trying to resist this force that called me to the water. Once I looked at the water, it was impossible look away. I could hear my grandmother's warnings, but that didn't stop me. I got into the water, and I was pulled down to the ocean floor as a faceless boy frantically tried to save me. Moments before death, I'd wake up.

The memory of the dream becomes fresh. My heart rate accelerates, and I feel faint. Sebastian catches me before I can hit the ground. He wears a fierce look of concern on his face. I suddenly begin to feel extremely hot in Sebastian's grasp as if there is fire, rather than blood, running through his veins. For a moment, I see strange symbols that look like embedded tribal tattoos moving on his skin, but when I blink, there's nothing there.

"I'm okay." My eyes flutter, and I shake off a desire to stay in his arms. *Why do I know his touch?* "I tripped," I lie.

He obviously knows I am lying but says nothing and lets me go.

"Willow may not be here, but I can be her surrogate and protect you if the need arises." This strikes me as odd. As he looks intensely into my eyes, it feels like he's someone else, someone I have known before.

"Thanks. Since I don't have a swimsuit, do you think I can sit today out?"

"Your togs are in the bag we got from the school store," he says, entering the boys' locker room.

Walking into the girls' locker room, I realize that I'll be wearing a bathing suit in front of everyone— including Sebastian. The other girls are donning brand-new, stylish bathing suits while I am the odd girl out wearing a school-issued, plain, royal-blue one-piece with gold lettering that reads "LHS."It isn't bad, just plain. I look over to Mandy, Aften, and Christa, who look like they went shopping together. Of course Mandy's suit is pink, Christa's is red, and Aften's is black, but they are all a similar style.

"Nice suit, Bijou," Aften comments sarcastically.Christa and Mandy giggle.

"Thank you," I answer, giving her a smile and posing. She sneers at me and walks away, Christa on her heels.

"Don't worry about them, Bij. I didn't waste my money on a bathing suit either." Kim is wearing the same suit as me.

"Hey, Bijou," Mandy says.

"Yeah?"

"You're new, so I'm only gonna say this once." Mandy briefly checks herself out in the mirror as she speaks. "Sebastian is mine, so stay away."

She smiles brightly like the psychopath she is and exits the locker room.

I am not totally confident, but I hold my head up high, walking out of the locker room until I see the pool. Everyone is lined up—females in one line and males in another. *Why are we lining up?*

I try to walk to the end of the line, but my legs won't allow me to move. I stand there, my heart beating so fast I think it might burst through my chest.

"Coach, this is Bijou Fitzroy, the new girl," Kim says, introducing me to a man about an inch shorter than me with an athletic build.

"I'm Coach Di'Vincent," he begins, but everything else sounds like the grown ups from a Charlie Brown cartoon as I look into the water.

"Is there something wrong with your legs, Ms. Fitzroy?" Coach Di'Vincent asks.

"Um, it's just that I can't swim."

"That's not a problem. I just want to see where your strengths and weaknesses lie, and then we can go on from there." He looks at me with no hint of sympathy. "The only one who is excused from swimming is Mr. Sinjin, due to his asthma."

Sebastian is definitely going to be no help to me, so his comforting words were indeed only words.

"Then I don't need to get in the water either because my weakness is that I can't swim at all."

"I promise you will be fine."

I want to cry but fight the urge. Mandy, Aften, and Christa are the first three girls to get in while three boys get in at the other end. They race back and forth, with Mandy coming in first and Christa last. Just as I try to escape to the back of the line, Coach Di'Vincent motions for me to go next. A little bit of relief comes when I look up and see Sebastian at the other end of the pool. He looks worried, but at least he's watching me.

I decide to try to emulate what I see the other girls doing. As I stand waiting for Coach Di'Vincent's cue to get in, I begin to feel the bizarre gravitational pull that was so prominent in my childhood dreams. It feels like there is some unseen force in the water calling me. When the whistle sounds, someone else takes the liberty of pushing me over the edge. Panic rises as I plunge into the water, the force of the push sending me to the bottom of the pool. I know I am in trouble. I unintentionally swallow the water—confident that darkness will soon ensue—letting myself fade into an enveloping darkness, and then it starts. Strange voices all around me, voices I can't understand, but there is one voice that overshadows all of the others. My eyes open wide, wanting to see the owner of the voice, but there is no one there.

Suddenly something comes over me. There's a rush of adrenaline that surges through my body. I plant my feet on the floor of the pool, preparing for takeoff.

Without another breath, I lunge out of the pool and into the air like a dolphin at SeaWorld. When I land back in the pool, the water has me in its grasp, but fear is no longer an obstacle. For the first time ever, I am home.

Once my head submerges, everything and everyone is irrelevant. My eyes are wide open. I see clearer here than I have ever been capable of seeing above water. By the time I get to the other end of the pool, I realize that I have yet to come up for air, and it doesn't bother me. I am actually inhaling and exhaling underwater. With my legs together—kicking as one—I am more comfortable moving underwater than I am walking on land.

When my head finally emerges, I am back where I started. *Did I imagine that I made it to the other end? How did I get back here so fast? And why am I not tired?* I feel rejuvenated and more vibrant than ever.

I climb out of the pool, recognizing the silence in the enormous room that was recently filled with echoes of laughter. Once again, all eyes are on me.

"I thought you said you couldn't swim?" Mandy says , looking at me like I have deceived her.

"Believe me, I'm just as surprised," I answer, wrapping an oversized, yellow towel around myself. "I've never swam a day in my life—well, until now."

She looks at me doubtfully, whispering something in Aften's ear that makes the girl snicker. I am confused and angered by her insinuation.

"What would be the purpose of lying to you?" I ask Mandy, defiantly turning away from her to avoid saying what I really want to say.

"Don't worry about them," Kim says, her voice concerned and earnest. "Mandy just doesn't like anyone else stealing her spotlight."

"I've never seen anything like it." Coach Di'Vincent looks at me strangely. "You made it back to the starting point before anyone else could even make the turn around."

"How's that even possible? I was underwater for forever." I try to make sense of it all, but I can't quite seem to comprehend what just happened. *Am I actually hearing voices now?*

"You swim like a fish," Coach Di'Vincent says.

Sebastian's face wavers between emotions, but the redness of his face indicates that anger is the most prevalent. "I'm sure this is all too much for her to process, so why don't you all back off and stop smothering her." His voice is protective, and as he speaks his eyes focus on Mandy, who is growing angrier by the second. Her emotions are volatile, making me physically ill.

The heavy feeling from before returns to my legs, but this time it spreads throughout my body, and then I am overwhelmed by darkness.

When I awaken, my classmates are all hovering over me.

"Give her some room, guys," someone commands.

"Are you okay?" Mandy asks with artificial sincerity.

"I'm fine." I finally manage, trying to stand up too fast and collapsing into a familiar grasp. It's Sebastian.

"Take it easy, Jewels," Sebastian says, trying to sound playful, but worry is written all over his face.

"Why can't you ever call me by my real name?"

"Well, at least I know you're coherent."

"Bijou, you had us all worried for a moment there," Coach Di'Vincent says while clearing the path of students who now surround me. "I think it was the adrenaline rush that got to you. You need to take it easy, but when you feel better, we should talk about getting you on the swim team. Oh, and Ms. DeVoe, I want you in my office, now. You never push someone into a pool. It isn't just mean; it's dangerous. She could have hit her head."

Mandy actually pushed me?

She looks at me with utter contempt as she leaves.

"Jewels, how are you getting home?" Sebastian asks as we make our way to the locker rooms. I'm kicking myself for the week I spent convincing Gigi to let me walk home from school.

"I'm walking home."

"Right-o! I'll give you a lift home," Sebastian says. "Wait for me in the junior parking lot."

* * *

I'm still a little shaken by what happened at the pool as I make my way to the parking lot. *How can I know how to swim?* It makes absolutely no sense. I've never been in a pool in my entire life. Gigi won't even let me anywhere near water, so how can I know how to swim, and so well?

My inner turmoil is distracted as I look across the parking lot to find the hooded figure, staring at me once again. I stop walking, halting traffic to the annoyance of many. I pull my cards out, afraid of what feelings may come.

"I hear you're possibly in the market for a bff." The voice startles me. I turn to find what looks like an extremely blonde, female version of Sebastian rushing towards me like a bolt of lightning that has escaped from the sky. "Someone needs to help you take that Mandy girl down."

"Where'd you hear that?"

"Besides the fact that the entire school is talking about Mandy trying to drown you, Bastian seems to think we'll get along. I'm Amina, Sebastian's twin sister."

"I would introduce myself, but you seem to know a lot about me already."

Sebastian's the yin to Amina's yang. She's open and outgoing without giving the impression that she's too cool. But like Sebastian, she's definitely one of the Others.

Just as I'm about to open up, I look across the crowded parking lot to find the hooded figure, staring once more.

"What is that dude's problem?" Amina follows my gaze. She links her arm in mine and I'm hit with a static shock and a vision of my cards flying through the air, but never landing on the ground. We pull away from each other quickly, which in turn knocks my cards to the ground in reality.

"You saw him?" I ask, shocked.

"Of course I saw him," she answers as we scramble to pick to collect the cards. "But forget about the creepy dude. What about the flying cards?"

"You saw the vision too?" I ask.

She simply nods.

We linger on the ground, staring at each other even though all the cards have been gathered.

"Is this some weird female bonding exercise?"

Sebastian's voice interrupts our staring contest and we both quickly stand.

"Your sister was just helping me," I rush to say.

"Bijou's seen him too," Amina says as her eyes wander with obvious paranoia. "The hooded bloke."

Sebastian's face hardens as he surveys the parking lot with hawk-like eye movements.

We make our way through the parking lot in silence. They're looking around and I'm looking at them, because for the first time in my life, I don't feel crazy. They've seen him too.

CHAPTER 3—NIGHTMARES

I'm riding in a car with a really cute boy and a potential bff and this isn't some scenario I've hijacked from an episode of *Buffy*. This is real life and they don't think I'm crazy. The horrifying thing about it all is that unlike the other girls in my P. E. class, I was ill-prepared for the pool and my hair looks like I've been electrocuted.

"I told you I saw someone," Amina says, punching her brother's arm from the passenger seat of the shiny, red Dodge Charger. "I should've bet you, Bastian."

"Mina, can you blame me for my skepticism?" he asks as he pulls out of the parking lot. "It wouldn't be the first time you've cried wolf."

"Wait, you've seen that guy before?" I ask, caught off guard by Sebastian's admission.

They look at each other briefly before Sebastian's eyes return to the road.

"About a week ago, I thought someone was watching me outside of our house, and the next day at school, I thought I saw a hooded guy, staring at me in the cafeteria," she says. "But Bastian didn't see it, so everyone thought I was lying."

"Everyone?" I ask.

"Our family," she answers. "We're pretty tightknit."

The idea of a family not keeping secrets from each other is unfamiliar to me.

"I've got you beat. I've seen him a few times before. I saw him about five or six times in New York," I recall, happy to finally be able to talk about this, but I'm still lying. I've been seeing him much longer than that.

"And your mother hasn't filed a restraining order?" Amina asks.

"Grandmother," Sebastian corrects.

Sebastian's gray eyes find mine in the rear view mirror. He seems to be doing this a lot. At every light, I find him staring, but I guess I'm doing the same.

"My parents are dead," I interject before Amina has an opportunity to ask.

Surprisingly, she doesn't apologize, and although it's faint, I can feel sadness and anger, coming from her.

But isn't she one of the Others?

"When no one believes you about what you see, you tend to stop telling them," I finally answer.

"Your eyes," Sebastian says out of the blue. "They're green. Weren't they gray earlier?"

"They change sometimes." If I were smart, I'd leave it at that, but I feel compelled to add a lie to justify the strangeness of it all. "My friend, Willow calls them mood rings."

"So, what's she like?" Amina asks.

"Willow's the best. She's loyal, smart, and loves weird things like me."

"No. I mean your grandmother," Amina corrects.

"Have you seen *Mommy Dearest*?" I ask.

The both nod.

"Take away the wire hangers and add the fountain of youth," I quip.

"Fountain of youth?" Amina inquires.

"She looks too young to be a grandmother. That's why I call her Gigi instead of Grandma."

Sebastian grunts.

"So, why'd you guys move here from Australia?" I change the topic to them.

"Our dad's a journo and got a job in D.C." Sebastian says, his eyes meeting mine in the rear view mirror once again.

"He means our dad's a journalist," Amina adds.

"I kind-of figured that one out." I laugh. "That's a coincidence. My grandmother's a writer as well."

I'm careful with my words, not giving away too much.

"Oh, does she work at a newspaper?" Sebastian asks, meeting my eyes once more.

"Uh no. She works in publishing," I answer, making sure not to make eye contact. "Fiction mostly."

"Is she famous or something?" Amina turns with excitement to see my face. "I'm a bibliophile. Maybe I've read something of hers."

Maybe this is how normal people get to know each other but they seem to be more interested in Gigi than in me.

"Oh she ghostwrites mostly, so her name wouldn't be familiar."

I'm becoming nervous, because every time I lie, they look at each other but say nothing.

"So back to the guy in the hoodie," Sebastian begins. "Don't you find it weird that someone has been following you around?"I pause for a moment before responding. *Why so many questions?* "I actually thought I was imagining it all, especially since my grandmother has never..."

"But that's not all, Bastian," Amina interrupts. "I saw something when I touched her-"

I interrupt. "Make a left into the development and my house is at the end of the cul de sac."

I don't want to believe that Amina saw what I saw, but then again, when I first touched Sebastian this morning, I felt the same electrical charge and saw myself drowning. Something that nearly happened today. Maybe this means I'm not so crazy after all, but it could also mean that something strange is unfolding around me and I could be in trouble.

* * *

In a development where the houses all look unsettlingly similar, ours stands out dramatically. Before moving to Maryland, Gigi hired landscapers to plant various evergreen trees to surround it in place of a generic fence.

The house itself is unnecessarily large for two people, but our backyard is a whole separate entity. The massive space is large enough to build two single-family homes. Gigi constructed a fairy-tale-like maze made of hedges, weird herbs, and who-knows-what-else. There is supposed to be a garden somewhere within the maze, but I don't have the nerve to try going through it. It's creepy.

As I climb out of the Charger, I feel their eyes on me.

"Your cat's huge," Sebastian says, breaking the silence.

"What cat?" I ask, following the direction of Sebastian's pointed finger.

By the time I turn, all I see is a shiny black Sedan, parked next to Gigi's red jag in the driveway.

"It must be the neighbor's cat," I say. "Thanks for the ride."

They wait until I make it through the door to pull off.

"I'm home," I call out to Gigi the moment I walk through the door. She pretends to be preoccupied in the kitchen.

I drop my newly heavy backpack on the shiny, wooden parquet floor, then quickly pick it up when an image of Gigi's reaction comes to mind.

She has always been particular about appearances. The house doesn't look like we've just moved in. It was decorated before we even got here. Lavish, French-accented rooms with brilliant vaulted ceilings. Most of our rooms have floor to ceiling windows accentuated by extra-long layers of red, orange, and brown-toned curtains, accompanied by furniture that is light in color with hints of red and brown accents.

"Oh, I didn't hear the door," she says pleasantly, examining my face and looking at my hair judgmentally.

She's lying. I saw the curtains shift as I got out of the Charger.

"So tell me, how was it?" she asks as I walk into the kitchen.

I reach for an apple, but she smacks my hand, pointing to the sink. "I picked these from the orchard out back," she says with pride. "Try some of the lavender lemonade. That's from the garden as well."

Gigi has a talent for making things grow. Every herb we consume comes from her plants and every herb has it's own ability. She plants basil for good fortune and beauty, honeysuckle for money and protection, jasmine for love and sweet dreams, and lavender forcalm. She's tried teaching me more, but I don't have the patience for it.

"School was okay. I think. Classes were fine, and I think I may have some potential friends," I explain, sounding a little too excited, while taking an oversized bite out of an apple.

"Bijou, that is very unladylike. Smaller bites. Anyway, did you meet anyone interesting?" she asks suspiciously.

"Gigi, I just told you I met some potential friends." She isn't old enough to be senile, so what is she really asking? "They're twins, they moved here at the beginning of the semester, and one of them had to show me around today. Happy now?"

This seems to spark her interest. Her finely arched brows cock, and she glances at me curiously, trying not to seem intrigued.

"What is it, Gigi?" I ask.

"No, that's interesting because no one's mentioned anything to me about any new families moving here—besides ours."

"So, you have spies now, investigating the comings and goings around here?"

"This is a small town, and I've been filled in on just about everything else, so why not this?" A crease forms in her forehead, alerting me that she is thinking of something else to ask. "Are they the ones who brought you home?"

"How do you know someone brought me home?"

I knew she was watching.

Her eyes narrow on me.

"School let out not too long ago, and you're already here, so you couldn't have walked."

She folds her arms over her chest.

"Yes, Gigi, Sebastian and Amina gave me a ride home." I take another unladylike bite of the apple just to annoy her. "Who's car is in the driveway?"

"Safe Harbor sent my new agent here," she replies, giving no further details. Safe Harbor is a literary agency that only represents best-selling authors who want to keep their true identities hidden. I've never understood what the big deal is about keeping such a stupid secret, but to each her own.

"Well, where is your friend or agent or whatever?" I ask.

"She went out back to take a call." Gigi dismisses the subject with the wave of a hand. "Why is your hair wet?" she asks.

I knew I should have gone straight upstairs.

I don't answer.

"I'm quite sure you heard my question, *ma petite*."

"I had swimming class today."

Gigi is instantaneously facing me. "Don't lie to me. I've seen your schedule; there is no swimming class."

I dig my schedule out of my backpack and shove it into Gigi's hand.

"The only course on this schedule that is remotely close to swimming is Physical Education."

"Call the school, if you want!" I am too exhausted to do this little dance with her.

"This schedule is misleading," she says in a voice that is an octave higher than her usual tone. "Since you can't swim, I'm sure I can get you out of this class. It won't be a problem."

I think about pleading with Gigi, but I know it won't help. Defiance takes over instead. "I don't want you to get me out of that class. I'll be just fine," I retort through clenched teeth, remembering her friend is near.

"I won't allow it! If you stay in that class, they'll all know..." She quickly turns away from me as if she has said something wrong.

"What will they all know?" I ask, almost afraid of what she might say.

"I have to finish up my meeting, and I have work to do, so just get started on your homework." Gigi's expression is unreadable. She is hiding something, and from her behavior, it's obviously important.

When I turn on my heels, Gigi begins to speak again. "And if you don't listen to me and drop the class, I can always take you out of school. You don't need the credits anyway; you're already ahead of those students."

This is one of the main reasons why Gigi and I clash so often. She thinks she knows everything! I close my eyes, clenching my hands into fists as if that will help stop the angry words I want to shout.

"I never complain about anything. I follow you around whenever the spirit moves you, never questioning your motives. I'm already a big enough outcast at school; please don't make me any more of a weirdo by requesting preferential treatment for me. I don't want to disrespect you, but I am going back to school tomorrow, and my schedule will be kept as is." I try to keep my voice as composed as possible.

She looks like she wants to strangle me. Any other person in this situation would be turning red in the face, but when Gigi becomes angry, her face strangely turns pale.

"You'd better watch yourself. I'm sure you need no reminder of how easy it would be to take your butt out of that joke of a school."

"You can't do that. I wish you-" Before I can finish my sentence, her hand flies across my cheek, cutting off my words.

She actually slapped me. Fury surges through me as though I am a volcano preparing to erupt.

"Bite your tongue, you spoiled little brat," she screams.

She is so overdramatic and superstitious. She is a firm believer in the saying, *be careful what you wish for*, so she flies off the handle whenever I wish for something. That's why she never puts candles on my birthday cake; she's afraid I'll make a wish. Still, she has never slapped me before.

My face is hot with rage. I want to slap her. I want to scream. Truth is, I don't know how to react. Tears sting my eyes, but I refuse to blink, knowing the floodgates will open..

"You didn't even let me finish," I say, pushing her away from me as she steps forward in an attempt to touch my face. "I wish I could leave and not have to see your evil face."

I run upstairs, silently wishing for some long-lost family member to show up and take me away. Anything would be better than this, but I can't help but feel guilty. Gigi could have such a wonderful life, maybe even love. She's worldly, beautiful, and fluent in many languages, but she can't be free because she's bound to me. Since my parents have been out of the picture, her whole life has revolved around me, and sometimes I think she resents me for it. But maybe I'm just overly concerned about her feelings because I'm suffering from Stockholm Syndrome.

My face burns and out of spite, I rip a leaf of her aloe vera plant before entering my room. As soon as I walk in, I know she's been here. For one, my clothes were all over my bed after this morning's rummage, and now everything's neatly folded or hanging in my closet.

Why does she do this? Can't I have one thing that's mine without her prying? If hanging my clothes was all she came in to do, I'd have no problem, but she snoops around. I know this because once I planted a fake diary in my drawer about a make-believe guy named Angel I met and fell in love with, and Gigi completely lost it. As much as I talk about Buffy, she didn't even pick up the fact that the boy I was obsessing over happened to be named after the love interest from the show. She seized the diary and interrogated me for hours about it. When she finally realized I'd made the whole thing up, she had the nerve to tell me I had a real future as a writer and moved on as if she hadn't invaded my privacy and lost it like a crazy person.

So my room looks like she wants it to look. Very Parisian and chic, with no personality. The only traces of me are my books and my clothes which are hidden behind the obscenely overpriced couture she buys me and I hardly ever wear. The most personal things I have are my books. The paperbacks are the ones I actually read, but I buy the hardcover books just to get the book jackets. I leave the actual books in random public places and use the book jacket to cover my real journals. Every strange thing that happens to me, every strange dream I have is written down. There must be about twenty or so. Right now, I'm using a Stephen King book jacket and Gigi has no clue. I don't want to be that person. I am a liar because of Gigi. When I first told her about my dreams, she told me I was having them because I watch too much TV. When I was five, I told her about feeling the emotions of others, she brushed it off and yet began to grow verbena, putting it in the water and anything else that can hide the awful taste, saying it will stop my hallucinations. About a year later, when I told her that sometimes my dreams come true, she told me that things like that happen all the time and it's called coincidence, and soon she began putting these weird herbs in a capsule for me that's supposed to stop all of the madness. I pretend that it works and tell her I don't dream anymore, so she doesn't think I'm crazy. It only makes me sleepy. When I was 10, I told her about the man in the hoodie. She said I was being paranoid, but less than a week later, she moved us halfway around the world. So I've stopped telling her things.

I lie to keep her off my back. I lie to stop her from using her superstitious remedies on me.

But I'm not hallucinating, and today proves it.

I take off my cardigan and catch a glimpse of myself in the mirror. There are deep red welts on my triceps. I take a closer look at the marks and there's no doubt that they're fingerprints.

It makes no sense though. They can't be from Gigi. She slapped me. She didn't squeeze my arms. But Sebastian did, when he caught me.

* * *

I don't go down for dinner. Instead, I head to bed early. Maybe in search of the faceless boy, but the moment my head hits the pillow, I'm not greeted by his familiar presence.

The rain pours down through the trees as if it is intent on purifying the earth, making it almost impossible to see the path. I walk, refusing to let the relentless downpour stop my journey through the overgrown foliage.I walk without hesitation or confusion as if I know this path, but as I look down, I realize something else isn't recognizable. My feet. My feet don't look like mine. They're someone else's. I'm barefoot, and I'm in dire need of an industrial pedicure. My feet and legs are enveloped by symbols—tattoos really, but they are so deeply embedded into my skin that what I see is more akin to a birthmark than something manmade.

This forest is wild, untouched by the hands of man. I close my eyes, continuing on the path, not by sight, but by sheer instinct.

Soon, I stop, quietly standing, utilizing each of my senses one by one. I hold up my right hand to the sky as if in protest. Then, slowly, I open my eyes. The rain ceases with a simple hand gesture.

I hone my senses and I can actually feel others near. I begin walking again, arriving at a clearing where three cloaked figures stand waiting. Waiting for me. But these aren't the ones I sensed. There are four others and their presence is strong.

I walk towards the three that stand in the middle of the clearing and I'm surprised to see them each holding babies. Before I can start to question them or their motives, I look down to find a baby in my own arms and I, as well, am now cloaked in a black robe.

Each figure places their own baby on the ground, and each baby crawls to various corners of the clearing as if their instructions have been foretold. They all look at me expectantly. My baby squeezes my finger, finally drawing my attention to her face. She is beautiful. In fact, she is the most beautiful child I have ever seen. Her oblong face is framed by hair blacker than a crow's feathers. Her smile is so pure, it breaks my heart and heals it in repetition. Her sun-kissed skin urges me to look into her eyes, but she closes them tightly, squeezing my finger tighter than before.

I carefully place the beautiful child on the ground and, as if on cue, she crawls to her spot in the clearing, completing the four points. But as I slowly rise, I notice the symbols on my legs and feet are moving, and as I looked to the other three cloaked figures, I notice all have their share of symbols moving about the parts of their bodies that I can see.

Soon I follow my baby to her place and the others do the same, pursuing their own children. Once again, I raise my right hand, gesturing to each child, then to the ground, next to where my child sits. The other three figures follow suit once more, only gesturing to their own children. When I look to the other babies, they now each carry the symbols of the figures that once held them. And when I finally look at my baby, she is overwhelmed by the symbols that once devoured my skin as well as the symbols that were once on the other three figures.

I wake up in a cold sweat. My hair and t-shirt are soaked and cling to my skin. I quickly remove the covers, inspecting my skin for the moving symbols from my dream. I'm awash with relief as I find nothing there. The symbols from my dream are the same ones I thought I saw on Sebastian's arms when he caught me mid-fall.

At least I didn't wake Gigi. She used to tell me that dreams are meaningless—an improper subject for a lady to dwell upon—but I don't believe that. I see them as riddles—ones seeking a resolution from the dreamer. *So what's the riddle I'm meant to solve?*

I dream nightly and they often vary, but I have never had one without the faceless boy, so why now?

He's always watching over me, always protecting me. He never changes. He's been the same since I was a child, and I know it sounds psychotic, but I think I'm in love with him. Although his arrival in my dreams usually signifies impending doom, I only feel safe when he's near. In my dreams, I'm sure someone or *something* is watching me. And though I never see it, his presence is always felt. Sometimes I'm being chased, and other times I'm drowning. Whatever the dream may be, there's always danger. But what I just dreamed was different.

At times, I think Gigi knows exactly what's going on,but she's in denial or something. For someone so smart, she can't be this oblivious.

When we lived in France, there was a woman who lived next door. She instantly took a liking to me. She always wore a smile on her face, but the smile never reached her eyes. Gigi told me it was because she wanted to have a baby but couldn't. One day we saw her, and I couldn't stop staring. I left Gigi's side, walked up to her, and hugged her so tightly that she began to weep. Gigi pulled me away while apologizing to the woman. That night, I dreamed about her sitting by a river, cradling a baby in her arms. She called me over to sit next to her. She was so happy. When I looked up across the river, the faceless boy was standing there, motioning me to leave. Once again, I felt like I was being watched. I turned around to see who was watching, but no one was there. When I turned my attention back to the woman, she was gone. A few weeks later I saw the woman, and she told Gigi that she was pregnant. I had never seen her so happy, except in my dream. Shortly after, we moved away. I never got to tell her goodbye.

There's a scratching sound emanating from somewhere in my room. I sit up in my bed, attentive and frightened enough to jump out of my skin.

I hear it again and it sounds like it's coming from my window.

I head over to my window, leading to my faux balcony that overlooks our backyard maze. I draw the curtains, exposing an almost full moon that makes the balcony and yard look enchanted. It's weird, but even though I have an aerial view of the maze, the hedges are so thick that I can't see beyond the greenery.

The scratching begins again and I look down to find a fat grey cat on its hind legs, scratching at the French doors of the balcony.

I exhale, unlock the latch, and open the doors.

The cat doesn't move at first. She stops scratching and sits there, staring at me with deep amber eyes that have flecks of gold in them.

"Who do you belong to, beautiful?" I whisper, bending to pick her up.

She willingly jumps up into my arms, nuzzling my face as if telling me she's happy to meet me.

I stand up in an attempt to close the doors, happy it was a cat and not a rat, when the songs of night are suddenly silenced. No night bugs. No nocturnal birds singing in unison to keep the company of the moon. Just complete and utter silence. For some reason, this bothers me more than the scratching did when it was still a mystery.

I take an apprehensive step forward, unsure of how much weight the balcony can hold. There's something moving at the far left edge of the maze. An animal, maybe.

I take another step forward, squeezing the cat as though it's stuffed. I focus my eyes, and the figure becomes clear.

It's him. The man in the hoodie. He's crouched down, head bent, broad shoulders rising and falling.

I almost wet my pants.

The cat purrs and he quickly stands, pointing at me.

I jump back, making the balcony creak. I shut the doors with the gray cat still in my arms.

My room is scorching hot, but it does nothing to stop me from barricading myself under my comforter, wishing none of this is real.

CHAPTER 4—TEACHER'S PET

I count sheep for hours before falling asleep again, but by the time the faceless boy finally makes an appearance, my alarm goes off. I'm up before the sun in an attempt to dodge Gigi before school.

After getting dressed, I eat a huge bowl of Fruity Pebbles to make up for missing dinner last night and pack up leftover spaghetti for lunch. This is pretty much my routine for the rest of the week. Run upstairs after school, sneak in the kitchen for leftovers once Gigi has gone to bed, and get out the door before she wakes. In all honesty, she could see me if she really wanted to, but I'm probably not her favorite person at the moment either.

Now it's Wednesday. The walk to school isn't a very long one, but it is indeed a cold one. There are no sidewalks, so if I'm not walking on grass, I'm walking on the road.

Thank goodness this isn't Manhattan.

The thing about leaving home so early is the sun hasn't fully risen, so my walk to school looks like this is Gatlin, Nebraska and the children of the corn will emerge momentarily with machetes and a Molotov cocktail, preparing to sacrifice me to "He Who Walks Behind the Rows."As the end of my walk draws closer, the smell of rotten eggs overwhelms me, and I begin to get the feeling that I am being followed. Without being obvious, I kneel to tie my shoe in an attempt to verify my suspicion, but there's no one there.

Even though I know I'm alone, I'm still unsatisfied. I stand all the same, still looking behind me. I turn forward in an attempt to continue my walk, only to bump into the hooded figure. I freeze in terror. Fear surges through me, and I feel a jolt of electricity.

His face is covered in black bandages that blend in perfectly with the black hoodie. His eyes are the only actual part of his body that's exposed. His pupils are red and elongated. The sclera and irises of his eye are displayed in shocking contrast to the black he's covered in, more yellow than a bad case of jaundice, but not quite saffron yellow. Sulfur. As yellow as sulfur.

I slowly take a step back as if moving too fast will induce him to grab me. He takes one step forward.

"Wh-what do you want?" I stammer.

He points a gloved finger at me.

Attempting to run past him is my only option. I've walked too far to make it back home, and I'm closer to school. But there's no point. He catches up to me, grabbing me by the arm and turning me to face him once more.

I feel like I'm going to throw up. He squeezes my arms tightly. I'm trembling like a Tickle Me Elmo toy, and it isn't from the cold.

"Let me go," I protest, fighting to break free, but his grasp is too strong. I kick him in his nuts, but he doesn't flinch. If anything, it only infuriates him, making him stronger. I continue to fight and his grasp becomes so heated, it feels like a live flame burning through my flesh. Fear soon turns to unbridled pain as I fight to get my hands to his face and dig my thumbs into his ugly eyeballs. This hurts him as he releases me to cover his eyes, letting out a piercing scream that sounds more animal than human. I kick him in his chest, knocking the wind out of him. Thank goodness for Gigi and those damn Krav Maga lesson. I take this opportunity to run, screaming at the top of my lungs.

"STRANGER DANGER!" It's the first thing that comes to mind. I scream it repeatedly as I run. I am hysterical and I don't dare turn around to see how close he is to me. I'm running so fast, it doesn't even feel like my feet are hitting the pavement and soon, I hear a car behind me.

I wave my arms even before turning around, but when I turn, the hooded man is nowhere to be seen, and I'm almost hit by a school bus that honks at me but doesn't stop.

I quickly move out of the way and continue running until I make it to the junior parking lot, dripping with sweat and fear.

* * *

I spend the thirty minutes before school starts in the bathroom trying to stop crying. My jacket is ripped and singed where he held me. I take it off, exposing burn marks on the arms of my sweater and welts on my skin quite similar to the ones I received at the pool last week.

I take off my sweater to examine the marks from the other day, but there's nothing there.

The most logical thing would have been for me to run into the front office, screaming bloody murder, but if I do, Gigi will find something else to take from me like she's done with swim class, or she'll or yank me out of school, and we'll probably move again. What's happening here is real, and I can't be hallucinating because these burn marks and the man chasing me are proof I'm not crazy.

I can't help but think of Sebastian. Every time I'm near him, there seems to be heat radiating from his skin, and not like a gross perspiration type of thing. This is more of a human toaster thing. His hands are always hot, and I think he burned me last week. Is he somehow connected to the hooded man with Satan's eyes?

If so, how? He can't be the hooded man, because that would mean he started stalking me when he was in elementary school, and whoever has been following me has always been a full-grown man ...or whatever *it* is.

Each time I close my eyes, I keep seeing those horrid yellow eyes and smelling rotten eggs. I wash my face with cold water as if the entire experience will disintegrate, but it does nothing more than calm me a bit.

The bell rings and I rush out of the bathroom without my cards in hand. The emotions hit me harder than that slap in the face. Excitement and angst. Deep sadness and then hate.

I look up to see Mandy with a smile as wide as the Cheshire Cat's.

"Stranger danger!" she yells in my face, with Aften and Christa following suit and cackling like two dwarf hyenas.

I almost run out of the building, but a warm—not hot—hand holds mine, stopping me from fleeing. Sebastian.

His crooked smile is bright, exposing dimples that match the one in his chin. His gray eyes stare into mine and it feels like everything's okay.

"Come on. Class is this way," he says, leading me in the right direction.Mr. Jennings' class doesn't seem like work at all. So far, we've discussed pieces of literature, only for Mr. Jennings to give us alternate details to the tales we've read. The atmosphere is very relaxed—there are a few desks, bean bags, and a couch for those who get to class early enough. His personality draws people to him, and although he's a cool teacher and well liked, something about him seems off to me. I still can't bring myself to fully trust him. Mr. Jennings greets us as we take our seats, then says, "According to the syllabus, you were supposed to finish *A Midsummer Night's Dream.*"

As he speaks, it's hard to determine whether that was a proclamation or question.

"Sheesh. Shakespeare in the 11th grade. How redundant," Mr. Jennings says as he paces the length of his desk, while going through his notes.

"Do you mean cliche, sir?" Sebastian asks.

"No. I mean redundant." He mumbles something, but I'm not close enough to hear.

Maybe I'm wrong, but shouldn't a teacher encourage students to take an interest in the material, instead of discouraging them?

He's a literary snob, just like Gigi. She hates this play as well as many others people consider great literature.The rest of the class seems as perplexed as I am. There are mumbles and a couple raised hands.

"Sir, I'm actually anxious to discuss the rest of the play as it sort-of ties into the story I'm going to tell eventually," Kim says, looking at Mr. Jennings with obvious scrutiny.

Mr. Jennings' jaw tightens as he takes a seat on the edge of his desk. He isn't as calm as he he usually is. In fact, even his appearance isn't as pristine as it was before. Although ever so slight, his complexion is a little lackluster as well.

A few others chime in, mentioning their favorite parts and rebuking others.

"Oberon was a control freak," Roland surprisingly adds. "If it weren't for him, none of the chaos would have ensued."

I'm not sure if I'm more surprised that Roland actually read the text or that he understood it. From our first encounter in the cafeteria, it seems like all he talks about is basketball and his theory about the correlation between gluten-free diets and small bust sizes, so the fact that he read Shakespeare with comprehension is shocking to say the least. Honestly, Roland turns out to be nicer than I thought at first. He always says "Hi!" to me before school and at lunch. And Kim is nice. The rest of Mandy's crew continues to be awful.

"Roland's right. Oberon was a misogynist, intimidated by Titania's strength," I add, quietly shuffling my cards beneath my desk. "He selfishly wanted to raise the changeling child as his henchman, while poor Titania wanted to raise the child as her own."

"You've been here for like a week and you've read the play already?" Mandy asks with a smile that is anything but sincere. "Freak," she adds through a faux cough.

"Duh! Did you read it?" I answer, returning her saccharine-laced smile. "I think it's one of Shakespeare's best works."

She counters by rolling her eyes.

Mr. Jennings' interest is piqued. His brow rises and he folds his arms across his chest, looking at me.

"So tell me, isn't Puck just as much to blame as Oberon?" he asks me.

"As much as I detest everything about Puck, he was simply following the orders of the buffoon king."

Sebastian laughs heartily, prompting a few others to follow suit. Mandy is shooting daggers at me with her eyes. Mr. Jennings is far from amused as well.

He's stone-faced, staring at me, agitated with conflicting emotions.

"Ms. Fitzroy, would you please stop shuffling?" Mr. Jennings' voice is low but forceful, and I am caught off guard.

"I'm sorry, sir, but it relaxes me." I continue shuffling.

"Mandy," he calls, suddenly standing. "What relaxes you?"

There is an air of affected civility in the classroom as no one is sure where he's going with this.

"I don't know," Mandy responds, but she sits up in her seat, and a malevolent anticipation radiates from her, like she's a toxic Barbie from Chernobyl. "Dancing relaxes me. Or maybe a good workout."

Now that Mr. Jennings is on his feet, he begins to make his way towards the back of the classroom. Towards me.

"And Mandy, you wouldn't start dancing in the middle of class to relax yourself, would you?" He's still looking at me.

"Only if Sebastian asks nicely." Her deadpan response has the class in an uproar.

Sebastian's brow raises, but he doesn't comment. He's watching Mr. Jennings like a hawk, not fidgeting, not shifting in his seat, still as cool as ever.

"Settle down," Mr. Jennings says to the class. He's finally standing before me in a menacing fashion. "Your cards please, Ms. Fitzroy."

A silence falls over the classroom that only increases the volume of the emotions surrounding me.

"I-I'll put them away." I stammer.

"No. You can have them after class."

"But they're mine." My voice is nothing more than a whisper. I think I'm going to cry.

"Oy. She said she'll put 'em away, mate." Sebastian's voice is authoritative and strong as opposed to my timid one.

"I suggest you stay out of this, Mr. Sinjin." He looks Sebastian directly in his eyes, but it only makes Sebastian stare back defiantly.

I struggle to put my cards in my satchel, but my hands are shaking.

In his attempt to grab my cards, his hand brushes against mine, igniting a searing pain that feels like I've been set on fire. A lightbulb from above us explodes along with the light fixture that once covered it, and sparks fly. This sends the class into a state of shock. A cry escapes my lips, but before I can let out a full blown scream, he retracts his hand, along with my cards, putting them in his back pocket.

The classroom isn't in darkness as there are other lights and it's sunny outside, but it is noticeably darker than before as my classmates make assumptions about what just happened.

"Mandy, please summon the janitor for me." She obediently rushes out of the classroom.

Is Mandy's name the only name he can remember? It's annoying.

"And Ms. Fitzroy, Mr. Sinjin, since you two want to challenge me in front of the entire class, you can think about it in detention." Well, I guess he remembers mine too. I can feel his triumphant joy as he changes the subject and makes his way back to his desk. "The library. After school. You'll have time to work on your stories to present tomorrow."

The light exploding was no coincidence. The first jolt of electricity occurred when Sebastian and I touched, the second occurred when Amina and I touched, and now this with Mr. Jennings. The one common factor in all of these incidents is me.

I'm silently wishing the Shakespeare discussion picks up again, because since no one is talking, their emotions are playing tug of war with me, and I'm going to implode.

My breaths become shorter and my heart is beating faster than when Buffy chooses to date a hot vampire over a real live boy.

I'm about to lose it when Sebastian's hand finds mine and holds on tight.

I don't know if my discomfort is written all over my face or if it's something else, something nameless and unexplainable that is happening between us, but he leans in and says, "Listen with your ears and not your heart."

As he stares into my eyes, he repeats it three more times, and all of a sudden I feel safe.

I close my eyes and three times I say, "Listen with your ears and not your heart."

The emotions are now nothing more than the buzz of a mosquito on a hot summer's night. I reopen my eyes and Sebastian pulls away, flippantly slouching in his chair and looking forward as if I'm no longer beside him.

"How'd you do that?" I whisper, but he ignores me.

"You may find this hard to believe, but Shakespeare's play is not as clever as you all may think." I'm finally back to reality, listening to Mr. Jerk—Mr. Jennings speak. "These characters aren't original, but based on people from throughout history and other, less popular works of fiction."

"I doubt that." Roland shakes his head in utter disbelief, extracting a devious smirk from Mr. Jennings. "Don't you think his plays would have been discredited by now if they'd been plagiarized?"

"But the existence of Shakespeare himself has been the topic of scholarly debates for centuries." Sebastian's voice brings a look of pure disdain to Mr. Jennings' face. "Some believe it was Christopher Marlowe that authored it all, the bloke who wrote, 'Was this the face that launched a thousand ships, and burnt the topless towers of Ileum?'"

"How many of you have heard of the Otherworld?" Mr. Jennings asks, disregarding the remarks of both Sebastian and Roland.

No one answers.

"Neverland. Oz. Avalon. Faerie. Since the beginning of time, humans have obsessed over the existence of a magical place parallel to the plane we occupy." The delight in Mr. Jennings' face can't be mistaken for anything else. "Humans try to name it, as they often attempt to do with things they can't understand, but the name is as simple as they come. The Otherworld."

As he speaks, his words weave a tapestry of enchantment and mystery around the room that intrigues us all into complete silence.

"The stories are as infinite as the beings that inhabit them. Fantastical with no end. So many names for the occupants, so in light of the stories you will be telling, I'll tell you one of my own to prove my point about Shakespeare."

"Who knows what a djinn is? And let me forewarn you that I'm not speaking of the blue creature in the lamp that Disney has misled you poor souls to believe will grant your heart's desire."

There are a handful of raised hands. Mandy re-enters the room with a janitor that I classify as one of the Others. He looks like he was an extra for the film *Grease*. Slicked back hair, rolled sleeves, black Chucks. All that's missing are the cigarettes.

"I know the movie was off, but isn't it based on the original legend of the creature?" Kim always has a way of wiping Mr. Jennings' smug smile off his face.

"You're right. The word djinn derives from the Arabic root word janna, meaning—"

I interrupt involuntarily. "To conceal or to hide." Jennings stops speaking with wide eyes as if I have done something wrong. "I'm sorry. I was just guessing. I didn't mean to interrupt."

"It's quite alright. You're absolutely correct." He continues with the lecture, explaining that any supernatural being whose identity is hidden is considered a djinn.

"The beings of the Otherworld go by many names. Some you're familiar with from childhood—mermaids, faeries, elves, genies, and more. Yes, these beings have individual names, but in all actuality, they are all djinn."

Before Mr. Jennings can continue, snorts erupt among some of the students.

"Do you find this funny?" He snaps. "Western civilization has packaged something the rest of the world fears and transformed it into something cute and cuddly so it won't make you uncomfortable. They have romanticized the djinn by turning it into a friendly, blue creature that resides in a magic lamp, granting wishes and calling it a genie. They have turned what most Africans and scholars refer to as Mami Wata into a singing girl with a tail and call it a mermaid, but if you were to encounter the real deal, it would be nothing to sing about."

He stops briefly, waiting for any interruptions, but no one speaks. We are all too afraid, but I still want him to continue.

Mr. Jennings explains how many cultures believe that once, the earth was just a single mass of land ruled by a very powerful and immortal race of beings. With so much power came the responsibility of maintaining peace, which in theory seemed to be a simple task, but it was harder than expected. Soon the race became divided into two groups. One group thought it was so powerful, it could misuse its magic, while the other group kept to the old ways.

Some people believe the wayward group was punished and stripped of its powers, making them mortal, which is how the human race was created. The ones that remained powerful, severing all ties to their lost brethren. Other cultures believe that these beings were always a separate race from humans. They are known for their trickery—stealing human babies and replacing them with the offspring of a mystical creature, as well as granting mortals' wishes but usually at a cost. As promised, Mr. Jennings gives us a frightening side to the mermaid myth. How they possess an unearthly beauty that lure people— particularly men—to their deaths. The one similarity that all these beings share is the ability to hide themselves, therefore earning them the title of the concealed.

"Like in Shakespeare's play, the Otherworld had a king and queen of it's own, the most powerful of all djinn. And like Titania and Oberon, they fought mercilessly until they eventually tore the Otherworld apart. Some believe the rift between the two is what left their world susceptible to humans slipping through."

There is something strange and dark about his delivery, prompting me to look around in search of signs that someone is in agreement with my notion. Sebastian's face has lost its mirth as he squirms uncomfortably in his seat. He and Mr. Jennings are having some sort of odd staring match. Sebastian looks like an animal ready to pounce on its prey, but no one else seems to notice.

The bell rings, marking an end to the oddest classroom experience I've had thus far.

"Now that you know of the Otherworld, I want you to start writing your stories," he announces as we gather our belongings to leave. "We'll draw names later this week and you'll start telling your stories next Monday."

The idea of public speaking already scares the crap out of me, but in this class, in front of Mandy and her Plastics, the idea seems unbearable.

"Can I please have my cards back?" I ask Mr. Jennings on my way out.

"You can retrieve them after detention," he says with a stern look on his face, practically pushing me out of the classroom and shutting the door behind me.

CHAPTER 5—DOOMED

I've never had a boyfriend, but I know what it feels like to be dumped by one. I've never been kissed, but I've experienced the lethargy that mono brings. And although suicide is never the solution, I know the pain of wanting to end it all. That's what I feel when I enter the cafeteria. Extremities of every high school experience. The sensory overload feels like the time I had two cavities and decided to chug down a banana Slurpee in under a minute.

Normally the cards help to block it all out, but today I'm out of luck.

"So, how much do you love me?" I'm relieved to hear Amina's voice as she grabs my arm—something she does daily—and leads me to our table.

"Heaps and heaps and heaps," I say, unable to stop myself from laughing at Amina's enthusiasm.

Amina and I have become fast friends. We eat lunch with Sebastian, so I never feel as out-of-place as I did on the first day.

"Because you love me and I you, I decided it was time for you to officially taste one of my world-famous sandwiches."

"Jewels, have you ever experienced food poisoning before?" Sebastian nudges his sister before appraising the lunch spread she's prepared.

"Shut up, Bastian." She scowls at him and smacks his hand. "If my food's so bad, why do you prefer it to Mum's?"

When Sebastian's around Amina, he's a totally different person. Open and playful. By himself, he's guarded and serious and all the girls throw themselves at him. I can feel the lust and angst when they're around him. It's annoying. Or maybe I'm just jealous.

Amina's sandwiches look like something Shaggy and Scooby would be proud of. "She makes all this stuff all by herself," Sebastian says casually, but it's obvious he's proud.

"Well, duh! She did say she made the sandwiches."

"No, I mean, she bakes the bread, grows the veggies when she can, and makes her own deli meats as well," he explains, trying not to smile as he prepares to take a bite out of one of the sandwiches. "The only thing she doesn't make is the Vegemite."

"He just smiled and gave me a Vegemite sandwich and he said," I start singing, thinking one of them will finish the song.

"Are you fifty, mate?" Amina laughs. "What teenager knows the words to that ancient Men at Work song?"

"Apparently the 16-year-old who knows I was singing a Men at Work song, mate," I say with a smile and a wink.

"Burn," Sebastian says between bites. "Good on ya, Jewels."

"Bij, Vegemite is an acquired taste, so there's none on yours," Amina says, placing a sandwich made of challah bread and all sorts of other delectables before me.

"This is amazing, Amina!" I say, after inhaling half of my sandwich. "How'd you learn how to make all this stuff?" I remember Gigi's words about my unladylike eating habits and chill for a moment.

"Trial and error," she says, taking some sort of dessert out of her bag. "I'm always stressed, and being in the kitchen soothes me."

"That's how I feel about my cards."

"Where are your cards anyway?" Amina asks with sincerity in her voice.

"Mr. Jennings took them from me in class this morning."

"And gave us after-school detention," Sebastian adds.

"For what?" Amina looks puzzled.

"Bijou challenged his theory on *A MidSummer Night's Dream*, so he seized her cards." As he speaks, he's looking at Amina as if I'm not there. "But Bijou wouldn't give them up willingly, and I defended her."

"Hey!" Kim joins our table and helps herself to Amina's spread, taking the other half of her sandwich.

"Oh, hey Kim," Amina says. "Why don't you take the other half of my sandwich. It's not like I was going to be eating it anyway."

Kim and Amina have this Lucy and Ethel thing going on, but sometimes I wonder if it isn't more of a Willow and Tara thing. Truth be told, I think they'd make a cute couple, but I don't want to assume anything.

"There's another girl missing," Kim says with her mouth full.

"Who's missing?" Sebastian asks, his voice serious and his eyes dark.

"Priya Kapoor. The girl who runs that *Spooksville* site about the strange things that happen in Sykesville."

"She's in my sixth-period Mythology class," Amina says as she begins to clear the table. "Mr. Jennings' class."

"Other girls have gone missing?" I ask.

"She's the sixth girl from Sykesville to go missing," Kim responds, finishing up the sandwich. "This one's better than the one you made last time.

Amina rolls her eyes, but Sebastian's face is serious. He's in full-on brooding mode.

"Were the other girls students here?" I ask, starting to feel a lot like one of the Scoobies with my questions.

"Three from Century High and now three from Liberty," Sebastian says, but his attention is somewhere else as he speaks.

"There's going to be a town hall meeting on Friday," Kim says. "I heard Mayor Parrish might announce a town curfew."

"Gotta go," Sebastian announces as he abruptly leaves the table.

Moments later, I see him running to catch up with Mandy and my heart plummets. Without him present, all the emotions begin to hit me once again. Whatever mantra he taught me earlier slips my mind.

I run out of the cafeteria without a word to Amina or Kim and head to the nurse's office.

Nurse Washington rocks. I tell her I have a migraine and she lets me sleep until the final bell rings. The tears probably help sell it, too. Her sympathy is so overwhelming that I end up hugging her after my nap.

All I can think about is Sebastian. How can he be friends with Mandy after all she's done to me? He's so hard to read. One minute, he's holding my hand, and the next he won't acknowledge my presence. *Are all boys this hot and cold?*

"Hey, Bijou!" Roland flags me down as I exit the office.

"Hey Ro-"

"Listen."

I roll my eyes, annoyed at the interruption. "It was really uncool for Jennings to call you out like that, so I found these in my locker and I want you to have them," he says, holding a full deck of cards out for me.

"Nah," I say, retracting my hand and putting it behind my back like a kid trying to avoid contracting cooties. I quickly realize how rude I'm being and try to make it sound better. "I'm on my way to detention now, so I'm about to get my cards back."

His green eyes are sad and I can feel his disappointment.

"It was sweet of you to think of me though," I say. "Wanna walk me to the library?"

His spirits instantly brighten as we begin to walk.

"So, there's this rave Friday night."

Boy, he's resilient.

"A rave?" I ask.

"Yeah, it's a party at Piney Run Park," he says scratching his head nervously. "The town elders are having a meeting about enforcing a curfew that night, so while they're plotting, we'll be partying."

I've never been to a party before. Not even as a kid. Who would invite me?

I think about saying no, but I don't want to explain how my grandmother is a freak show who pulled me out of P.E. just because it involved a pool so she definitely wouldn't let me go. So I fake it. I'll figure it out later.

"Sure! Why not?" I say, leaving him behind with a big goofy smile as I enter the library.

* * *

I walk into the library with my head held high. So what if Sebastian likes Mandy? I'm not going to let him think it bothers me because it doesn't.But why her?

The library is not what I imagined it to be. It isn't grand like the ones in New York or London. I can't get lost in it like I did at Bibliothèque Nationale de France. But this one is mine. For the first time, I will have a library card and there will be a record of my existence other than being a strangely familiar face to someone I may have seen some time ago.

I find Sebastian, engulfed in whatever's on the screen of a computer. His face is serious as he concentrates.

"Jennings was in here a few minutes ago." He looks up. His eyes still brooding. "He wants us to continue doing research for our stories. We're both up tomorrow."

Great, that's all I need: public speaking in a class where Mandy is present.

"Did he leave my cards with you?" I start to get anxious.

Sebastian shakes his head. "Listen with your ears and not your heart. Remember?"

"Thanks, but I'm okay right now." I sit down next to him, taking my notebook out.

"It's cool that you speak Arabic," he says, watching me with raised brows.

"I don't speak it.""Well, you did earlier and you just understood what I said." His thick brows furrow and he looks at me with renewed interest.

I have no idea what he's talking about, and I'm still too angry with him to care. "Sebastian, let's just work on our stories."

He sneaks a peek at me, then looks back at the computer.I try to sneak a peek at what has him so intrigued on the computer. He gives me a quizzical look and parts his lips as if he's about to speak, then clamps them shut.

"I don't know about you, but my I've written my story. I'm more interested in what's happening here in Sykesville."

"What is it?"

"This has happened before," he says, his attention back on the computer screen. "Almost seventeen years ago."

"What happened seventeen years ago?"

"The girls disappearing." He clicks on Priya's blog. "And seventeen years before that seven more girls disappeared and were never found."

"But only six girls are missing," I say, a chill coming over me as Sebastian scrolls through the photos of girls who were snatched away from their families.

"Which means there's one girl left," he says, his voice grim. "It looks like Priya has done a pretty good job with theories."

"Let me see," I say, grabbing the mouse from him. "According to Priya, all of the missing girls are Geminis, come from single family homes, and have some sort of psychological disorder. That's not much to go by. But why was she so invested in this?"

He clicks on the website's "About Me" section and we both read silently.

Priya's birthday is June 21st and she lives with her dad. She knew there was a possibility that she could be next. The website is comprised of post after post of strange happenings, even in between the seventeen years. Priya was obsessed with this stuff. Her writing is good, but her last posts read like the ramblings of a crazy person. She thought she was being followed and that members of the town council had been possessed and were somehow involved in the disappearances of the girls, which is why they were trying to downplay it.

"Man, I thought I was crazy, but I've got nothing on Priya. Maybe she'd been binging on too much *Supernatural,* because this 'Invasion of the Body Snatchers' theory is nuts."

"Priya takes Seroquel?" Sebastian says randomly, showing a selfie of the beautiful Priya Kapoor, with her long dark hair, big brown bloodshot eyes, a bindi on her forehead, a pill on her tongue, and a bottle of prescription meds in hand. "What's that?"

"It's used to treat bipolar disorder," he says.

It turns out Priya has been blogging about her mental health problems, too. It seems like over-sharing to me, but I feel guilty about calling her "crazy."

Sebastian seizes his mouse from me, motioning for me to use the computer before me. "Hey, what about the hooded guy you and Amina saw? Do you think he could have something to do with it?"

I hug myself, feeling for the holes caused by the scorch marks.

"What is it?" His gray eyes are cloudy and inquisitive.

"I saw him this morning, on my way to school."

"And?"

"He attacked me, but I don't know if what I saw is real." I pause to look at Sebastian, but his expression, as well as his emotions are lost to me. "I'd never seen his eyes until today. The pupils were red and elongated. Everything else was as yellow as sulfur and he smelled like rotten eggs."

I shut my eyes tight as if doing so will wipe my memory clean.

"Sulfur," Sebastian repeats.

"Yes. Yellow like sulfur."

"No. Sulphur smells like rotten eggs." His words are deliberate as if to emphasize a point.

There's silence as we both turn back to our computers. It's driving me crazy, not knowing what he's thinking, and for the first time ever, I want to know what someone else is feeling. What doesn't make sense is how much I want to tell him every little quirk I have, but he'll probably run. And who would blame him?

Sebastian changes the subject abruptly. "Don't you find Mr. Jennings' behavior odd?I mean, you clearly were having some sort of panic attack, and it's like he wanted you to lose it."

I'm not looking at him, but I feel his eyes piercing through me. "It wasn't a panic attack."

"Then what was it?" His insistence is annoying.

I still can't look at him. Why are we back to this?

"I can't be open with you if you can't be open with me, Jewels."

"Don't laugh. Okay?"

He holds his hand up, making a strange gesture.

"Is that the Star Trek thingy?" I ask, perplexed. "I'm not a Trekkie."

He laughs. "It means scout's honor, Jewels. With all the Buffy pop culture references, I would have thought that one was easy- peasy."

"Lemon squeezy," I respond, my face red from the fact that he's caught the Buffy reference and hoping he hasn't figured that my version of Willow is a stolen fabrication.

"When I'm around people, I believe that I can feel their emotions." I finally look at him, and he's no longer looking at the computer. His full attention is on me, and he's looking into my eyes as if he's in search of something lost.

"You mean, you're an empath, like Professor X and Jean Grey. What am I feeling right now?" he asks, taking my hand as if it will somehow amplify his emotions.

"It doesn't work on you," I say, still holding on to the warmth of his hand.

Disappointment etches across his face, making his cleft chin ever more pronounced.

"You're one of the Others, Sebastian."

He quickly retracts his hand and looks at me with so much scrutiny, I want to run out of the building and never come back.

"What does that mean?"

"Don't mind me. I'm crazy. I have the meds to prove it too." I say, turning in my seat, looking at Priya's site on my own computer. For some strange reason, I type Mr. Jennings' name into the search bar.

Sebastian has other plans. He pulls my seat in closer to his, making the wheels squeak and garnering a shh from the librarian. "Stop deflecting. What kind of pills are you taking and tell me what that means to be one of the Others."

His smoldering gray eyes meet mine and it's as if I'm spellbound and compelled to speak. I take out my days of the week pill pack and hand them over to him.

He picks one up, examining and sniffing it.

"Smells herbal. These aren't prescription. Where'd you get them from?"

"My grandmother knows about herbs and traditional medicine, so when I get sick, physically or mentally, she prefers the natural route to fix me."

He looks at me with confusion before replying. "So this grandmother of yours is a writer and an herbalist?"

he snorts. "And you just believe her and believe you need to be fixed? No questions asked?"

Even though Gigi annoys the hell out of me, she is my grandmother and the only person who's ever had my back. How dare he question her intentions? I find myself growing increasingly angry, but truthfully, I'm not sure if the anger is directed at Sebastian, Gigi, or myself. Regardless, he isn't going to let this go.

"Fine. Look, for me, there are generally two types of people in this world: the Typicals, whose feelings can't be hidden from me, and then there are the Others, like you. I can't feel anything from the Others, which should be a relief because the emotions make me go crazy. But with the Others, even though I don't feel anything, my instincts usually tell me to run." He flinches as though he's just been stung.

"But it's different with you," I assure him, reaching for his hand. "I don't want to stay away."

"You said there are generally two types of people," he says this, ignoring my not-so-subtle come on. "So do you meet people that don't fit into either group?"

"Well yeah, like Amina." His brows furrow and he parts his lips to speak, but I continue speaking instead. "She's different. I can feel what she feels, although it's not overwhelming."

"That can't be right. Amina and I are twins, so whatever you see in me should be the same with her, right?"

"I don't know what to tell you. That's what I see and feel," I say with a shrug. "I don't know if it's right or wrong, but that's what it is."

There's an awkward silence between us as he allows me to roll my chair back to its rightful place. What is he thinking? Probably that I'm crazy and he should have let Mandy drown me. "I believe you, you know?" he says.

I quickly turn, hoping I'm not hearing things.

"The other day, in the office, when we first touched, you saw something, didn't you?"

I nod.

"I saw it too. Someone drowning," he says with eyes so sincere.

"And then Mandy tried to drown me." I look away from him, unsure of what he's feeling or what's going through his mind.

"The same thing happened with Amina, right? She mentioned something about a vision."

He's asking too many questions now, but what did I expect when I told him I can feel the emotions of others? "We saw my cards flying. That's all."

"The cards help silence the emotions, don't they?"

I nod anxiously, a tear leaving my eye. I lift my hand to wipe it away, but Sebastian beats me to it, letting his warm hand linger on my cheek. I close my eyes as if to somehow record this feeling, this moment into my memory.

"There's more. Earlier, when the man attacked me,—" I don't know how to verbalize it, so I show him the finger-sized burns in my jacket as well as my scorched skin.

As if right on cue, the room begins to swelter and I look around for the hooded man. Besides the librarian, there are maybe two other people in the library and they are nowhere near us. The heat is coming from Sebastian.

"You don't think you should have come into the building running and screaming?" His voice is low but angry.

"Well, there wasn't exactly any evidence of a man chasing me, and besides, what was I going to tell them? 'His hands were so hot they burned a hole through my clothes'?" He looks angry. "I'm not trying to end up in a mental institution."

"You're not walking to school anymore." He says it as a proclamation and not a suggestion.

I laugh and back away, turning my chair back to the computer.

"More research and less talking," the librarian says, prompting us to focus on the computer screens.

"I'm serious, Jewels. I know what I'm saying. It's not safe."

"You know absolutely nothing, and you don't tell me what to do."

Who does this boy think he is?

"I know that you're sheltered. I know that it's probably just been you and your grandmother your entire life, so you insert bits and pieces from television shows into your life and make up stuff about your best friend Willow to make yourself seem more interesting." I'm embarrassed and angry at his audacity all at once. "But you're the most interesting person I've ever met. I just want you to be safe."

I'm not sure if I should run away in shame, yell at him, or be blushing, but just as I'm about to speak, something on my screen catches my eye.

"Sykesville is a town of secrets, run by those who ensure that the strange occurrences aren't brought to light. 17 years ago, seven 16-year old girls from Liberty High School went missing and were never found. The town made it seem like they ran away. They weren't friends. They were barely acquaintances. The only thing they had in common were the fact that their birthdays were on or around June 21st, the summer solstice. Now, nearly 17 years later, it's happening again, and I'm not going to let it go unnoticed."

"My birthday is on June 21st," I say, pointing at the screen. For the first time since meeting Sebastian, I am utterly cold. "I could be the seventh girl."

"Amina and I will bring you to school and take you home from now on." He looks at me like a parent looks at an insolent child.

"I'm not a fragile thing, you know," I respond as I continue to deflect my focus to what's on the computer screen. "People always think they know what's best for me when they have no idea who I am or what I'm capable of."

"Whether you're fragile or not, everyone needs someone watching their back."

"Check this out," I say, disregarding his declaration, but definitely willing to take him up on it. "The summer solstice is the longest day of the year, and it says it's the biggest in-between. Whatever that means."

"Oy. There's a site about in-betweens," he says, turning his screen towards himself and away from me as I try to see for myself. "There are many instances and stories of humans entering the Otherworld and vice versa, but in reality, there are only specific times and places when this can occur—known as in-between times and places. They are the most unstable, like equinoxes , dawn, the turning of the seasons, birth, marriage, and death. Each of these times represents a major change in life. For example, midnight is neither one day nor another, and the seashore is neither sea nor shore. Where one thing stops for another to begin."

"Summer solstice is an in-between, isn't it Sebastian?"

He looks at me. His eyes are dark and sad all at once, as if in silent warning, but he says nothing.

My heart sinks as the painful realization that I may be next to disappear begins to take shape in my mind.

"Detention is over." Mr. Jenning's voice destroys the moment, bringing us back to reality. "Ms. Fitzroy, your grandmother is here waiting for you."

"Oh no! You called her?" Gigi is going to murder me. If she lost it over me taking a required course, imagine what she'll do about my insubordination.

"I didn't call her. You, my dear, didn't call her to tell her you'd be late, hence the explosion in the office." Mr. Jennings looks like he's in a rush to leave as he drops my cards on the table. "I hope you two are ready to present tomorrow."

Without awaiting our responses, Mr. Jennings rushes out of the library.

"I don't have a cellphone. I couldn't have called her even if I had wanted to."

"Do me a favor, Jewels," Sebastian says as we make our way out of the library.

"What's the favor?"

"Stop taking those pills." He stops me and holds my hand as he says this. "I'll explain later, but please do as I say."

I stare into his gray eyes and nod, not only because I can't shake the feeling that Sebastian knows a lot more about the missing girls, the Otherworld, and what's going on with me than he's saying, but because, if I wasn't sure before today, I am completely in love with Sebastian Sinjin.

CHAPTER 6—SEBASTIAN

There are people who enter a room and command it by their mere presence. That would be Gigi, if only she'd simply enter a room and keep her mouth shut. With all the class she claims to possess, she has the temperament of a bulldog.

We peer into the glass doors that lead into the front office to see Gigi draped in Gucci, with black Louboutins that make her look like she's seven feet tall.

"Who are you? The secretary? You are an incompetent little thing, aren't you?" The thing about Gigi is that she doesn't have to scream at you to make you feel insignificant. Her tone is leveled, but there's an icy edge to it as she interrogates Mrs. Reaper, while Mr. Jennings finds his way to the woman, who almost looks like she's shrinking by the second. "Isn't it your job to alert a parent if their child won't be making it home on time?"

"Mrs. Fitzroy, I'm Mr. Jennings, Bijou's homeroom and first-period teacher. I'm the one responsible for Bijou staying after school." His voice is diplomatic as he smiles at her. "She did nothing wrong. I just wanted her to work on her presentation with Mr. Sinjin and there wasn't enough time in class."

Why is he covering for me? One minute, he's going off on me for no reason and now he has my back? It doesn't make sense.

I turn to look at Sebastian who is so stiff as though he's paralyzed from shock.

"That's your grandmother?" He manages to ask as I notice the students and teachers that are lingering around to watch the fiercely beautiful and frightening Lilith Fitzroy terrorize the administration.

"Uh huh."

"You insignificant little man," she addresses Mr. Jennings. "What gives you the right to keep my granddaughter here without consulting me first?"

The shock that hits me comes from Mr. Jennings and everyone else that has gathered, which unfortunately includes Mandy and the rest of the cheerleaders, the baseball and softball teams, Amina and some others.

"I can understand your fear, especially with all the missing girls." Mrs. Reaper says. She should have scurried away when Mr. Jennings showed up and took the heat off her, but her little admission has turned an angry Gigi into an irrational witch.

From English to French and back to English again, the expletives that escape Gigi's mouth make the jaws of everyone in earshot drop, whether they understand or not. After her rant and threats to sue Mr. Jennings, Liberty High, and the Carroll County Public School Board, she flies out of the office like a bat out of hell. She stops before me and is about to chastise me, but her eyes fall on Sebastian and she's completely speechless.

With eyes wide, she stares at him as though any sudden movement will cause some catastrophe. Sebastian looks at her with pure disdain, his shoulders broaden and I come to realize how massive Sebastian truly is. It looks like Xena is about to attack Hercules. His golden skin in stark contrast to her porcelain complexion, but both shine brightly in the school's lobby in an intimidating fashion.

"Gigi," I call to her, breaking the trance.

"Allez! Dépêche-toi!" she says, strutting out of the building as if nothing weird has just occurred.

* * *

The ride home is nothing but warnings to behave myself at home and school and to stay away from the boy with the ponytail because he looks like trouble. At home, I eat my dinner in haste, anxious to do more research. I do everything to appease Gigi, even though, while at school, she made sure to have my schedule changed, so instead of swimming last period, I am now registered for weight training. I smile, say thank you, and pretend to take my pills before leaving the table for my room.

Because I'm not allowed to have a computer of my own, I wait for Gigi to go into her study before stealing her laptop from her bedroom.

I need to know more. Why are girls with my birthday and mental health issues disappearing from this town? It can't be a coincidence that we moved here now. *Can it?*

I revisit Priya's site to search for info on in-betweens but don't find what Sebastian was reading. It isn't there at all. Instead, I exit the website and scour the web for info on in-betweens. I don't find what he read either, but there are things about in-betweens, so he wasn't wrong, but I'm beginning to think he wasn't reading at all, because he never typed in those words. He was only using his mouse. Was Sebastian already privy to this information?

I shake my head, unsure if I'm ready for the conclusion I will draw if I continue this line of questioning. On a whim, I type "djinn" into the search bar. After pages of colorful Wikipedia pages and fanfiction about Aladdin and magic lamps, I change my search to "djinn+otherworld+inbetween" and stumble upon a website entitled "Concealed Things and Where to Find Them."

"Not all djinn are made of smokeless fire." That one line catches my attention. The hooded man, who burned me, and Sebastian both felt like they had fire running through their veins in place of blood.

"In-between times and places are the gateways to power and the supernatural world; thus, the human world is more susceptible to the beings of the Otherworld at these times and places. This is a good thing for the djinn, but not for the humans because they sometimes slip through accidentally or may even be lured in by some of the less-than-friendly inhabitants of this hidden world. All djinn have the ability to manipulate their element, and each has different kinds of powers, shapeshifting being the most common."

It's hard to take some of this stuff seriously, especially when many of the people telling these stories look like they're the offspring of Uncle Daddy and Auntie Mommy, but the site is detailed with full names, locations, exact dates of disappearances and theories of what may have happened. There are images and video footage that I'm sure are all doctored, but I click on a link that reads *Prophecy* and my skepticism subsides.

"When the day lingers longer than it is intended to stay and before the earth has completely spun, a child will come forth, stealing powers meant for the sun. To one from here and one from there, it shall be born and shall be lost but impossible to stay hidden. For it is impossible to dim the light from the sun."

What does that even mean?

Something Sebastian mentioned comes to mind. The summer solstice is the longest day of the year. It's the only day that lingers longer than the others. All of the missing girls were born on or near the solstice.

I continue through the page. It's a bunch of riddles that are nearly impossible to decipher, but it lists a few book titles and the name of a bookstore on Main Street in Sykesville, A Likely Story.

I close the tab to be greeted by tabs left open by Gigi. Youssra Bellaz, Katerina Harasemchuk, Lee Sang Hyun, Emily Patterson, Leila Wolf, Priya Kapoor. How can the names of the missing girls be on Gigi's laptop when she supposedly just learned about them after school today?

She hasn't used her laptop since we've been home, which means she knew about them before Mrs. Reaper said anything.

The hairs on the back of my neck rise as I read the details of each disappearance. The similarities between me and the girls. Dead parents and being raised by one family member. Mental health issues. June 20th and June 21st birthdays.

Sykesville is a hotbed for supernatural activity and then it hits me, Sykesville itself is an in-between. Sykesville and Eldersburg are neither here nor there. Did Gigi not do the research before buying a home in a town that was now looking like the gateway to hell? Or was moving here just fuel for her creative fire?

Gigi, please don't tell me you moved us here to exploit the disappearances of these girls for the sake of a good story to write about.

As I lie in bed, I can't help but think back to what happened in the pool, as well as Sebastian's ever-changing behavior and the heat he exudes.

I ponder the subject for a while until I drift into a dream that I haven't had in awhile. A dream about the water.

I am on the beach alone, but this time I'm not afraid. The sand is white and hot, the sun slowly beginning to kiss the horizon. As I walk toward the water, the sky begins to change, as does the mood. The full moon instantaneously replaces the sun, making the ocean glisten and the beach brighter and more beautiful than before.

I can't take my eyes off the water. There is no fear when it calls to me. This time I am intrigued. I don't bother removing the white, cotton dress I am wearing. As I begin to walk forward, I feel like someone is watching, then I realize that he is by my side. He quickly grasps my hand as if he is afraid of something, but I'm not. We walk together into the water, splashing around until we hear animals in the distance going wild.

I look at him, realizing that his face still isn't visible. I reach for his face, but he dodges my touch. Once again, the feeling of being watched returns. He holds my hand tighter, and we begin to run further into the ocean. Something jumps in the water after us. He utters the words "Don't let go" as we go under and begin swimming deeper. He holds onto me tightly as we get closer and closer to the ocean floor. I look over to him and can see that he is not as comfortable as I am underwater. He is terrified. I begin leading him to the surface. When we finally emerge, he says the same words to me, "Don't let go," as if he knows something is going to happen. Slowly, his face becomes clear. It's Sebastian!

Just when I am about to speak, something begins pulling him away. I hold onto him as if I am hanging on to my own life. He never screams, but fear is evident on his beautiful face. Whatever holds him is extremely strong because I am losing my grip fast. Suddenly, I see a pair of familiar eyes, but they are different somehow. Almost malevolent. It's Gigi, pulling him away from me. My hand flies over my mouth in shock, letting go of Sebastian, and he disappears.

I wake up screaming into my pillow. *What is happening to me?* I have never been able to see the boy's face in my dreams. How can the boy be Sebastian? *Well, I thought about him so much when I was awake that he probably followed me into my subconscious*, I think to myself nervously.

The gray cat jumps into my bed and I sit up, extremely alert. It keeps coming back, and I don't mind the company. Feeling a sudden chill, I decide to check my window, knowing I had shut it earlier. Like I guessed, it's closed. As I peer out of the window, I sense a presence, something or someone watching, waiting. For a moment, I can swear I see a figure standing between the trees, but as I look more intently, I see nothing more than shadows.

The images from my dream flash in my mind as my subconscious tells me I should be afraid. I yearn for sleep once more—only to be able to see Sebastian's face—but fear of the one who took him away from me forbids sleep to return.

* * *

As promised, Sebastian and Amina are waiting for me a few houses down when I begin my walk to school. The conversation in the car is light, with talks about the rave and Sebastian's eclectic taste in music.

"Bastian, how about this?" Amina giggles as Sebastian blocks her from changing his favorite song. "We'll take turns. Today, you can have your Paul Kelly, I'll have the next day, and then Bijou can have the day after that."

Sebastian ignores Amina, turns the music up and begins singing at the top of his lungs, "In the middle, in the middle, in the middle of a dream. I've lost my shirt, I've pawned my rings. I've done all the dumb things."

"Seriously, Bastian?"

He taunts her, smiling widely and pinching her cheek. "I threw my hat into the ring," he continues singing.

Amina is annoyed, but soon enough, she joins him in singing, "I've melted wax to fix my wings."

* * *

First-period brings new fear as I now remember the homework I forgot to do. Sebastian shakes his head and mumbles an expletive. Clearly, he's forgotten as well, but Mr. Jennings calls his name and he doesn't protest. I sit in the back of the class in a last ditch effort to not fail or get another detention. "When the day lingers longer than it is intended to stay and before the earth has completely spun, a child will come forth, stealing powers meant for the sun. To one from here and one from there, it shall be born and shall be lost but impossible to stay hidden. For it is impossible to dim the light from the sun."

My heart nearly stops when Sebastian begins to speak. That quote was on the website. Sebastian is speaking without the help of a book, phone, tablet, or paper. He's speaking from memory.

"This was the prophecy that the Oracle of the Otherworld foretold, sending the djinn into reproductive frenzy. No one truly understood what this meant, but it didn't stop them from guessing. The djinn are divided into elemental groups of earth, wind, fire, and water, so it was popular belief that the 'here and there' of the prophecy meant that the child would be born of two different elemental groups. This mixing of elemental groups was a rare occurrence because the outcome was always unknown and potentially dangerous. But this new prophecy changed that, producing all types of creatures. Some were extremely powerful, some considerably weak, while others were born mortal.

"For some, the birth of this child was thought to be a blessing, but to others, the child's birth was a threat. Many wanted the life destroyed before it could ever live. Fear of the unknown was too strong to be overlooked, even if this child could bring an age of peace never before seen in the history of any world. A child so divine that its beauty would be both feared and unmatched."

Sebastian's delivery never falters. This isn't the tale of someone unprepared. This is a story he knows and knows quite well. He's looking at Mr. Jennings as he speaks as if in defiance or as if they're fighting some silent war that none of us are privy to.

"So many questions arose concerning what the child's powers might be, but the Oracle said nothing except that the child would have abilities beyond comprehension, making the child an outcast.

"The king and queen of this world were known to be the oldest of all the djinn. With age came great power. The female was the most powerful of all Mami Wata, and the male was the most powerful djinn of all. They were the ruling monarchs over all the Otherworld.

"The king had the ability to possess the bodies of others—a task no other known djinn could achieve. Like water, the queen was dual-natured, possessing the ability to grant wishes—giving people bottomless wealth and luck—but also possessing the ability to be frightfully vindictive and evil. The one thing these two had in common was that they both kept their true gifts secret.

"Everyone assumed that this child would be the offspring of these two beings. So, they were married. Years passed and no offspring were produced. Centuries passed. Nothing. People were beginning to doubt the prophecy or their ability to produce this child. Until one day, the queen announced she was pregnant. The beings of the Otherworld were euphoric, showering her with gifts and surrounding her at all hours. The vain and materialistic queen revelled in the attention.

"When the baby was finally born, the Oracle was brought in to see the child, but she soon realized this wasn't the prophesied child. The baby was not the king's spawn. When the queen hadn't been able to conceive a child for the king, she became desperate and went to the vilest djinn, Zina, for help. Zina was powerful, known for feasting on the blood of humans and djinn alike, and feared by many. He agreed to father the queen's child and let her pass the child off as the king's spawn, but at a cost. Some even believed him to be more powerful than the king, so the queen thought that the prophesied child could be born of this union. The king was outraged and left his wife at once, his anger spreading across the realm. He wanted nothing more to do with her after her betrayal and the failure of their experiment. The queen, on the other hand, was in love with him, and was devastated. She felt that if she couldn't fulfill the prophecy with the king, then she would allow no one else to fulfill it. She became vengeful and hell-bent on killing newborn babies so they wouldn't have the chance to fulfill the prophecy.

"She killed both human and djinn babies alike, encouraged her elemental counterparts to lure men to their watery deaths, and urged the switching of human babies for djinn babies, because if she couldn't fulfill the prophecy, she didn't want anyone else to either. It was chaos."

Sebastian shudders noticeably and is about to continue when Mr. Jennings interrupts, "That's enough, Mr. Sinjin. Take your seat."

Mr. Jennings' anger is palpable and unexplainable. Maybe he's read the prophecy quote from "Concealed Things and Where to Find Them" as well and is angry at Sebastian's plagiarism.

Sebastian salutes him with a smirk as he takes his seat, leaving the entire class confused.

CHAPTER 7—STORYTELLER

Sebastian's story and behavior leave me with no time to concoct my own story, so when Mr. Jennings calls my name, I panic, wracking my brain for ideas. "Good luck, Jewels," he says.

I head for a fidgeting Mr. Jennings. Once again, he's looking a little worn around the edges. Maybe he's sick or something.

I think hard and decide to use Gigi to my advantage.

"Mr. Jennings, the cards actually help with my anxiety. My grandmother insists on me using them to keep the panic attacks at bay," I say with puppy dog eyes.

He nods, giving me permission.

I face the class, close my eyes, and begin to shuffle, soon noticing that one of my cards is missing. I shuffle nonetheless, allowing my memories and imagination to take over, and one of my dreams comes to mind.

I clear my throat and the words begin to flow.

"It was nearly the end of June, during the worst part of the infamous rainy season. It was a time when nature made all things possible. During this season, the rain washed away the negativity and brought a fresh start. But it was no secret that along with the beautiful greenery and the elaborate array of exotic flowers came unexplained phenomena. "The rainy season is a time of growth, and the people of the villages knew that along with new plants and wildlife came mysterious creatures...creatures as old as time, whose presence most would like to forget. There were always disappearances and mysteries this time of year that were never solved.

"This particular year, all the disappearances were of women of childbearing age and infants. The townspeople were in a state of panic and confusion, unsure of how to protect their families, or if it was even possible to do so.

"There was an enormous amount of pressure placed on the town's leader, Chief Musa, so he went for a walk in the vast forest to consider his options. He was so caught up in his own thoughts that he didn't notice that he had been followed.

"A voice said, 'Do you always talk to yourself when no one's present?'

"Chief Musa's heart almost stopped when he heard the voice, but when he saw the face of his beautiful, doe-eyed daughter, all of his worries went away, and he embraced her.

"Chief Musa's sad, brown eyes always had a twinkle in them as he looked at his daughter. He was known for being a strong and stern man, but his daughter, Femeni, had the power to melt his heart. Whenever he'd look at her, he would see the face of his deceased wife and couldn't bear to look away. 'I'm just thinking out loud, Princess,' he said. 'Now it's time for me to ask the questions. Didn't I tell you it's not safe to come into the forest alone?' He grimaced as he looked at his very pregnant daughter. "It is no longer safe here."

"Biting her lip, Femeni tried to fight back a smile and to avoid eye contact with her father. 'Well, technically I'm not alone,' she argued, putting her hands gently on her belly; she was due any day now. 'I wanted to talk to you in private, so when I saw you leave, I followed you.'

"The chief sat on the ground and motioned Femeni to sit beside him. She stubbornly shook her head from left to right and her endless cascade of wild hair moved fiercely with the wind. Her hair was long, thick, as dark as night, and it spilled onto her luminous, copper skin. She pointed to her flowing, white linen dress, a symbol of her marriage status and said nothing. He stared at his daughter for a moment, amazed that his once mischievous child was now a married woman, well on her way to motherhood.

"Ah, I forget. You can't sit while wearing white," he said.

"The chief was happy that his daughter had found a man whom she loved dearly, even though he was foreign to their land. Many people were against Femeni's marriage to Alieu because no one knew of his origins.

"Although the chief was known to be the wealthiest man in the village, Alieu had arrived at their village with unimaginable riches. His skin was fair, in contrast to many of the inhabitants of the land. He had green eyes that sparkled like emeralds, hair so black that it appeared blue in the scorching African sun, and an accent that was unfamiliar to the locals and all of the foreign merchants who frequently came to trade or do business in their land. He was almost too perfect and beautiful to be human, and that generated much speculation about him."

"You so did not write this story," Mandy interrupts.

I can't decide whether to ignore her or defend myself. Why would I plagiarize a story and recite it when I would probably be caught?

Mandy looks angry, but why? I can feel it.

"Be quiet, Ms. DeVoe!" Mr. Jennings sounds more angry than I am. "You may continue, Ms. Fitzroy."

Mr. Jennings' face conveys no emotion, and, even though he defended me against Mandy, he doesn't smile at me. Instead, he looks like he's deep in thought.

"Alieu and Femeni seemed to be a perfect match," I continue. "She had turned down suitors who had come from distant lands to ask for her hand in marriage. Her beauty was revered for its ethereal qualities that could convert the most eloquent man into a blubbering idiot. Femeni knew the strength of her beauty as well. When she met Alieu, she fell in love with his charm, and they were married in a month's time.

"Many of the village elders were suspicious and blamed him for the strange happenings, even though they had no proof. Although disappearances were common during this time of year, other mysteries were also becoming more ubiquitous. Occasionally, some of the missing people would turn up with no recollection of their time away. Many children were behaving as if they weren't themselves, people were seeing strange and unspeakable things, and there was unnecessary bloodshed. Soon war had spread throughout the country and it was no longer safe.

'What would you like to speak to me about?' Chief Musa asked his daughter.

"When he looked up at her face, there was an apprehensive edge to it. She dodged her father's glare and bit her bottom lip.

'Is there something bothering you, child?' he asked. The concern in his voice was rapidly becoming fear.

"Whenever Femeni was upset, everything about her would change. Her mystifying beauty became threatening, something to fear rather than admire. Her wrath was a force to be reckoned with. When things didn't go her way, she would throw terrible outbursts until the situation favored her expectations. But this time, she looked defeated.

"'Papa, I think something is wrong with me,' she began as tears escaped her slanted eyes and stained her face.

"'Is there something wrong with the baby?'

"'The baby is fine,' she answered.

"The chief was still worried but did not wear the expression on his face.

"'Something has been happening to me nightly.' Femeni lifted her long, luminous, black hair to expose her neck and shoulders to her father. They were covered in deep scratches and bruises. It was gruesome.

"'I'll kill him!' he almost growled, jumping to his feet.

"'No, Papa, it wasn't Alieu.'

"'Well then, who did this to you?' he asked. He started to reach for his daughter, but recoiled.

"Femeni was about to speak when her father placed a single finger against his lips, signaling her to keep quiet. The chief stood and pulled her along.

"She followed her father deeper into the forest. When they finally stopped, she realized that she had been taken to the Great Tree.

"Femeni took a few cautious steps around the familiar tree, wondering why she had been brought here. She knew that the tree served as the site for gatherings of importance. It was the tallest and oldest tree in the forest, and the space surrounding the tree was like no other. Not only did the tree provide shade from the sun's smoldering rays, but many of the elders believed that the spirits of their ancestors resided in this tree, listening to the petitions of those in need, and sometimes—if you were lucky enough—the spirits would appear to you in animal form. So people often left food under the tree as an offering to the spirits.

"'Do you know the importance of this tree, Princess?' the chief asked his daughter in a coarse, but forceful, tone.

"'Of course,' Femeni grumbled, annoyed by her father's riddles at a time like this.

"The chief stood still. His dark eyes were miles away now. 'Have I ever told you that this was the site of your birth?'

"This caught Femeni's interest. With all of her father's never-ending stories, this was one she had yet to hear.

"'This tree is sacred. It offers protection from any being—human or other—which may wish you harm.' Chief Musa put his hands in his hair in anxiety, still not focusing his eyes on Femeni. 'It's the only place in the entire forest where no harm can come to you, especially on a day like today—the solstice.'

"Puzzled, she stared intently at the far-away expression on her father's worn face. She suddenly began to understand his reasoning, and fear slowly began to creep up her spine.

"'Now you can tell me everything,' he exhaled, finally focusing his eyes on his daughter.

"She frowned, touching her protruding belly. 'Every night, since the rain began, I've been having the same dream. I'm running through the forest, and there's something after me.' She paused briefly, wrapping her arms around herself as if she were cold and reliving the dream as she spoke. 'Suddenly, I'm approaching the beach. They're almost catching up with me, and I'm running as fast as I can. Something grabs my leg, and I fall down. They're attacking me, and I can't stop them. Their scratches are burning. Then I hear a voice coming from the ocean; the voice is telling me to jump in, so I do.'

"She paused again as if to catch her breath. 'The water seems to soothe my cuts, but then I notice that I'm sinking to the ocean floor. I finally find the face attached to the voice that invited me in; she's beautiful with hair almost like mine and wearing a dark pendant resembling an eye. Her skin is darker than Alieu's but shimmers just as bright. She has dark, hypnotizing eyes, but I can't see her legs. She wants to help me, but then a menacing voice begins to pierce my ears, and she panics, trying to push me to the surface, but something keeps grabbing me from below. When I finally awaken, my hair is wet as if I had really been swimming.' Femeni raised her hands to cover her face and began to shiver fiercely.

"Chief Musa held his daughter as she wept in his arms. He was at a loss for words. He felt so helpless. 'Maybe you scratched yourself in your sleep, and your hair was wet from sweat.' He paused briefly and then continued, 'I mean, the description of the woman you just gave me is that of your mother; it was just a bad dream.' Even as the words left his lips, he knew this was not the case.

"Femeni became stiff in her father's grasp. Her hands were clenched into fists, and she pushed him away. Her smooth, copper-toned face contorted as she shook her head in denial and disgust. 'You know I couldn't have given you a detailed description of a woman I've never seen. She died right here under your precious tree giving birth to me. I wish she would have taken me with her.' Without giving him a chance to reply, Femeni turned away from her stunned father and ran, not knowing where her feet would take her.

"Eventually, Femeni stopped running and wrapped her arms around her belly as if to ask the baby if it was okay. She suddenly gasped, noticing a bright light further ahead.

"'Am I seeing things?' she asked herself.

"She was bewildered because she had grown up exploring this forest, but this was a sight she had never seen before. The sky suddenly darkened, but off in the distance was what looked like a pool of diamonds. She squeezed her eyes tightly shut, hoping that when they reopened she would be able to make sense of the situation, but the vision never changed. Femeni moved closer to the blinding sight. The colors became so vivid and clear. It was a lagoon. "Surely no one knew of this lagoon. The area was untarnished as if it had never been touched by the tainted hands of mankind. It was like nothing the human mind could ever dream of, home to overgrown plants and nameless colors. Femeni knew she had never been there before, but something about the place seemed vaguely familiar. She slid out of her cotton dress and got into the crystal-clear water. Femeni had always felt an unexplainable pull toward water but was never allowed to embrace it. She was always told to stay away from water—without any explanation—which only prompted her to slip out to the river when no one was watching. She could swim as fast as the fish, and like the fish, she could swim underwater for long periods of time without emerging for air."

As I tell the story, I begin to realize how similar the story of Femeni is to my life. *Oh, the power of words.* I probably would never have made this connection had I not spoken the words myself. Maybe I have based the character of Femeni on myself.

Noticing how impatient my audience is growing, I continue with my story.

"The water was a refreshing escape from the thoughts that had previously boggled her mind. In fact, Femeni had never felt so carefree and unrestricted as she swam alongside colorful tropical fish and friendly bottlenose dolphins. The dolphins were the most enchanting subjects in the lagoon. The glow of their white bodies underneath the water was breathtakingly beautiful. As time eluded her, she watched while the dolphins played—jumping and peeking out of the water.

"While she was being entertained by her new aquatic playmates, a captivating, harmonious sound broke her concentration. It was singing coming from near the coral reef. She did not understand the language, but the sound was alluring and pulled her closer.

"Following the voices, she found three beautiful women singing playfully. Femeni couldn't help but notice the similarities between her and the three women— the unnaturally long hair, although theirs were lighter hues than her own; the lighter than normal skin, although they were different complexions; and the captivating eyes that forbid you from looking away.

"Something about the women drew her closer, compelling her to embrace her belly as if to reassure the baby that everything would be okay. The minute she touched her protruding belly, the baby began to kick as if in warning. That did not stop Femeni from moving forward; she could not tear her gaze away from the three intriguing women.

"Suddenly something was pulling her from below. She fought, but it was no use. Whatever was pulling her was unnaturally strong. She sank below the surface and was paralyzed as she laid eyes on the culprit. It was the beautiful, dark-haired woman wearing the pendant, the woman from her dreams—the one who tried to protect her.

"She pulled Femeni along, trying to lead her away from the deception of the three others. For a while, they seemed safe until one of the women appeared before them. Femeni noticed something that she hadn't noticed before. They all had sapphire tails instead of legs. She knew instantly what they were, but fear prevented her from acknowledging it.

"Terror and alarm rose in her chest, but she did not fear the dark-haired beauty; it was the fair-haired ones she feared as she faced them. The moment Femeni and her companion tried to get away, the other two women appeared at their sides, stopping any further movement. Suddenly, an intense pain gripped her abdomen. At that moment, she knew the baby was on its way.

"Femeni could not fight because the pain was crippling. She was no help to her protector who had been bound by the other two. The pale-haired woman who seemed to be in charge violently pulled Femeni to shore. Everything went dark as she fought hard to stay conscious. It was a battle that she could not win.

"When Femeni awoke, she found herself under the Great Tree. 'It was only a dream,' she thought to herself. There was just a dull pain. She sighed, lifting her hand to find the pendant that she thought only existed in dreams. She quickly sat up, reaching to embrace her belly for reassurance, suddenly realizing what had actually happened. For the first time in nine months, she was completely and utterly alone. The one thing that had brought her comfort in times of chaos had been taken from her.

"She screamed. The villagers came and surrounded her. When she explained her ordeal, no one understood what happened. The villagers couldn't tell if she had gone mad or if she were speaking the truth. A search party was sent by Chief Musa to look for the newborn baby. In the midst of the confusion, one question circulated amongst the villagers, 'Where was Alieu?'

"Femeni slowly began to slip into darkness. The last words leaving her lips were, 'As long as I still have life in me, I will never stop searching for my child.'"

As my story comes to an end, I continue shuffling my cards, unwilling to face their feelings as I notice a plethora of facial expressions. "That was creepy," I hear someone whisper from the back. I look to Mr. Jennings to see what he thinks, but he doesn't look at me; his facial expression is indecipherable.

Sebastian looks pale. He looks at me as if he is seeing something new, and rushes out of the classroom.

"I thought that was excellent," Kim finally announces, prompting others to give their opinions.

"But I feel like it's incomplete," Roland chimes in. "I want to know what happened to the baby. Did it die?"

"That would have been a happy ending," Mandy says. My confidence is slowly dwindling. The bell suddenly rings, almost startling me into a heart attack. Mr. Jennings doesn't say anything to the class. No assignments, no farewells, nothing.

"What a horrible story," Mandy says. Her pinched face fights to expand as she tries to smile. Her face is as tight as a forty-five-year-old divorcee who gets weekly Botox injections.

"You shouldn't smile so hard, Mandy. Your face might crack."

I try to walk past her, but she puts a hand up in resistance. The hand is light, but a sharp pain sears through my chest as if her slight touch is a massive punch. She wears a smile, but there is something disturbing about it that makes me step back.

"You know, I always felt like your name doesn't suit you." She stops to read my reaction. "I've always had this theory about names. Everyone is born with a true name, and if you spend your life with the wrong name, then you're eternally lost. Don't you agree?"

"What does that have to do with anything?" I ask, confused by the randomness of it all.

"Just food for thought."

"Ms. Fitzroy, I would like to speak with you briefly," Mr. Jennings announces, still not looking at me.

I stand as Mr. Jennings still sits uncomfortably on the black couch. Tension fills the air as I wait for him to say something. The late bell rings, and he finally speaks.

"Don't worry. I'll write you a pass for your next class."

I nod in acknowledgment and wait for him to begin. *Did he think it was that bad?*

"Bijou, I'm going to ask you one time and one time only. Where did you hear that story?" His voice is accusing.

I am appalled. He actually thinks I stole someone else's story, trying to pass it off as my own?

"It's my story."

"I find that hard to believe. I know that story."

Let me rephrase that. I am beyond appalled. I am angry.

"It's my story," I say slowly through compressed teeth. "It's a dream I had a long time ago."

He finally looks in my direction, studying my face while avoiding eye contact. "If you say that the story is yours, then I have no choice but to believe you." He starts to smile in an attempt to lighten the mood. It is forced and inauthentic.

He is studying me.

"You're incredible." His voice is barely audible, but I hear him clearly. I'm not quite sure I understand the look on his face. His eyes are glassy, and he looks as though he wants to smile, but his jaw tenses, and he closes his mouth instead.

Why does he look like he's fighting back tears?

I stand there staring at Mr. Jennings for a long period of time as if willing him to look me in the eye again. His eyes lock onto mine, and I hold his gaze; he is transfixed. As we stand face to face—staring at each other—I feel as if I am in control until his face transforms into a blur. I'm not sure if it is real or not. As I look harder, the face begins to unveil itself. It contorts into an evil grimace, giving him a fiendish appearance. The pupils of his once pleasant, brown eyes are vertical, red slits; his brass skin is as white as the dead. He is hideously beautiful but devastatingly frightening, a nightmare that is impossible to look away from.

I shake my head, breaking his gaze, but what I thought I saw is no longer there; it is now just Mr. Jennings.

I stagger back. I feel like I'm going to be sick.

Am I losing it? Or is there something about this town—this school—that's sending me over the deep end? First, my nightmares plague me more than before, and now I'm hallucinating.

Could it get any worse than this?

I hurriedly assemble my belongings and run out of his classroom.

CHAPTER 8—SURPRISE

Ever since seeing Mr. Jennings' face transform before my eyes, I have come to dread going to school. Sebastian has been avoiding me. Amina picks me up for school in the morning and takes me home. Sebastian still sits next to me in Mr. Jennings' class but says nothing more than hi. Even at lunch, he sits at Mandy's table now.

Things are changing rapidly and I don't understand why. There's a new element to my dreams. There are piercing screams from all around making my ears bleed, pleading and begging for help. And then there is one voice. A single voice silences all the others, whispering into my left ear, stirring a fear within me that turns my blood into ice. Soon, Bijou, I'll be near." I never see the face that belongs to the bittersweet voice.

I sit up in my bed, looking all around my room. "It was only a dream," I have to keep repeating to myself.

My eyes sting. *Was I crying?* The cryptic rhyme replays in my mind. "I'll ease your pain and wipe your tears. Soon, Bijou, I'll be near."

* * *

Since moving to Sykesville, I've discovered why people call it *beauty sleep*. My eyes are now home to dark circles, giving me an eerie resemblance to an extra from *The Walking Dead*. I know I'll once again be subjected to all sorts of speculation and questioning.

"Wow! You look like death," Roland *poetically* points out as he passes my lunch table. "You okay?"

I just nod and mumble something, and he goes away. I drop my head down onto my crossed forearms on the table.

"What's wrong, Jewels, not getting enough shut-eye?" Sebastian's voice is nonchalant, but there is a hint of concern in his breathtaking, smoky-gray eyes.

"Oh, you're talking to me now?" I roll my eyes at him and put my head down again.

"Why are you sitting with us today?" Amina asks as she approaches the table with two lunch bags, instead of three, handing one over to me.

"None for me?" He's wearing his crooked smile and being playful as if we're supposed to fall in line, now that he's ready to talk to us.

"Anyway." Amina ignores him. "Have you figured out what you're wearing to the rave?"

"Not a clue, but I'm not even sure how I'll get away tonight," I say, opening the homemade antipasto Amina's made for me.

We carry on a conversation, purposely ignoring Sebastian, who has to buy his own lunch.

"Have there been any new developments about the missing girls?" I ask, causing Sebastian and Amina to look at each other instead of me.

"Louder, Jewels. I don't think they heard you in Auckland." Sebastian looks around as if people are listening.

"What? Isn't it common knowledge that six girls are missing?" I take a bite of my food, savoring it before continuing. "I mean, isn't that why they're having a town hall meeting tonight?"

"Yes, but you don't want the wrong people to hear you asking questions." Sebastian sticks his fork in his disgusting looking meatloaf and it gets stuck. Amina, being Amina, pushes her lunch near Sebastian, handing him an extra fork to share with her.

"What do you think of Mr. Jennings?" Sebastian asks me, changing the subject.

"He's weird and he hates me. Why?"

"I'm not quite sure he hates you, but he has it in for me."—Hey, Mandy!" Amina and I look at each other in horror as Sebastian calls *Teen Witch* over to our table. She saunters over to Sebastian, and, for a moment, it looks like she's about to sit on his lap, but she settles for resting her elbows on his shoulders. Of course, Christa and Aften follow her to our table. "How long has Mr. Jennings been teaching here?"

Pulling away from Sebastian, Mandy looks agitated by the topic at hand.

"I don't know," she shrugs. "He's always been here, for all I know. Why?" I can feel her guard go up when Mr. Jennings' name is mentioned.

"No reason," he says casually, but I know better. There is more. "Everyone in our class seems to really like him, but he doesn't seem too close to anyone. Well, anyone but you. The only name he ever seems to remember is yours."

"I haven't really noticed," she answers smoothly. She's lying, and you don't have to be an empath to notice.

"Yeah, Jennings is cool, and he's made a total turnaround," Kim joins our table and the discussion.

"What do you mean?" Amina asks anxiously, looking briefly at her.

"It's just that he was always a no-nonsense, by-the-book kind of guy. Now he's so laid back and cool." Kim's face scrunches together. "Well, except when it comes to you and Sebastian. Man, does he have it in for you two. Come to think of it," she adds, "it's weird that he's even teaching a course on Mythology when he's always been an AP Comp teacher who assigns boring essays to write and non-fiction books to read. Now we're reading and writing fiction? Cool, but weird."

"That *is* weird," Sebastian says. He and Amina share another one of their silent but telling looks.

"Maybe it has something to do with Emily going missing," Kim says.

"Emily Patterson?" I ask. Mandy's eyes narrow on me, as do Amina's and Sebastian's.

"Yeah. Did you know her?" Kim asks.

"No, but I read online about her going missing."

"Oh, well Emily is Mr. Jennings' step-daughter, but he's raised her since her mom left years ago.

"He doesn't seem very distraught." The gravity of my own words hit me after it's too late. Someone kicks me under the table, but I'm not sure if it's Amina or Sebastian.

I'm about to open my big mouth once more when I notice a shadow cast over me. I turn to find Roland lurking again.

"Hi Roland," I say, trying to break the ice.

"Hey, Bijou." He takes a seat beside me as if speaking to him first was an invitation to sit. "Are you still going to the rave tonight?"

"That's the plan." I take a huge, final bite of my lunch, making Amina cringe, before remembering I'm having a conversation with a boy who's actually kind of cute. Note to self: take smaller bites next time. His nervous energy and anxiety are suffocating me. I open my water bottle and chug half in a nanosecond.

"So, we're still going to hang out there? You know, together?"

With wide eyes, I look at Amina, who is making all sorts of foolish hand gestures behind Roland's back and mouthing, "Say yes!" Her twin, on the other hand, is turning fifty shades of red, and for that simple reason I agree.

Roland leaves the table excited, and I look over at Aften, Mandy, and Christa. All three of them are shooting emotional daggers at me. Aften's face is red. The petite girl, who had once seemed so slight in her cheerleader's uniform the other day, now looks very forceful and aggressive as she runs her fingers through her chestnut-colored hair. She has completely stopped eating her lunch and will not look away from me.

If there were any doubts about Aften's feelings toward me, this moment has just made them blatantly clear. She despises me.

"And so what do you and the galah have in common?" Sebastian's voice is laced with disdain.

"That's what I plan to find out tonight."

* * *

Approaching the house after school, I notice the garage door is open with Gigi's car halfway in and halfway out. *She's never this careless.*

Peeking into the garage, all I can see are two boxes that Gigi has been nagging me to unpack since we moved here, but no sign of Gigi.

She would have told me if she weren't going to be home.

The house is eerily quiet. Too quiet. Gigi always leaves music playing in the house to give intruders the impression that someone is home.

Panic and guilt wash over me. I have been avoiding Gigi so much lately. If anything has happened to her, I will never be able to forgive myself.

Going through the first floor of the house, nothing looks out of place, but I have the odd sensation that I'm not alone.

I slowly and quietly make my way up the stairs, my heart beating so rapidly it sounds like a snare drum. All of the bedroom doors are shut except for Gigi's. I peek inside and freeze at the sight I now face.

Gigi's room—which never has any objects out of place—is in complete disarray. There are papers everywhere, open drawers, and the bed is unmade. I slowly step into the room to see if I am actually alone.

Looking under the bed, checking her closets, behind her layers of curtains. There's no one here.

I don't know what to do next. Should I call the police? What if Gigi had been looking for something and just didn't have enough time to clean up after herself? *Yeah, that was it!* I wouldn't want to call them unnecessarily.

Gigi has a cell phone now. I begin shuffling through my backpack to find the number that I should have memorized about a month ago. A piece of paper on the floor catches my eye.

It's a birth certificate. Mine. It reads that my mother's name is Lilith Fitzroy.

My legs begin to go numb as I read her name. I squeeze my eyes shut, hoping that by the time they reopen, it will all be a lie. This has to be some kind of mistake. According to this piece of paper, Gigi is my mother, and I wasn't born anywhere near France. It says that I was born in Monrovia, Liberia at John F. Kennedy Hospital.

Liberia? Why would she lie about something like this? The only thing that isn't a surprise to me is my date and time of birth—June 21, 2001, at midnight.

My stomach begins turning in knots. My mouth is suddenly overwhelmed by a bitter taste. I feel like I am on a merry-go-round as the room begins spinning. Too many thoughts and questions. I'm going to be sick.

I run dizzily for Gigi's bathroom and collapse on the cool linoleum tile. Several things begin happening at once. Sweat envelopes my hair as I convulse violently, soaking my shirt.

I taste this morning's Belgian waffles and cranberry juice rapidly making their way back up my esophagus. My eyes open so wide that I think they might pop out of their sockets as I blow chunks onto the floor, with only a few rounds making it into the toilet. It's like I have vomited everything that I have eaten in the last week.

After a while, I return to the mess of papers in her room. *This can't be right. Gigi can't possibly be my mother.* Although, it would make a lot of sense.

She never speaks of my parents, and every time I bring them up, she politely changes the subject. Maybe that's why we moved around so much. Gigi can't be anyone's grandmother. What have we been running from for all these years? Who is Gigi really? Should I be afraid?

There are so many other papers, including numerous deeds to houses and properties all over the world.

I thought this was the first home Gigi had ever owned.

I find a tattered, red scrapbook that peeks out from between the king-sized mattress and the box spring. The book is thick and extremely old.

There are newspaper clippings and legal documents dating back to the 1600s. My heart stops as I spot three different documents with names that catch my eye. There's Lilitu Fitzpatrick, born December 17, 1902, Lily King, born March 28, 1950 and Lilith Fitzroy, born July 26, 1978. No date of death for any of them.

Who were all of these people? And why did Gigi have their belongings? I had always felt that Gigi was keeping something from me, and this definitely confirms all of my suspicions.

My hands tremble as I put the papers aside to look through the scrapbook. There are all sorts of pictures, pictures not from our time but from long ago—before everything became digitized. The first photograph is dated 1902. There is no mistaking that it is Gigi's face in every single photo.

This can't be right. How can this be? It is definitely Gigi, and her face is the same as it is today. I can't stop shaking my head. Turning the page makes me even more certain. Another photograph dated 1908 holds the face of Gigi. She looks exactly the same as she does now. Her face is caressed by a cascade of pale curls. She's wearing dozens of bangles on each arm, standing confidently barefoot with her hands on her hips. She seems so different from the guarded Gigi I know today. The same confidence is still present, but she appears carefree in the picture.

This has to be a joke, or maybe even some sort of storyboard for the novel she is working on.

Maybe she knew I would find this. If Gigi is trying to scare the hell out of me, then bravo. Mission accomplished. I am freaked!

But a joke this intricate is out of character for her, so I know this is wishful thinking. Gigi wouldn't be this careless. Someone had been here searching for something. *Did they find it?*

Sitting on the floor, I begin to rock back and forth—a habit that annoys the heck out of Gigi. *I need to think.*

If Gigi is, in fact, fine and knows nothing of this supposed break-in, she will definitely make us run again. But I can't leave. I need answers, and my instincts are telling me that my answers are here in Sykesville.

I am sure if I ask, Gigi won't give me the answers I seek. She will somehow convince me that I misunderstood the things that I've read, and that answer is unacceptable.

I decide to clean Gigi's room, putting everything in its rightful place. Hopefully, she won't notice anything. I have to act as if nothing has happened, but can I do that? Who is this woman I once thought was my grandmother?

Just as I finish cleaning the room, the doorbell rings. I give the room a quick last inspection, hurrying to the window. It is Sebastian and Amina.

What are they doing here?

The doorbell rings repeatedly as I stumble downstairs toward the door.

"We wanted to see if everything is okay." Amina is all smiles as I open the door. "On our way home, I mentioned to Sebastian that I thought I saw the man in the hood not far from your development and he turned the car around."

I don't feel like speaking because speaking would require me to open my mouth, and opening my mouth would allow me to cry.

"You've been crying," Sebastian cuts in.

"Is everything okay?" Amina asks, rushing to my side. "Your hair looks like hell." Sebastian stands as if planted, his eyes never leaving my face.

I bow my head to avoid looking at them. And then the pain finally hits me, and the numbness fades. I feel nauseous as the confusion of my discovery replays itself in my mind, but I refuse to cry. *Preposterous. Why should I cry anyway?* I'm not even sure of what I'd found out.

"I'm just not feeling too good, and my grandmother isn't here." I stop, touching my stomach as though it aches.

Sebastian stares down at me, his thick eyebrows pulled together with concern. "Where is your grandmum?" he finally asks.

His question makes me cringe. "I have no idea. She wasn't here when I got home," I answer, looking away from his questioning eyes. "Which is really unlike her," I feel compelled to add.

And then it happens. I hate crying in front of people, but I am no longer in control. What will I tell them now?

They both look at each other, concern written on their faces. Amina comes to my side as Sebastian studies me. They just let me cry.

"What's wrong, Bijou?" Amina asks lovingly.

I think about lying but then reconsider.

"Well, when I got home, my grandmother wasn't here, so I began to worry..."

"What's so odd about that?" Amina interjects.

"Let her talk," Sebastian reprimands.

"She usually tells me when she's going to be out, and she-she—" I can't stop repeating myself.

They don't urge me to continue, but Amina looks as if she is trying extremely hard to restrain herself.

"I went to her room, and everything was turned upside down. It was horrible."

The twins look at each other.

"Take us to her room," they say as one.

They follow me upstairs in silence and it's killing me. What's going through their minds as we walk through the corridors of our house?

When I open her room door, the gray cat is lying on her bed like it's her own.

"I thought you said you didn't have a cat," Amina comments, heading for the cat, who hisses and runs out of the room.

"She kind-of won't go away."

Sebastian walks around the room, inspecting it from top to bottom.

"You said your nan had money, but you didn't say it was anything like this," Amina says, examining a ring with a rock bigger than her nose.

I shrug.

"There's nothing wrong with the room. I don't get it." Sebastian bends to look under the bed and mumbles something else that I can't make out.

"I cleaned it up because if nothing's happened to her and she comes home and sees that someone broke in, she'll make us move again. There's more." I open my satchel, pulling out the red scrapbook. There is a part of me screaming stop, but I ignore it, almost relieved to share this burden with them.

My hand trembles as I hold the large book in my hands. I think about saying something to pre-empt what they're about to see, but in order for them to have an unbiased opinion, they need to look with no preconceived notions.

Sebastian looks puzzled as he receives the tattered book. Amina stands a safe distance away as if afraid of what's inside.

"Just open it," I instruct, refusing to say any more.

The air grows thick with anticipation as I watch their eyes linger on each page. Amina's eyes widen as she reads. Sebastian's face is just a blank canvas. I expect to see him flinch at the various photos of Gigi from year to year with the same youthful face. He doesn't.

He never even bats an eye. He stands there, straight-faced and emotionless. It is nerve-wracking and strange to watch. Amina looks like she's itching to say something but waiting on Sebastian to react.

Suddenly, his interest is diverted away from the book of pictures and twisted information.

Silence.

"Where did you get this?" He looks away from me for a second, and then his eyes return.

"It was right there, on the floor with all these papers."

"So, no one else knows you have this?" The emotionless palette that had been his face only moments earlier is now faltering, and the dark and brooding presence that I sense beneath Sebastian's cool exterior has devoured him. The same chiseled face looks at me, but nothing is hidden beneath the surface at this moment. What I had sensed and maybe even feared is now in plain sight.

"No. No one but you two," I stammer. "So what do you think? Do you think my grandmother is crazy or maybe she's my mother?"

"You need to stop asking for our opinion and decide for yourself what you believe," he says. "One thing is for sure; these pictures look extremely authentic."

"So, I'm supposed to believe my grandmother is either some master criminal with various aliases, or over a hundred years old, or she's my mother?" I look at Sebastian, who seems to be fighting something within himself, and Amina, who looks like she's on the verge of telling me something. "Yeah, I highly doubt that."

"As of now, the whole book is subject to anyone's opinion because you know only bits and pieces of a puzzle."

I hadn't expected Sebastian to handle it like this. I expected him...well, quite frankly, I don't know what I expected him to say.

"You're coming with us," Amina declares abruptly.

"Pack a few things. I'm going to take a look around to see if there's any sign of forced entry," Sebastian instructs.

"Okay, Officer Sinjin." Amina salutes. "Come on, Bij, I'll help you get your things together."

In my room, it's obvious Amina is trying her best to distract me from real life by taking an unusual interest in my things. She is ranting about what she is going to borrow from my closet and where she'll wear it. When her eyes land on my bookshelf, she's intrigued by how many first editions it encases.

"Wow, you sure do have a lot of Anastasia Powers novels," she comments. "Is she your favorite author or something?"

"Or something," I answer shortly.

"What do you mean?" she asks, picking up a paperback copy of *The Old Ones* by Anastasia Powers.

"That's Gigi," I say pointing at the book she's holding.

"What? Your grandmother is one of the Old Ones?" Amina asks, looking at the book's blurb. "But that's just a novel."

"Huh? I mean, my grandmother is the author. She uses Anastasia Powers as a pseudonym."

Amina's jaw drops open, then shuts as she unsuccessfully searches for the right words to say. Instead, she settles for some sort of squeak that possibly means "okay."

She begins to help me pack my overnight bag, searching for something new to talk about, but nothing seems quite right. "Maybe she was looking for something and didn't have time to clean up before she left."

I look at Amina, but I am too drained to argue.

When we get back downstairs, Sebastian is there waiting.

"Did you find anything odd?" I ask.

"Nothing odd," he answers. And how would he know anyway? He's never been here before.

"Jewels, what kind of writer did you say your grandmum is?" Sebastian asks, his tone suspicious.

Amina proceeds to tell Sebastian about Gigi's secret identity. After they learn who Gigi is, I want to hear someone say that maybe what I saw has something to do with a book she's working on, but no one offers me that particular theory.

I leave a note, telling her where I'm going, in case she returns.

CHAPTER 9—WELCOME TO THE HELLMOUTH

I am broken. My edges are jagged with pieces missing, so no matter how hard I try to put myself together, I will never be whole again. I've never been prone to ulcers, but it feels like hot lava has erupted within me and is melting my insides. I'm sweating bullets and it's only 60 degrees outside.

I'm alone. Everything about me is a lie. I have no identity. If Gigi is my mother, what reason would she have for pretending to be my grandmother? It makes no sense. My mind begins to wander to dark places, but I shake it off before the thought fully materializes. The more I think about it, the more I realize what I'm feeling is fury, and it's strange because it's my own emotion and not the unwelcome emotion of someone else.

Sebastian and Amina are trying their best to distract me from worrying, but their attempts are futile. They offer to take me to their house, but I don't want to sit around, not doing anything. I want to know what's happening here. Why are girls my age disappearing? Where's Gigi? Will I be next?

I close my eyes, trying hard to connect the dots between this overload of information and how I fit into the equation. Then I remember the website, *Concealed Things and Where to Find Them.*

"Sebastian, how far are we from downtown Sykesville?" I ask, speaking for the first time since I got in the car.

"About five, ten minutes," he says, sneaking a look at me in his rearview mirror. "Why?"

"Can we go to Main Street? I wanna check out a bookstore."

He nods. Amina is looking at him, but he doesn't look at her.

* * *

Main Street is unlike any place I've ever been. There are no chains or franchises. Each shop has its own niche. There's a shop that sells nothing but yarn and knitting tools. We stop at another that sells hot dogs that represent each major city in America.

Once, we leave the hotdog shop, my eyes are set on the bookstore a couple blocks away, but as we make our way down the street, the intoxicating fragrances from a small shop vie for my attention. Unwined Candles.

Before I can suggest us going into the store, Amina silently enters, not waiting or asking if Sebastian and I will follow.

It's a candle shop that makes handmade soy candles in reused wine bottles. The store is breathtaking. It looks like an artist's loft. There are paintings and canvases with works-in-progress and there's a couple making candles on-site while identical twin boys, no older than seven or eight, write something about an open mic on a display chalkboard. There are candle displays all around with various scents, but one seems to be overpowering the rest. Sandalwood.

It smells like Sebastian. Earthy and sweet.

I pick up a candle, close my eyes, and inhale deeply.

"You're lucky. We just restocked Sweet Sandalwood today," says a stocky man with tattoos, wearing a Wu-Tang Forever T-shirt and a friendly smile. "It usually sells out the same day we stock."

"It's really nice," I say.

He looks in my eyes, and for a moment, I see flashes of a younger version of him in a blue and gold football uniform. He's on the field and arguing with someone that looks a lot like a younger version of Mr. Jennings. He's in a uniform as well. I quickly break eye contact, for fear of seeing something that might haunt me. I stagger a little, shaking my head as if it will help to ground me.

From the look on the man's face, I swear he's seen something as well. He shakes his head and his smile is gone, replaced with a grimace and furrowed brows.

"Did you go to Liberty High School?" I ask.

"Class of 2001. But how'd you know that?" He's smiling once more, but it doesn't reach his eyes.

2001 is the year the girls went missing.

"I go to Liberty," I begin. My eyes search Unwined in a panic, falling on a painting of a lion, wearing the blue and gold jersey.

I quickly point to the painting as my heart rate normalizes.

"Ah." His smile returns, along with the sincerity it held prior to eye contact with me. "You're a Lion."

I nod, returning his smile reluctantly.

"What? You don't like Liberty?" He fishes.

"It's fine." I pause briefly, in search of fitting words. "I'm just the new kid. You know how that is."

"Never been the new kid. Born and raised in Sykesville." He says, his voice sympathetic. "But I know it must be hard going to school with kids who've known each other since kindergarten."

"It is very hard." I open up. "And now there's all this stuff with the missing girls. It's scary."

"Yeah. It's just like before." His voice trembles a little as he speaks.

"This has happened before?" I ask, playing coy, not wanting to look like I'm prying.

He hesitates, looking around as if he doesn't want the wrong person to hear.

"Yeah. 2001, before Century was built, seven girls from Liberty went missing, the ground shook, and it all stopped. No more disappearances, but they were never found."

"What do you mean the ground shook?" I ask, unable to act uninterested.

"There was an earthquake on June 21st. I remember, because this is Maryland and we never have earthquakes, and it was graduation day."

What does this all mean? For some reason, my eyes are focused on the ground and I notice dried-up paint splatter.

"Take it."

"What? The painting?" I ask, caught off guard.

"No. The candle you're holding and constantly sniffing." He laughs. "Sweet Sandalwood. Just know you have friends at Unwined."

I hadn't noticed I'd been perving over the candle.

"I'll pay for it." I grab my bag in an attempt to purchase a candle I'm not even sure I wanted to buy to begin with.

"No. I insist." He takes the candle out of my hand and wraps it before I can argue any further, and I can't help but wonder what he saw after looking into my eyes that made him want to be so generous.

Just as I'm about to leave Unwined, my eyes fall on a woman, frantically painting on a canvas that takes up most of a wall, far in the back of the store. She's petite, wearing paint-splattered overalls. Her massive brunette ringlets look like they haven't seen a brush in some time, but not in a bad way. More of an artsy chic.

"Who's she?" I ask.

He looks back at the woman, smiling warmly.

"That's Dodie Hemisphere. Unwined's artist-in-residence and Sykesville's own Boo Radley. She's semi-famous, you know?"

"What's she famous for?" Amina interrupts with a hot dog in tow.

"Her art. She's been commissioned to paint for royalty and her work hangs in galleries around the world, but people tell all kinds of stories about her. Some say she's crazy. Some say she's over eighty but doesn't look a day over thirty. I just call her mom." He smiles. "Go talk to her. She knows all about the disappearances in this town."

Her back is turned to me as she works, and I approach her.

"Come to hear the rantings of a basket case?" She doesn't turn to look at me, but she knows I'm there as she paints. "Someone's always disappearing from this town, but they only care when the number is great."

I'm taken aback by the forceful voice of the petite woman. It sounds like she could command an army. She is highly alert, and as she paints with one hand, she constantly taps her hand on her side with the other as if keeping a rhythm that she can only hear.

"Your son says you know about disappearances here in Sykesville." My voice trembles as if I'm afraid of her or afraid of what she might have to say. Sebastian and Amina are closely watching as I approach her.

"It was a few years before I met my husband and had my David." She pauses and briefly looks over to the the guy who gave me the candle. He nods as if giving her permission to continue. "I was a little older than you, an artist, but none of my work was selling at the time, so I got a job waitressing and bartending at Poe's in downtown Sykesville. I worked seven days a week, which didn't leave much time for me to paint much of anything. And besides that, the atmosphere at Poe's wasn't very inspiring. One night, while working my shift, I met a guy. I mean—don't get me wrong—I met a lot of guys, but something about this guy was special. It's hard to put into words what was so different about him...well, besides the fact that he was more beautiful than any man I'd ever seen. There was something inhuman about him."

She doesn't hesitate to tell her story. Still painting. Still tapping her side.

"Anyway, on the first night I saw him, we didn't speak to one another, but night after night he'd show up on my shift, always alone, always quiet, always watching me. One night, it was rather slow, so I sat at the bar, sketching, and he began talking to me. I remember thinking his voice reminded me of rain— soothing. He took a look at my drawing and guessed I was an artist. He told me he saw something special in me...that I could be great. I only laughed, but his face remained stern. He asked me what my heart's desire was, and I told him I wished I was as he saw me. After that night, we began dating, and that's when things started getting weird.

"I started having these odd dreams of a door made of vines and no knob, in the middle of nowhere, a door placed in our reality leading to another world. It was the kind of place you'd expect to see if you were tripping on acid. I can't really describe it any better than that. After the dreams, I began to paint better and better. I no longer needed the job at Poe's because my paintings were headlining in galleries around the world. I felt I owed it all to my good luck charm.

"He told me he only wanted one thing in return. A child. So I thought, why not? We were happy, and soon after, I became pregnant. She was the most beautiful baby ever, with yellow ringlets and dimples so deep they could hold water. One day, he took us out to a strange clearing for a picnic. I knew I had never been there before, but it was still so familiar. I remember thinking, as we ate, that I had never tasted food so good. Then he stood up, holding the baby, thanked me, and walked away. I didn't understand at first, and I just lay there on the picnic blanket, watching them walk off. Eventually it clicked, but they were far off. I cried out his name as I ran after them, but for some reason, no matter how fast I ran, I couldn't catch up to them. He never turned to acknowledge me.

"After running for a while, I could no longer see them, but I saw a familiar sight that I had only seen in dreams, a sight I had brought to life through my paintings. There was the door I had seen, night after night. I stepped through the door without thinking because thinking was going to cost me my daughter. Stepping through took me to the world I had been dreaming of. Some of it was so gorgeous, but there were things there so ugly I still have trouble forgetting. Creatures so abnormal that even monsters in fairy tales are cute and cuddly in comparison.

"My mind fell to pieces. Words couldn't possibly describe the horror that I encountered there. I was chased and attacked. None of the terror stopped me from searching for my baby, but it was no use. She was lost to me forever. I looked and looked for what seemed like hours. My feet were bloody, and the last thing I remember was seeing the door that brought me to this other world, but I don't remember ever walking through it.

"Anyway, when I woke up, I was lying in my bed, but what I didn't count on was the fact that I had been gone for some time."

"How long were you gone?" I ask.

"Years," she says plainly. My baby was gone, and there was no record of the thing that took her ever existing."

"That's not possible," I say, knowing that it's quite possible, because Gigi has done it.

"No one even remembered me being pregnant, let alone remembered seeing my baby. All of the pictures of them were somehow gone, along with all documentation. All that was left of my baby was the portrait I painted of her. If you've ever been to Patterson Mansion, I'm sure you've seen it."

A huge part of me wants to believe her, but how can an entire town forget she even had a baby? Especially this nosey town. I look at her, feeling sorry for her, but not knowing what more to say.

"I'm not crazy. That's what happened. My mistake was falling in love with a man who wasn't even a man. They're among us, and they take our children and erase our lives." As she ends her rant, she turns to face us, but when she does, her eyes widen, and she points an accusatory finger at Amina. I swear I feel her mind and heart shatter simultaneously. "It's you!"

She grabs Amina. Amina's eyes are wide as Dodie, who is no bigger than Amina, holds onto her for dear life.

"My baby. My baby." Dodie sobs uncontrollably and within seconds, I am crying. Whether she's crazy or not, the emotions she's feeling are real and potent as joy slowly intertwines with pain.

Amina looks mortified as Sebastian and her son try to tear her away from Amina, which causes a scene.

"My baby. That's my baby, Dave. She's your sister!" she shrieks through cries, her face a dark shade of red.

"No mom. It can't be. The numbers don't add up. This girl's in her teens." Dave tries to soothe his mom, but she refuses to be comforted as she fights to find her way back to a now sobbing Amina.

"Sorry about this, mate." Sebastian is visibly sympathetic as he apologizes to a confused Dave, who is too concerned with calming his mother to acknowledge Sebastian or notice us leaving.

* * *

"What the hell was that, Jewels?" Sebastian asks, once we're outside again. His voice is angry, deep and raspy like someone who's already experienced a whole lot of life, so nothing really surprises him anymore. "Why were you questioning them about the missing girls?"

"That guy, Dave was at Liberty in 2001. That was 17 years ago, when the other girls went missing, Sebastian." He's holding onto Amina, who has been stunned into silence. A first for her. "I mentioned it and he told me his mom knew about disappearances. That's all."

"Stop asking random people questions. You never know who they are and what their intentions are."

"You don't know everything." I'm thoroughly annoyed with him at this point. "And for the record, that woman may not be emotionally stable, but she wasn't lying. I could feel it."

"So Amina is her missing toddler that was stolen years ago." He stops walking. I stop to look at him, his eyes are dark and I can tell he's angry because his eyebrows look like they're on the verge of connecting when he's mad. "And where does that leave my parents and me, Amina's twin?"

"I didn't say she was right about Amina being her daughter. I meant I could feel her anguish. Whatever the case may be, she believes all that stuff really happened to her."

"I know what you mean." Amina finally speaks. She's hugging herself as if she's cold. "I felt it too. She really believed what she was saying."

Sebastian picks up his pace, leaving Amina and me behind.

"Did you see what she was painting?" Amina asks, her voice fragile and changed.

"No. I was too caught up in what she was saying." Even though I was talking to Amina, my eyes were still on Sebastian, who stayed close enough to hear our conversation.

"There were four hooded figures, each holding a baby. Before she went berserk, she was drawing these weird symbols on the babies."

My heart rate accelerates as Amina describes my dream in 140 characters or less.

"You gasped, Bij. I heard it." Amina searches my face as we walk.

At this point, withholding information isn't helping me. Sooner or later, I will have to trust someone. I choose Amina.

"Not to freak you out or anything, but the other night, I had a dream about what you described. Only, in my dream, those symbols were moving."

"It feels like hell is opening up to swallow the world and we just happened to be at the center of it all." Amina shivers noticeably, her voice unsteady as she speaks. "We move here and girls start disappearing, we start having shared visions, and hooded men are following us."

"Welcome to the Hellmouth."

As awkward as it feels, I put my arm around Amina's shoulder and we walk to the bookstore in absolute silence.

CHAPTER 10—LISTENING TO FEAR

A Likely Story isn't what I expected at all. It isn't dark and ominous like something you'd find in Sunnydale. It's inviting, with posterized signs of new Young Adult releases and smiling faces all around. To be honest, it seems unlikely I'll find anything helpful here.

The truth is, I feel like I need to be immersed in something, anything that will take my mind away from what I found in Gigi's room. Somehow I'm starting to believe Gigi knows something about what's happening in Sykesville, and it's the reason why we're here. I can't wait for her to be forthcoming with information, so I need to dig, but I can't do this on my own.

Sebastian heads for the comics section, while Amina follows me as I search through genres.

"What exactly are you looking for?"

"So there's this website, *Concealed Things and Where to Find Them*. It talks about in-between times, the Otherworld, and this prophecy about the sun lasting longer than it's supposed to. I thought about it, and that must be referring to the summer solstice. The site also talks about djinn and some kid being born, stealing powers meant for the sun."

Amina stumbles, coming to a complete stop at the section that reads, *Town History*.

"Prophecy?" Amina's voice doesn't sound as fragile as it once was, and even though I can sometimes feel what she feels, at this moment, there's a fierceness and glow radiating off her that screams Other. "Bijou, what exactly did this prophecy say?"

"When the day lingers longer than it is intended to stay, and before the earth has completely spun, a child will come forth, stealing powers meant for the sun. To one from here and one from there, it shall be born and shall be lost but impossible to stay hidden. For it is impossible to dim the light from the sun."

She's looking at me as if she's seeing something new. Her eyebrows furrow much like her brother's, only not so dramatic.

"You remember it verbatim?" There's a level of surprise in her voice that dances on the verge of fear and disbelief as she looks at me.

From the look on her face, it's one of those odd things about myself that should remain private. I shrug.

"Anyway, the site says that there are books here about the djinn, the Otherworld, and supernatural occurrences."

With eyes wide, Amina grabs me, pulling me toward a confused looking Sebastian as she looks around suspiciously. "Are you crazy? You can't talk about that stuff in public."

There are about 10 other people searching for books throughout the store, and none of them seem the least bit interested in anything we have to say.

"It's not like any of it's some big secret. There's an entire website devoted to it, so they must have wanted someone to see it."

She closes her eyes, shaking her head. "And maybe that's what they wanted-"

"Someone to come looking." Sebastian seems to finish Amina's sentence as she nods in agreement.

"Hey, there's a staircase," I say, leaving them to discuss conspiracy theories as I rush toward a sign that reads, *Rare Books*.

I descend down the spiral of stairs, arriving at what looks like a busy café. Music plays quietly in the background. There are tables set with rich purple and yellow cloths. Scented candles are lit throughout. It seems a little too dim for reading.

Every set of eyes is on me, but none of them make direct eye contact. They stare, then whisper amongst themselves as though I have food on my face or something. I catch a glimpse of myself in a hanging mirror, but there's nothing irregular about it. I don't think I'm just being paranoid. I almost turn to head back up the dizzying staircase when I see a beaded entrance that holds more books.

The moment I take the first step on the path to the curtain, the pain starts. The various emotions of hostility, curiosity, envy, and hunger hit me square in my face. I am definitely not safe here, but when has that ever stopped me?

Things are changing because everyone's emotions are affecting me. I touch my bag in search of my cards, then decide against it out of fear of drawing more attention to myself.

It takes everything within me to stop me from running to the entrance, but running will definitely make them aware that I know something, and my instincts scream that it would be a huge mistake. So, I walk at a normal pace as I make my way through the beaded entrance where the pain finally subsides.

The books in this section aren't like the ones upstairs. There is nothing crisp or new about any of these. In this room, paperback is not an option. These books are ancient. Everything has a hardcover with hundreds of aged pages that look like they've been to hell and back. There is no classification for the books in the overcrowded room.

"Expect the Unexpected," I say, as it is written all over the walls.

"So you do speak Arabic." Sebastian's voice startles me. I didn't realize they'd followed me down the rabbit hole.

"No. Why do you keep asking me this?"

"Because you just spoke Arabic." He raises his brow at me. "توقع ما هو غير متوقع."

"You're just repeating what I said. 'Expect the unexpected.'"

Sebastian and Amina look at each other, but don't say another word. Why is it that they're acting weird and I'm still the one treated like I'm crazy?

I don't dwell on their weirdness. I came here for answers and I feel like I'm getting close. As I look through the aisles, the titles range from *Aquatic Creatures* to *The Book of the Night Children*. There are books on lore and legends from all over the world, but it doesn't seem much like a bookstore down here; it's more like a library. All of the books are used.

Then one book catches my eye: *The Hidden People*.

The three of us sit there on the floor, skimming through pages of the book with no table of contents. The book tells stories of people who once lived in the same space that we live in, only on a different plane. People who weren't actually people, some humanoid and some so different that they could never blend in with humans unless they were powerful enough to don a glamour.

"That's an interesting choice."

The heavily accented voice is low and enchanting. She smiles. Her teeth are too white. Her thick, dark hair is done up in a curly mess of a bun. Her dark eyes glimmer and her skin glistens like it has been dipped in pure milk chocolate. She is scarily pretty, but something is off about her. She isn't Typical, but she isn't exactly like the Others either. If evil could be personified, it might be her. Hate, envy, jealousy, and every other ugly emotion I've ever felt before radiates off her like the sun's rays. The only other person I've ever encountered with so much animosity towards me is Mandy, but how can this woman hate me when she doesn't know me?

"It's quite interesting," Sebastian speaks up, even though she was clearly talking to me. Her eyes stay on me. "We're taking a folklore class and looking for supplemental material."

Sebastian's voice is protective. He stands, but he doesn't tower over her like he does with nearly everyone else. She's almost as tall as he is.

"It's more than just a book. It's a survival guide. It just may save your life." She never stops smiling as she speaks, her honey-coated voice as venomous as a viper. "Well, if not your life, at least your grade."

Looking at the back of the book makes me jump to my feet sporadically—a hundred and twenty dollars.

"Yeah, this is one survival guide that I can do without," I sigh, handing the book to her.

Upon placing the heavy book into her delicate hands, I ever so slightly brush the palm of her hand, making my vision blur.

Darkness surrounds me, sending me into a trance. A dream would be good, but no, this is the stuff that nightmares are made of.

A scantily clad girl runs barefoot through a dark forest. The darkness that envelops this forest is thick and seems to be chasing her. Her skin and clothes are dirty, and her arms are covered in cuts and bruises, but beneath the dirt, her golden skin glistens. She looks like she has been tortured. Her shockingly red hair is cut in strange places, and she keeps throwing her hands up to touch it as if it has recently been chopped off.

Casting furtive glances over her shoulder hinders her, causing her to fall repeatedly. The more she runs, the more I notice that her feet are barely touching the ground. She flutters in the air briefly, then lands back on the ground gracefully, but she has no wings.

There is light ahead. She slows her pace and hides behind a huge willow tree as she spies a group dancing around a large fire in the clearing. They sing and dance merrily, a sight that would make you want to join in, until you see them for what they truly are. Some have elfin faces on adult bodies. Others are no more than three feet tall with grotesque faces, and some are so tiny that they look like fireflies that have had too much caffeine. The rest look human, though they are anything but.

The music calls to her, even though it is obvious that she tries to fight the urge to move. Her feet begin to trudge forward, and once she steps into the clearing, their eyes land on her.

She stumbles over something, and when she looks down, there are seven teenage human girls bound together with tears streaming down their faces, pleading silently for help.

Just as she attempts to go to them, a short, shirtless, hoofed man with ram's horns and an executioner's mask stands before her eyes and utters one word: "Sleep!"

I gasp for air, and once again, I am standing before the mysterious Hershey-skinned woman, with Sebastian yelling at her.

He never yells.

"Now, for the last time, who are you?" he asks her.

"And like I told you before, I'm trying to make a sale. So, I'll ask again, how much are you willing to pay?" she asks, her voice more menacing than Sebastian's.

My eyes flutter, probably making me look like an idiot.

"Are you okay?" Sebastian rushes to my side, where Amina has been all along.

"I'm okay, but why are you yelling at that woman like that?"

He hesitates before speaking. "She was being way too aggressive for my liking." He smiles, but it's one of his nervous crooked ones. "We should get going. The party's started already."

I am overcome with fear for the girl in my vision. She was so afraid. It was like she was at the point of insanity, and I felt everything she felt. I felt how they felt as they looked at her. It reminded me of the way I was perceived as I walked through the café to get here.

"Not many people here can speak, let alone read Mandingo," she says, drawing all three sets of eyes to her. "Are they offering West African languages at Liberty now?"

Prickly heat penetrates the back of my neck. I raise my hand in an attempt to touch my birthmark, but Sebastian's hot hand catches it, holding onto it tightly.

"We never told you what school we attend," I say, my defenses fully up as I look at her with rebellious eyes.

"Lucky guess. You're either from Liberty or Century." The woman laughs nervously. "But understanding Mandingo, now that's an accomplishment."

"My mom speaks it," I lie, unsure of what to say to this woman, who keeps pressing the issue.

I try to sound as calm as possible, but I am not okay. How is it that the book is in a completely foreign language, and we can't even differentiate it from English? I look at the book once more. I mean, I really look at it this time. The words begin to scramble, and the script is indeed foreign—a language that I am quite sure that I have never seen until now.

That was more than a lucky guess.

"Anyway, we're closing up soon. There's a Town Hall Meeting tonight." She pauses. "What if I told you I want to give you this book as a gift? You know, for free."

I slowly begin backing away from the strange woman with the almond shaped eyes and the menacing smile.

"Nothing is free, so thanks for the offer, but I really must go."

What is it with Main Street? Why are they always trying to give me free stuff here?

"I'll take it," Sebastian says, startling both Amina and me.

With pursed lips, she reluctantly hands the book over to Sebastian, making me think the offer was mine and not his.

I hurry up the staircase with the twins behind me.

"Why did you take that book from her, Sebastian?" I ask, turning to look at him and bumping into someone instead.

It's her—the petite girl from my vision with the unusually red hair, only now, her hair is in a spiked pixie cut.

Relief washes over me when I realize she hasn't been hurt by the man in the executioner's mask that put her to sleep in my vision. But relief subsides and is replaced by sorrow when her hand mistakenly touches mine. Our eyes meet, and I am briefly hindered by a sharp and crippling pain.

She pulls away from me, leaving me wondering whether the pain I felt was emotional or physical. Whatever sort of pain it was, it was certainly pure torture, and no human being should have to endure anything like it.

I look at the girl who stands submissively before me—examining her. She's one of the Others. Her beauty isn't the only dead giveaway. She has a grace that would put the most talented dancer from Juilliard to shame. She has the effervescent glow they all have— the one that sets them apart from the Typicals. Her childlike face may hide her emotions from others, but based on what I saw in my vision, she shouldn't be okay. Her large emerald eyes tell a story of suffering that no one should ever have to endure. I feel pain coming from her, but it's faint now.

Why is this happening when she's one of the Others and not one of the indescribable ones? I can feel what she's feeling. But why?

"Were you able to find everything you needed?"

The tiny redhead keeps her voice low as she speaks. Probably so that witch won't hear her. Her eyes never leave mine. She never even blinks. No one has ever been able to look me in the eyes for this long without looking away in fear or disgust. Well, besides Sebastian and Amina.

It's weird. It's as if she is trying to speak to me with her eyes, only I'm not getting the message.

"Not really, but I like the vibe of this place."

"You can't be serious," Amina blurts out with zero regards for anyone who might hear. "I mean, upstairs is cool, but downstairs is like the entrance to the Hellmouth."

Every time one of the Sinjin twins make a reference to Buffy, I'm embarrassed by my pathetic story about my best friend Willow, and I'm grateful that I found the kinds of friends who didn't call me out on it right away.

"Your friend is right." The short woman with the spiky hair cocks a naturally arched eyebrow, examining me now. "I wouldn't think you'd like it here."

"How would you know what to expect from a complete stranger?" Sebastian asks, standing between me and the girl with the elfin face.

When her eyes fall on Sebastian's face, she reaches for it, but he catches her wrist.

"After all that's happened, you've found each other." Her voice is nothing more than a whisper as tears roll down her cheek.

"Guys, we should go," Amina says, pulling on me and Sebastian, who seems just as anxious to leave.

I'm not going anywhere.

"What do you mean, we've found each other?" I distance myself from Sebastian and Amina. "Who are you?"

"I'm no stranger," she says, sobbing through tears. "Where's the other one? There should be four."

"Four what?" I ask.

Her face changes. The tears stop, replaced by shock and confusion.

"No. No. No. You're supposed to know everything." She begins pacing like a crazy person, talking a mile a minute. "There isn't enough time. They're all here.

You'll never be ready. It wasn't supposed to happen this way."

"Oy Jewels, blind Freddy can see that this one's off her rocker." Sebastian pulls my hand, but I break free.

Amina is nervous and I can feel it without looking at her.

"Listen, you have to get ready." She rushes to me, grabs my hands, and looks into my eyes. "The four of you. Something's coming and if you're not ready, missing girls will be the least of everyone's worries."

"She's madder than a cut snake, Bij. Let's go. Now." Amina's voice is frantic.

"Once all is exposed, chaos will ensue, and the hunter will become the hunted. For only they can stop the end. In the beginning, there were four. Four, who gave birth to the elements. Four, who were tasked to protect the human realm. Four, with the answers to the questions the Chosen will seek. Four started it all, and four will stop the end. The giver of life, the bringer of death, the creator of the everlasting, and the master of all." Her words tumble out like clowns from a clown car. No form, just rushed and clumsy. But why?

"What does any of this mean?" I'm the only one humoring her, but I can feel the urgency from within her. What she's saying is important.

"Tell Sedia, we had it all wrong. She was only the messenger. It was foretold before any of us came to be."

"Wait...how do you know Sedia?" Sebastian is now back in defense mode, furrowed brows in place, and his jaw has tightened as if on cue.

"Who's Sedia?" I ask.

"She doesn't know anything," the crazy girl says, closing her eyes as if she's in pain.

"Hawah, you're not bothering Ms...I didn't get your name, beautiful," the dark haired woman interjects, standing behind the pixie-like girl who I now know to be Hawah. "I'm good at guessing names, so let me give it a go. You look like a Hazel."

I pause briefly as she smiles a sinister smile. The petite redhead is pleading for help with nothing more than her emerald eyes but remains silent. And of all names, why Hazel? A memory that I had buried deep within the darkest corners of my mind begins to emerge, but it is somehow suppressed.

"No, she's no bother at all. We were just on our way out. It was a pleasure meeting you both."

I don't give her my name. With all of the *crazy* unfolding around me, who knows what a name can do? I look down at Hawah once more before turning. Once again, her eyes call out.

She wants to say something, but there is no chance of that happening, especially now that *Cruella* has her eyes on us.

"I think we have a copy of the book you were looking for," Hawah speaks unexpectedly.

The woman looks from me to Hawah and back again with accusing eyes.

"And what book would that be?" She stares at Hawah, ready to pounce.

"*The Old Ones* by Anastasia Powers," Hawah answers without hesitation.

My whole world seems to stop as the words escape her lips. Of all the books, of all the authors in the world, why Anastasia Powers? This can't be a coincidence. If I wasn't guarded before, her reply changed that in seconds.

"Well, ring our new friend up, Hawah, so she can be on her way. I hope this isn't the last we'll be seeing of you."

I give her a hint of a smile, following Hawah to the register. Sebastian and Amina wait near the exit, watching keenly in complete silence.

"Your friends may not know it all, but they know much more than they're telling you." Her voice is a high-pitched whisper, but it holds conviction; she kind of reminds me of Amina. It looks like I am being preached to by a twelve-year-old. "You have to be ready because there's a bigger threat than we all thought, and you won't be ready until you are four."

I look at her because one moment she seems sane and sincere, and the next she seems to be missing a few screws.

"Anyway, your total comes to nineteen fifty." Hawah's volume elevates, speaking now as she would with any other customer.

"I don't need this—"

"Trust me, you do! This is the hardback collector's edition, and this must be your lucky day because it's the only one in existence, so take it!"

I feel like a contestant on a whacked out game show, being bullied into spending twenty dollars on a book that I can recite word for word.

CHAPTER 11—BEER BAD

In my limited experience, I've naively believed people only lie as the last resort, but that can't be any further from the truth.

Everyone who I've ever met has lied to me. That can't possibly be the last resort.

I stuff the book into my satchel and exit A Likely Story, no longer feeling sad or confused. I'm pissed.

I walk behind Sebastian and Amina as we make our way to the car and they talk about everything but what just happened in the bookstore. They're carrying on about the party, and how we're going to be late if we don't hurry. I feel myself growing angrier by the second.

"Bij, I bet you 20 dollars Mandy will be wearing pink at the party," Amina quips.

I say nothing and by the time we get to the car, I can take no more.

"Who's Sedia?" I ask.

Surprise, surprise, they're both quiet. Amina looks at Sebastian, who's looking at his boots.

"No. Don't look at him," I shout. "Look at me."

They both say nothing.

"Man, I was so dumb to think I could trust you guys. I'm not going anywhere with you."

I storm off, not knowing my way, but I'm not getting in a car with those two liars.

"Jewels, stop." Sebastian is following me, but I will not turn to acknowledge him.

He grabs me by my arm, turning me around to face him. His eyes are dark, but they give away nothing. I hate that I can't feel what he's feeling.

"Sedia's our mum," he says, his eyes serious.

"Bastian, I don't think we should be doing this out here." Amina's voice holds a level of fear I've never felt from her before.

"Get in the car, and we'll explain."

Sebastian steps aside, motioning me to get in the car. I reluctantly oblige.

"How did Hawah know your mother's name, and what did she mean when she said you guys know more than you're telling me?" I blurt out the moment Sebastian starts driving. "Do you guys know her?"

"We've never met her before," Sebastian says.

"Then how can she know who you are? How did she know to give me an Anastasia Powers novel? And what is up with all this crap about the Chosen One? It was mentioned on that website and Hawah just mentioned it now."

We're not getting anywhere. They aren't answering any questions and Amina keeps pinching Sebastian anytime he tries to speak, so he drives us to the rave in silence.

* * *

The night air has a chill, so I curl up under Sebastian's discarded leather jacket. Just as I am getting comfortable, I see the signs that read "Piney Run Park Parking."

I was so looking forward to this rave, but with all that's happening, how can I really enjoy a party?

It doesn't take long to find our way to the excitement as the light from a bonfire illuminates our path. The site is beautiful, but then again I am a bad judge because everything about the night fascinates me.

I get lost gazing at the stars for so long. I don't notice that only Sebastian and I are left standing.

"Where were you just now?" Sebastian fishes.

"Nowhere. Just looking at the stars," I reply.

It's hard staying mad at him. Why deny myself my only pleasure?

"Beautiful, eh?"

I nod, looking at him briefly. His face is serious.

"You look beautiful tonight, Jewels," he comments, still looking away from me toward the sky. "In fact, you're glowing."

I think I actually stop breathing when he says this. Maybe I heard him wrong, but I refuse to ask him to repeat it for fear that I'd misheard him.

"Um, thanks."

"I mean, you always look good, but it's just...I mean it's just that I never really see you outside of school." The words transform into gibberish.

"Where did Amina go?" I ask, trying to break the ice.

"Not sure. Shall we join the festivities?" he says, offering me his arm.

Maybe he just feels bad about keeping me out of the loop, but I'll enjoy the attention while it lasts. And besides, it will annoy Mandy.

The party is in full swing. I didn't think there would be this many people. It looks like most of the upperclassmen are here. The music is loud and fast as people collide and gyrate while others drink and smoke.

"Now this is a party," Amina says, appearing between me and Sebastian, acting as if everything is okay.

"Where'd you come from?" I ask, watching her trying to force her brother to dance with her.

"Just checking things out."

Sebastian is trying hard to push his hyperactive sister away when Mandy appears.

"Bijou. I see you didn't bother to change your clothes." Mandy appraises me with disgust.

I look down, remembering I'm still wearing the flared jeans and long sleeve crop top I had worn to school.

"Mandy. I see pink is still the only color in your wardrobe," I reply, noticing Amina's open hand and dimpled smile.

"Pay up, Bij," she taunts as I begrudgingly dig in my pocket for the 20 dollars I owe her from the bet on Mandy's apparel.

"Sebastian, did you—" But before I can complete my sentence, I watch Sebastian follow Mandy off into the crowd.

"Bij, I know you like my brother, but honestly, you shouldn't. He runs hot and cold," Amina says out of the blue.

"I don't understand."

"One minute he's like this, and the next minute he's like that," she explains. "Don't get me wrong, I love my brother more than words can even begin to describe, but you'll be better off forgetting about him."

I don't respond at all. I see Roland and a few kids from school at a cooler with beers, and they look like they don't have a care in the world. Without another word to Amina, I head over to Roland and do something I never imagined myself doing.

Upon seeing me, Roland's face lights up, and I find myself wishing Sebastian would have the same reaction, but I quickly shake it off.

"Bijou, you look great," Roland says, taking a sip out of a beer can. "Did you do something different with your hair or put makeup on or something?"

No. I think I threw up and cried my heart out after finding out that I've been lied to my entire life, but no biggie.

"Not really," I say with a smile. "Can I have one?" I ask, pointing to a beer.

His eyes widen as he looks at me, speechless.

"Well?"

"Uh yeah." He hands me a can of a lukewarm beer. "It's a local brew. Good stuff."

I don't care if it's local or from Timbuktu. I just want an escape from reality. I pop open the can and chug a beverage that tastes like what I'm guessing hot cat piss tastes like. I drink it all.

"Whoa. You're a pro," he says in awe. "Want some more?"

I nod, accepting another and another. Within what seems like moments, I'm dancing with Roland, gyrating like everyone else. His hands are all over me as we dance, and I'm not stopping him. I just want to forget everything. Sebastian. Amina. Gigi. The missing girls. Mandy. Everything.

I'm spinning and my eyes can't focus. Emotions are attacking me and I'm hearing things. Their conversations all sound so close you'd think they're all whispering in my ear at once.

I'm burning up. No, now I'm freezing. My inner temperature fluctuates every three seconds. I'm drenched. My hair is wet as if I've been dunked in water. I fight my way out of the crowd, my clothes soaked and my throat dry. I head to the cooler once more, but this time, I opt for water. Everyone's faces are blurred. My heart is racing and I feel like my brain is going to explode. I dig my hands in my back pocket for my cards as I'm moments away from tears, but before I can grab them, I hear my name.

"Bijou. Bijou. Bijou." It's being said in a taunting manner like a kid would say "olly olly oxen free" in a horror movie.

I try following the voice, bumping into a few people whose faces I can't make out.

"Gross. Watch where you're going," a girl says. Someone bumps into me, tripping me.

"I'm sorry," I say, but I think I'm nowhere near the girls I bumped into.

"Bijou," the voice calls again.

"Who's there?" I call, backing away, knocking over the table with the keg and falling to the ground. I'm drenched. The spilled beer seems to be seeping through my pores. I feel even more drunk than before.

"She's wasted," a guy says as others laugh. I get up, running away from the laughter. I'm embarrassed, wet, and drunk. When I stop, I find myself in a clearing, away from the crowd.

"Bijou." I hear my name being called again, followed by whistling.

The sound intensifies, and I don't know which direction it's coming from. I cover my ears but it's no use. The voice sounds like it's in my head. Just as I'm about to write this off as the antics of a drunk empath, I see the hooded man standing less than five feet away from me.

I take off, running as fast as I can while intoxicated, but he's gaining on me. The alcohol is clouding my vision, so I'm sure I look like an idiot, but it doesn't matter. I feel him behind me, and I know he's close. The moment I decide to turn and look, I trip and fall, stumbling down a hill.

It takes a moment, but I jump to my feet, aching all over, and he's here, standing right in front of me.

"Do you know what is said of whistling in the dark?" he asks in a hushed tone that makes the hairs on the back of my neck rise.

He's never spoken before. He has an accent and a voice that sounds like sandpaper rubbing against my eardrum.

"My friends are pr-probably looking for me by now," I say cautiously, my words slightly slurring.

Even though he's standing right before me, I cannot see his face, only his terrifying eyes. He begins to whistle.

"Ce billet doux est toi, mon bijou." I sing the words in tune with his whistling, unsure of where the words are coming from.

"This love letter is yours, my jewel," I finally translate. Where have I heard this song before?

"So indeed, it is you!"

I say nothing in return.

"You still offer me no answer to my first question," he says. His voice is disturbing.

"What question?" My voice is raw as if I haven't spoken in a long while.

"Do you know what is said of whistling in the dark?" He sounds as if his patience is worn.

"No, I don't," I answer hesitantly.

"Whistling in the dark is an invitation for the djinn to enter," he says in a whisper.

"The djinn? They're not real." As the words leave my mouth, I know I am wrong.

"They're as real as you and me," he answers, reaching out for me. "It's my job to protect you, so don't be deceived by others."

"Help! Sebastian! Anybody! Help me," I cry.

He grabs my right wrist with hot hands. I fight to break free, but it's no use. He's too strong.

"Let go! You're hurting me." The heat from his hand burns my wrist so badly I begin to think I will see smoke. I yell Sebastian's name once more through tears.

He frees one of his hands and waves it before my face. I feel myself becoming drowsy.

"Who is Sebastian to you?" he asks.

My lips begin to move and words are coming out, but I'm speaking so fast I can't comprehend much of what I'm saying. It sounds like gibberish. My mind is foggy and I finally say in English, "but we call him Sebastian."

"What did you just do to me?" I ask.

His grip tightens, grabbing me by the back of my neck to pull me closer. But something makes him scream in absolute horror, forcing him to release me from the chokehold.

He screeches—obviously in some sort of pain—as an imprint of an eye is branded on his hand.

I run, but my legs won't move as fast as I will them to. Although I can't hear him pursuing me, I can feel his presence near. The smell of sulfur is strong.

My legs are tired now, and I am completely out of breath. I stop running, resting my hands on my knees— my breaths coming rapidly. I realize that I am back where I started at the site of the bonfire, and the man is nowhere in sight.

I cough violently. My heart rate accelerates. I need to sit. I plop down beneath a huge weeping willow, far enough away from the party, but not too far, leaning against its trunk. How ironic. I feel like crying but refuse to let the tears fall again.

"Ce billet doux est toi, mon bijou." I keep repeating it to myself. Where had I heard that before? Thinking about my odd experience brings back another feeling— pain. I grab my wrist. It is red and it stings horribly. I have the urge to whistle. There is a part of me screaming to fight the urge, but I ignore it. I begin to whistle the tune quietly, then louder. All of a sudden, the once quiet forest is going crazy as insects buzz, deer run frantically, and the night birds that were out of sight leave the comfort of their trees.

What is happening? I'm hot again. I gather my hair up in a bun with a rubber band.

I don't know whether to stay put or to follow suit with the animals.

"Why are you out here by yourself?"

I look up to see Sebastian towering over me. The moon gives his skin a luminous sheen. He looks ethereal. Not human.

"How'd you know where to find me?" I ask, almost afraid to hear his answer.

He hesitates briefly, as if trying to get his story straight. "Someone saw you on the path, so I came looking for you."

I stand, staring at Sebastian with contemptuous eyes, contemplating my next actions carefully. I do not believe him, but I am afraid to voice the truth.

He touches my face, his hand is warm. I close my eyes, welcoming the warm sensation his touch brings. Without thinking, I lean in closer and kiss his lips hard, making him gasp a bit. I pull away quickly, unsure of what his gasp meant.

Before I can say anything, he plants his warm lips against mine, wrapping his arms around my waist. I don't know what to do with my hands. I think about putting them in his hair, stopping inches away from his head. I think about putting them around his neck, but I stop myself mid-flight. So here I am being kissed by a boy that I am falling hopelessly in love with and making a complete fool of myself because I look like I am flagging someone down with my hands. As if Sebastian knows what is going through my mind, he grabs my arms and wraps them around his neck without ever removing his lips from mine.

The heat I usually feel from him seems to transmit from his lips to mine. A burst of intermittent images surge through my mind. Every moment we have ever spent together is displayed, but it isn't as I saw it. It is through Sebastian's eyes. Yes, he saw me as strange and out-of-place, but in his eyes, I am beautiful.

Then something happens and all of my experiences with the hooded man, the shared vision with Amina, and the vision I had about Hawah replay.

When he finally pulls away, I am flustered.

"Jewels, have you been drinking?" he asks accusingly.

"I'm drunk," I misspeak. Crap. "I mean I'm not drunk."

"You smell and taste like a brewery. We're leaving." His voice is authoritative and angry.

The euphoria of the kiss wears off as I remember the fact that he'd found me, even though I am no longer on the path.

"Sebastian, I strayed from the path, so how did you know that I was in this particular spot, under this particular tree, at this particular moment?"

"You gave him my name, Jewels. Do you know what you've done?" he asks sharply. His eyes become glassy as if tears will fall.

I shake my head.

"You gave him my name, Jewels." With eyes closed as if he's in pain, he repeats, "You gave him my name."

"Have I missed something?" I'm so confused right now. "Why haven't you answered my question, Sebastian? How did you find me?"

"I saw everything. The hooded man. You, running and calling for me. And you, giving him my name. The kiss showed me everything," he says. He isn't smiling or being playful. "I saw what you saw." His voice is quiet, but I can still make out what he's saying. Although I can hear him, his voice is no more than a whisper. "Moh was right. It isn't safe anymore."

"Who the hell is Moh, and why isn't it safe?"

His eyes shoot up at me in shock. "You understood that?"

"Of course I did. You weren't exactly whispering." Sebastian's look of shock slowly begins to transform into something else.

"But I wasn't speaking English," Sebastian says quietly, turning away. "It's time to go."

"I'm not going anywhere with you. You never answered my question," I say. The hairs on the back of my neck begin to rise once more, but I'm afraid to ask again.

He stops walking, but he's looking at the ground, refusing to look at me.

"What are you asking me, Jewels?"

"You heard me whistle. Didn't you?" He's still looking at the ground. "Look at me, Sebastian!"

He says nothing which makes me panic. I leave him behind, taking the path back to safety. I know he's following me, but I don't turn to acknowledge him.

When we get back to the site, everyone is still partying. Amina stands in the middle of a crowd, reenacting a story of some fight she had been in. She has the whole crowd captivated as she jumps around. Mandy and her girls watch from a distance, disgusted. Kim is Amina's wing woman for the night, which doesn't seem to be going over well with Mandy.

"What is that, the Eye of Providence?" Kim calls out to me.

"I'm not sure what you mean."

"Your tattoo? Is it the Eye of Providence?" she replies.

Sebastian conspicuously snaps the rubber band that holds my hair together, covering the once visible birthmark.

"What's your problem?" I scream at him, fighting the urge to smack him.

"You had a bug in your hair."

He walks on, pulling me along with speed.

"Isn't Amina coming with us?"

"No, she'll be fine," he answers.

By the time I spot Sebastian's car, Mandy and company are already heading our way. I really don't have the energy to deal with them.

"Leaving so soon?" Aften mocks, walking toward me. The group of girls that follow her laugh at a joke that I do not care to pay any attention to.

Ignoring her, I lean on the car and begin shuffling my cards absentmindedly.

Of course, Mandy is in Sebastian's face. Only this time, he doesn't seem to be paying her much attention. He looks worried, which makes me feel uneasy.

As I watch the interaction between the two, Aften bumps into me, knocking the deck of cards out of my hand.

"Oops," she yelps sarcastically, cupping her wolfish mouth as she suppresses laughter.

"You evil little—" I want to slap her. My hands are idle, making me susceptible to their various emotions. My first instinct is to lash out at her, but instead, I bend to pick up the cards before I do something I'll regret.

While picking the cards up, I notice an upturned card in front of Aften. While reaching to touch the card, a sharp pain pierces my brain and I see her, wearing the same denim romper she's wearing now, but she's unconscious, and bleeding from the head.

"Oh my—" I quickly try changing the expression on my face before anyone notices.

"What the hell is your problem? You saw something with your creepy little cards, huh freak?" Apparently, she had seen my face.

I know telling her the truth will label me a bigger weirdo than I already am, but not telling her the truth will leave her predisposed to whatever danger she may be facing.

"Just spit it out," Aften says with a nervous laugh. I can see in her eyes that she is worried.

"I don't know what you're talking about."

She speaks with authority, but I can hear the vulnerability in her voice. "Bijou, or whatever the hell your name is-"

"It's just a feeling I have, but Aften, you need to be careful tonight." I can't look at her. I know how crazy I must sound, but could I really tell her that I think she might die?

"You're so full of it. You're just trying to scare me because I pushed you." Her voice is losing its force, and she knows it, so she pushes me again. The hatred and fear she embodies hurts more than the physical pain she inflicted on me. Her emotions become a conduit, igniting the internal flame that had only been a spark before.

That's it!

I push her back.

"Now we're getting somewhere," she says, shrugging off her jacket like she's Floyd Mayweather or something.

"I'm tired of restraining myself. If I were you, I would be very careful of what you do or say to me," I snarl, surprising myself.

"Oh is that a threat, Little Orphan Annie?" She's unflinchingly cruel.

"Trust me, that's no threat. It's a warning." I don't know where the words, or the authority behind them, come from, but everyone within earshot is silent.

Aften just stands there silently staring. The crowd dies down, and I now only feel what Aften feels. She is terrified.

"Jewels, get in the car, now!" Sebastian speaks through clenched teeth. His eyes are on fire, full of rage and compassion all at once.

I obey.

They all stare at the car as we drive off. I should have felt relieved to be leaving the park, but I am worried.

"Why did you say those things to Aften?" he asks almost immediately.

"I wasn't trying to scare her. I saw something."

"Yeah, but people see things all the time; that doesn't mean it's real."

"Maybe if we were talking about someone else, but things I see usually aren't that far off." I have said too much.

He pulls the car over on the shoulder of the road and just sits there staring at the steering wheel. I want to ask him why he stopped, but I am afraid to.

"Jewels, is Aften one of those special people you spoke of before? The Others?" he asks, still staring at the wheel.

"Take me home, now! I don't want to talk to you about this anymore."

"Answer my question, and we're on our way."

"Aften's not one of the Others, but I saw something horrible happening to her when the card landed in front of her."

Silence.

I fold my arms across my chest and look out of the window. Being in such close proximity to Sebastian, I'm reminded of the scent from Unwined. Sandalwood. It doesn't smell like cologne. It's natural.

Maybe it's just my imagination, but whenever he is near, my senses seem to heighten.

"How much do you know about your past?" he asks.

"Apparently not much," I answer.

He ignores my snark.

"Jewels, there's a lot you don't know about me and Amina." He stops briefly, holding both of my hands delicately but tightly. "There's a lot that you don't know about yourself."

I try to yank my hands away from him, but he won't let go.

"Earlier, when you showed me the scrapbook, I wanted to tell you all of this, but—"

"But what?" I ask hesitantly.

"Where do I begin?" He turns in the uncomfortable seat until his entire body faces me. "Jewels, you already know what happened to your mother. In fact, you carelessly told the whole story to Mr. Jennings' class the other day."

He looks at me, probably trying to figure out what is going through my mind.

"Wait, the story I told in class was just that—a story."

"No, it's not. You, telling that story in such a descriptive and passionate way just confirmed all of our suspicions. You're the one we've been searching for."

"No, no, no! Don't you even try it! That story isn't real!" I try opening the door, but the child lock is activated.

"I swear to you on everything that's important to me; it's real." He pauses briefly. "I wasn't sure until you showed me the pictures from the scrapbook. Your grandmother is the one who took you from your mother."

"That's a lie!" I speak through clenched teeth. My throat burns as I try to speak. "My mother died giving birth to me, and my grandmother has raised me ever since." I probably sound naive, but I still try to stand my ground.

"I don't want to frighten you, Jewels," he begins, choosing his words carefully.

"We're well past the stage of you frightening me. Now you're really pissing me off. I don't want to hear any of this. Let me go, Sebastian!"

"There are some really bad elements out here that either want to use you or want you dead. If you don't wise up, their mission will be accomplished." He pauses briefly, shaking his head. "I just don't get you."

"You don't get me? You're the one trying to tell me my grandmother killed my mother and also wants me dead, and yet you don't get me. You really need to sit back and re-examine the situation."

"You saw the book. Lilith is not your grandmother. Is it natural for anyone to live that long without aging?" His words seem to be drifting further and further away as I begin piecing things together. "She's dangerous, Jewels!"

"You know what, Sebastian, just stay away from me," I say, unlocking the door manually.

He jumps out of the driver's seat and starts following me.

"It's too late for you to be walking out here alone."

"Okay Sebastian, since you know so much, how do you know all this stuff about me and my family?" I turn, standing face-to-face with him.

He hesitates momentarily.

"Tell me, Sebastian," I insist.

"You know," he says in a low growl that brings a chill to the night air.

"Say it, Sebastian," I whisper.

"I'm the thing meant to watch over you... to make sure you're safe."

My stomach turns at his deliberate choice of words. He said thing, not boy or person, but thing.

"No more talking. Just leave me alone. I wish you would take me home," I say through clenched teeth, not wanting him to continue.

Sebastian stops dead in his tracks. The mask has fallen, and a darkness in his eyes takes up residency, but there is something else there that distinctly resembles a hurt child.

"As you wish." Sebastian puts me over his shoulder. I'm shocked by the speed of it. I kick, scream, and protest. He carries me to the car and plops me into the passenger seat of the Charger.

Without another word, he tears down Route 26 like a bat out of hell. He doesn't acknowledge my presence. Throughout the rest of the ride, I can't stop thinking about everything he said. Could he be right? There are so many questions Gigi has refused to answer. The strength of Sebastian's words seems to hit me even harder as the cold breeze blows in my face. The evidence is there, but none of that stuff could be real...could it?

What about Sebastian? How does he know so much, and what about the incident in the woods tonight? I can't swallow. Each time I try, it feels like I am trying to gulp down a giant, bitter pill. It is like a fairy tale gone horribly wrong. If he is right, I am more peculiar than I could have ever imagined.

I'm not happy to see my house when we arrive.

"When you really want answers to the questions you ask, you know where to look." He stops briefly. He doesn't look at me as he speaks. "Just be careful not to ask the wrong person."

Without another word, he pulls off with speed.

As I walk into the house, my mind is preoccupied with Sebastian's last words. I sit on my bed pondering them until I drift to sleep.

CHAPTER 12—TABULA RASA

My mind is clearer when I wake the next morning, but I am shrouded by a feeling of dread and uncertainty.

There is no sunshine, just darkness. I struggle to differentiate between my dream and the events of yesterday until it hits me; for the first time ever, I had slept a dreamless sleep.

Gigi!

I was so out of it when I got in last night that I went straight to bed. I didn't even shower, which is a big no-no in this house.

I jump out of bed. The smoke from the bonfire has saturated my hair and clothes. I think about spraying perfume on myself, but it would take the stench from worse to ridiculous.

"Gigi?" I call out, dashing out of my room.

No answer.

"Gigi?" I call, checking around her apartment-sized room.

Still, no answer. No Gigi.

I run downstairs, checking the living room, the dining room, the kitchen, and every other room.

Nothing.

Gigi never came home.

All the anger and animosity I felt for Gigi yesterday immediately disintegrates. I don't care who she really is. All I know is that she has done nothing but protect and care for me.

I need to call her.

I run back up to my room. Two minutes after dumping out the contents of my various bags, I finally find the lavender piece of scrap paper that Gigi had written her number on.

Grabbing our landline, I dial the number with hesitant fingers. I can't help but be fearful of the answer that awaits me on the other end of the line.

It rings and rings, but Gigi doesn't answer. I hang up and dial again, wandering into the hallway.

Upon leaving my room, I hear a ringing sound coming out of Gigi's room.

I breathe deeply, walking into Gigi's bedroom. The ringing continues and it's coming from under Gigi's bed. All of the air suddenly escapes from my lungs.

If Gigi's phone is under the bed, then where is Gigi?

My blood runs cold as I kneel on the hardwood floor. The fear of what I might find along with the phone makes my throat go painfully dry.

Gigi's black Chloe bag.

Why would she leave her purse here?

I grab it and lunge for the steps.

Had the bag been there yesterday?

I sink onto the living room floor, dumping out the contents of Gigi's bag. Never in my life have I been permitted to even get a stick of gum out of her bag. I thought she bought the oversized and overpriced bag because it was stylish, but seeing it filled to capacity makes me doubt my previous assumption.

Why does she carry around all of this crap?

I have never seen so many compact mirrors in one bag. I'm sure her reflection is the same in all of them.

The bag is completely empty now but still feels oddly heavy. I plunge my hand into the bag one last time, and this time I feel something under the silk lining.

At this point, nothing really shocks me, but finding this much hidden cash would alarm anyone. All hundred-dollar bills. There has to be about twenty thousand dollars here—maybe more.

I know Gigi is loaded, but who in their right mind walks around with this much cash on them?

I sit there on the floor in complete and utter silence. I don't know what to do or who to call.

Maybe it is time for me to call the police.

Suddenly, my attention is diverted away from the phone that I grip tightly in my hand. There is an annoying scratching sound.

The familiar lump in my throat returns, and I know I want to cry. I feel helpless and more alone than ever before.

The scratching intensifies. My eyes wander as I frantically search the room. I am making myself dizzy. It feels like I am running around in circles. Determination is the only thing that keeps me from fainting or crying.

I stop myself, finally realizing where the sound is coming from.

The sliding doors—the doors that lead to the deck. I had totally forgotten.

The doors are hidden behind layers of drapery. No wonder it is so dark in here. Gigi is usually up by sunrise to open the curtains, inviting the light into our home.

Putting discouragement aside, I quickly push back the elaborate draperies and vertical blinds.

It's the gray cat, standing on its hind legs. Its eyes are well defined and leering at me from the other side of the glass doors.

I unlock them, half expecting the feline to attack me. Instead, the seemingly aggressive, gray beauty gets down on all fours and turns, gracefully prancing off the deck.

What was all the commotion about if you were just going to run away?

A chill goes through my body as my bare feet touch the deck. I quickly notice that the cat has gone through a newly acquired gap in the boards.

As I start toward the gap, I notice blotches of crimson on the sharp, uneven edges of the wood. The fear doesn't hit me until the cat returns to the deck and jumps into my arms.

The blood on the deck doesn't belong to the cat.

A morbid tremor makes my hands shake violently. I yearn for my cards.

The gray kitty grows restless in my arms and begins to hiss.

I drop her before she decides on taking the hostile approach of scratching me. I don't need anything else drawing attention to my face.

She runs off the deck once more, stopping in the grass to look back at me.

It almost seems like she wants me to follow her.

She begins pacing in circles impatiently, so I follow her down the steps and into Gigi's fairy tale-style garden.

The garden is beautiful from a distance, but being this close to it is disturbing. I don't know what Gigi could have had in mind when she designed it. *Why would anyone put such an intricate hedge maze in a residential backyard?* The maze is made of cypress trees, and the entrance has a wooden door within a hedge, covered with rose vines.

As I step through the entrance of the maze, my surroundings noticeably darken. The afternoon sky looks like twilight, and the moon places a spotlight on the maze. The hedges that once matched my five-foot-seven stature are now suspiciously taller. This has to be a hallucination.

I close my eyes tightly, hoping the sun will return when they reopen, but no such luck. Instead, the wind picks up, carrying small voices that seem to be coming from the hedges. I can't make out what they're saying. It just sounds like a bunch of gibberish. They have to be coming from the neighbor's kids.

I turn quickly to run out of the maze, but the entrance is gone.

How can that be?

I haven't gone anywhere yet. This is exactly where I entered, and I haven't taken more than two steps into the maze.

"She's here. She's here." This time I understand the voices clearly.

"Who's there?" I call out. There is no reply, just more whispering, accompanied by childlike laughter, though something within me knows that the laughter is not coming from any child.

I catch a glimpse of the cat's gray tail turning a corner.

I follow, trying to keep up as the feline turns each corner like a pro, but it is impossible as I attempt to avoid the prickly vines and thorns that seem to be reaching out for me like outstretched hands.

I've lost the cat and keep running into dead ends.

Why did I even follow the stupid cat anyway?

I grow tired and I stumble repeatedly. I sit on the ground, my back against the seemingly growing hedges, and begin to cry. I pull my knees against my chest and hug them tightly, rocking back and forth. The voices begin again, this time coming from all directions. Now they are louder and feel like they are closing in on me. I sit still, my eyes wide, looking from side to side. From the corner of my eye, I catch a glimpse of an elfin face protruding from the hedge. When I turn to look, there is nothing there, just laughter.

I freeze with fear. There is definitely something out here.

The wind scatters my hair, but putting it in place is the last thing on my mind. I need to calm myself. I came out here for one reason—to find Gigi—so I need to be strong enough to face whatever I may find. I sit with my back against the hedge and close my eyes, trying to envision the events of the last twenty-four hours. I need my mind to drift to a quiet place. A place with no fear, no doubt.

Suddenly, the peculiar voices that had surrounded me are muted, and all I can hear is the tranquil whisper of the wind combing through the trees' leaves. I sit there, breathing, trying not to think, only listening to the wind. The newly calm atmosphere allows my mind to drift away from the fear that had smothered me only moments earlier. I now only hear and feel the movements of nature.

As I press my back against the cypress, all of the worries seem to exit my body. I feel as light and carefree as the wind.

After a while, the sound of the wind seems to change once more. Now, there is a chorus of soft-spoken voices. It isn't confusing like before.

My body seems to be getting heavier. There is a feeling moving through me that has never been present in my waking state, only in dreams. I feel powerful.

Although my eyes are shut, I am more conscious of my surroundings than ever before, noticing each individual sound. The whisper becomes louder and clearer, becoming the lead vocalist of nature's soundtrack, rather than the soft hum of background vocals. The menacing laughter that was once in the forefront is now nothing more than a muffled undertone.

The voice returns again, "Run. He's here too." The voice is so familiar, but I know I've never heard it before in my conscious state.

I inhale deeply, opening my eyes. Various scents I hadn't noticed before swirl around me: roses, honeysuckle, hawthorn, and lavender.

Lavender. Gigi smells like lavender. I have to get up. I can't lose her—not now, when it seems like I am losing everything, including my mind.

As I stand barefoot on the cool earth, the pain from my cuts is numbed. My eyes catch sight of a figure staring at me from a few feet away. This time, it isn't a man wearing a hoody. This is a man wearing an executioner's mask, like in the vision I had in the bookstore. He doesn't have hooved feet like the person in my vision. He's wearing pants and he's barefoot, but when I look at his eyes through the holes of the mask, they are the same yellow eyes of the hooded man.

"Run," the little voice says, it's diction clear and crisp this time. With renewed strength, I take off, running as fast as I can. The maze seems to open up. No more dead ends. I turn to see if he's behind me. When I do, there's a wall of trees, which is impossible, since it's where I came from.

There are slender bare footprints in the ground. A sense of encouragement surges through my body as I follow them, never looking up and never reaching another dead end. I catch sight of the misty-colored feline that got me into this mess. I follow her, this time running, not paying attention to the ever-growing vines, and not thinking of the masked man, who seems to have been swallowed by the maze. As I follow, the slender footprints end, and now there are only paw prints. I wonder if I am going the wrong way until we come to a narrow door made of vines.

A prickly pain runs down my spine, but this time it isn't from the thorns. It's fear.

The door has no knob. I remember Dodie Hemisphere's story. She described a door that looked like this one.

Why would she place a door here without a knob? And why would she have thorns growing across a door? It's like she doesn't want anyone to enter.

As I draw closer to the door, it slowly begins to open. The chattering returns, but I tune it out. I never even touched the door, yet it has opened for me as if it has been awaiting my arrival.

I feel no apprehension as I enter the enchanting center of the intricate maze. On the other side of the door, the sun gleams brightly, as if it is the first day of summer. I stand there in awe at the beauty that now faces me. My eyes immediately fall upon a glorious fountain with a statue of a mermaid at its center.

Drawn to the statue's beauty, I can't help but move forward. Tropical fish of various colors scatter as they feel the vibrations of my approach, but when I place my hand into the water, they all come to me willingly, their colorful hues dancing across the sparkling water.

The chattering gibberish returns and quickly brings me back to reality.

I look around, appraising my surroundings. There are mirrors all over the place, even at the bottom of the extravagant fountain.

The garden is sprinkled with accents that make it even more enchanting: rosebushes that seem to go on forever, lavender with a fragrance so intoxicating it could calm the nerves of the most troubled soul, and sunflowers so tall they seem to be sniffing me and not the other way around. There is a small playhouse with a miniature table, complete with a porcelain tea set.

As if she would ever let anyone's child come here. Gigi hates children.

The maze is large, but how can all of this fit at the center of it all?

In the midst of such beauty, my heart is heavy and overcome with an ominous weight. Something is happening while I stand, appreciating what appears to be a sinful pleasure. I can feel it. I am surrounded by nature, but something feels very unnatural about it. And to make matters worse, I am enveloped by the sensation that I am being watched.

I turn to find the gray cat perched on the steps of an arresting ivory gazebo that seems too outstanding to be here.

When I begin making my way toward the gazebo, the cat leaves its place, revealing a dark stain on the otherwise spotless marquee. Logically I know what it will be when I examine the blemish, but my heart still holds an ounce of optimism.

Just as I feared; it's blood. Looking at the feline once again, I know it did not come from her.

My heart pulsates as fiercely and loudly as a drum as I climb the steps to find Gigi lying motionless on the gazebo floor. Her face is hidden under her long, blond hair, which is crusted with blood. The cat just stands there now, staring at me as if waiting for my next move.

I drop to the ground and hold Gigi in my arms. I sweep her long, blond hair aside, exposing her perfect face. Normally, Gigi doesn't look like she could be anyone's grandmother, but at the moment, her usual fair skin is pale and chalky, and her small rosebud mouth has transformed into a colorless slit. I know the blood is coming from somewhere on her head because it stains my clothes as I hold it to my chest. This is no time to be helpless. I need to think logically to help Gigi, if I can.

Checking her pulse makes me lose all faith.

Nothing. She has no heartbeat. I sit there, looking at Gigi's lifeless body. All of my life, I had complained about being alone, and now I truly am. I decide to give CPR a try anyway, but nothing comes of it.

I don't know when the tears begin, but by the time the familiar lump becomes present in my throat, my face is already drenched.

Pain, regret, and loneliness eat away at my insides. I have nothing. No one.

I can't let go of Gigi. I sit leaning over Gigi's unmoving body, washing her face with a shower of tears.

And then I see it. She gasps deeply for air. Her eyes bulge and her chest rises violently, snapping her head up.

She's alive.

I don't understand what is happening. She had no pulse, so how can this be?

Her face is soaked from my tears as if her head had been dunked in water. She is disoriented, eyes searching for a focal point and then they land on me.

Her face twitches as if she is trying to smile but winces in pain and stops.

"Oh, Gigi!" I have never been so happy to see her open her eyes. All of the anger and resentment I had ever felt disintegrates, and I embrace her as tenderly as I can.

"What happened to you?" I am rambling. "I have to call an ambulance to—"

"No!" she cuts me off.

I didn't think she'd be capable of speaking at this point.

She raises her cold hand to weakly caress my face. Her touch is doing something to me. I watch as Gigi transforms before my eyes. The filmy layer seems to melt away, exposing the bewitching lapis lazuli eyes that I love and admire. The alabaster complexion that men swoon over is coming into sight, and her lips have blossomed into the pouty mouth I know so well.

What is happening?

Soon the voices return but this time at full volume. This time there are multitudes of little people with elfin faces walking toward the gazebo and exiting the lavender-covered playhouse. Some tall, some short, some supernaturally beautiful, some grotesque enough to give you nightmares for all eternity, and others too tiny to make out their facial features as they hover in the air. I hear splashing coming from the fountain, but I refuse to look for fear of stupefying myself any further.

I am scared stiff. They are speaking amongst themselves whilst moving in on us slowly.

"Gigi, are you seeing this, too?" When I look down at her, she is smiling and looking at the crowd that surrounds us.

The look in her eyes tells me that from here on out, nothing will ever be the same again.

A lone tear escapes as a feeling of dread stings my eyes. Her eyes contort, becoming the red menacing eyes that had taken Sebastian away from me in my dream. I try blinking, but it is impossible. I am weak and spellbound.

My body becomes heavy, as do my eyelids. I try fighting the urge to close them because I know that if I do so, my body will shut down as well.

It's no use. I am becoming weaker and weaker. The voices are only silenced when Gigi begins to speak in Latin, "*Et nunc est insania factum est deletur. De terrore somniorum, sive qui insipientes estis nunc scio mihi, cum motus sit incorruptibilis. Repone insipiens veritatem somnia. Tabula Rasa. Tabula Rasa. Tabula Rasa.*"

Gigi sounds like an old smoker, singing a lullaby. Her voice is raspy, making it sound like a witch's spell from Grimm Fairy Tales.

I murmur it in English as if I'd been instructed to do so, "Madness has taken place and now must be erased. The horrors you now know will be replaced with senseless dreams or disintegrate. Replace the truth with senseless dreams. Blank Slate. Blank Slate. Blank Slate."

Darkness surrounds me, and I no longer see or hear the strangeness that my life has become.

CHAPTER 13—BEWITCHED, BOTHERED AND BEWILDERED

The sun's rays seem to be on a mission to blind me before I can even make it out of bed.

My body feels terribly heavy, and I can't quite seem to shake the feeling that something is missing.

Even the usually soft, black jersey sheets on my bed seem too harsh. Everything is off. Pushing the sheets aside, I begin making my way out of bed, almost falling from dizziness as I sit up in my bed. My head pounds, feeling like it will explode.

Why am I such a masochist? I should just stay in bed like any other teenager would do on a Sunday morning. But something inside my head—maybe the drum line that won't cease—compels me to stand at attention.

Besides the massive migraine, I feel like I'm not seeing things clearly. Everything around me seems hazy and I'm overcome with lethargy.

"We thought you'd never wake up"

My heart almost bursts through my chest as the deep and raspy voice startles me. This is usually the part in the horror movies when the girl slowly turns to find the killer skulking with a sharp cleaver in hand. I hold my breath as if that will somehow stop whatever fate awaits me.

Turning in the direction of the murderous voice, I scream when my eyes fall upon a silver-haired freak, sitting in my old rocking chair.

"Who the hell are you and what are you doing in my room?" I yell, jumping to my feet, in an attempt to pounce on him, but I fall instead.

The *Silver Surfer* rushes to my aid, and I make a feeble attempt to hit him that only makes him laugh.

"Lilith said you were feisty." His voice is vaguely familiar. The gravelly tone and the accent remind me of Sebastian, though this one is more aristocratic. British maybe.

"And you would be?"

"Niko. We're family. Well, sort of. No blood relation."

"You're either family or you aren't." I steady myself, getting to my feet, rushing past him and out of my bedroom.

"Gigi!" I scream, clumsily running down the stairs. *Why is my balance so off?*

There's a lot of commotion. I think I've stepped into The Twilight Zone. My house is lively. There's a bald, clean-shaven man with flawless dark skin playing the piano while a pale little man with red hair sings some ugly song. A beautiful redheaded woman, draped in jewelry and as tall as Gigi, is wearing a flowing green maxi dress and dancing around like it's the most beautiful thing she's ever heard. Relief washes over me when I find Gigi in the kitchen, preparing a breakfast spread fit for a king. There are three different types of bacon, sausages, poached and scrambled eggs, Belgian waffles, French Toast, pancakes, fresh fruit, and fresh juice.

"Who the hell are all these people and why does the house look like the circus has come to town?" I ask, taken aback to find Gigi, who never lets her hair hang loose, looking like an ethereal goddess. Her hair is no longer tamed in an intricate bun. It's free, beyond waist length. She's barefoot and wearing a white camisole and white linen pants. She's not even wearing a bra. Her appearance is in stark contrast to Gigi's usual affinity for Parisian chic.

She's laughing wildly as she hands a tray of food to a timid but beautiful, petite girl with skin like bronze.

"Gigi?" I say her name with uncertainty because I'm utterly confused.

"You're awake, ma petite chérie." Her voice comes out so sharp, my immediate reaction is to cringe. She rushes toward me to hug me, catching me off guard. "We've been so worried about you."

Gigi is different. Her face is paler than usual and she has bags under her eyes and a bruise on her forehead that she's tried to cover with makeup. For the nearly 17 years I've known her, she has never looked like this.

I'm trying hard to remember how I got into bed and why I'm wearing this god-awful red silk pyjama set that I've always hated.

"You were worried about me and yet you left a strange boy in my room, alone, watching me from a rocking chair like Norman Bates. Can you say creepy?"

"You're so dramatic. Don't you remember? I came home from the town hall meeting on Friday night and found you passed out on the deck. You were burning up. You slept straight through Saturday."

She checks my forehead. I'm not sure if it's out of sincerity or if she's putting on a show for these people.

"You may not have a fever anymore, but I think you should stay home another day." Her brows furrow momentarily but relax as her eyes fall on Niko.

"Two things. One, I never get sick. And two, it's Sunday. Where would I be going? Unless you've become religious while I was sleeping and we're going to church."

"Bijou, it's Wednesday. You've been sick since Friday and in and out of sleep."

"That's not possible. I don't remember being sick. And if I was so sick and passed out, why didn't you take me to a hospital?" Gigi is lying to me. I know it. I fold my arms over my chest and look at her skeptically. She's fidgeting and gets back to preparing food, but I'm not letting this go.

"You know I don't believe in hospitals. Everything we need can be found in nature, and it worked because your fever is gone." She sounds so chipper and fake. "But I do think you should stay home for the rest of the week. I've already talked to the school, so they'll understand."

"I'm not missing any more school. Who are all these people? We never have company."

"They're family." She's being short with me now.

"You said we don't have any family, so where did they come from?" I follow her from the kitchen to the dining room and back again. I'm not letting her off that easily.

"Well, that's what people say when they aren't on speaking terms with their family, Bijou."

"No. They say, 'We have family, but we aren't on speaking terms.'"

"Look!" she screams at me, slamming her hand on the surface of the island table. She finally turns to face me as she speaks. "I've made peace with my sister, so she's come with her husband, step-son, my brother, and her maid to help prepare for your seventeenth birthday party."

I'm taken aback by all of this. A party? This is coming from the woman who once told me birthday parties are for fools seeking validation from even bigger fools.

"So who's the fool in this scenario? The celebrant or the party thro—"

"Finish that sentence if you want to pass out again," she threatens. "You still don't look well enough to return to school."

"I don't feel sick at all. Disoriented, yes. Sick, no," I say. "Why can't I remember anything? Maybe you poisoned me with all your magical leaves and hocus pocus, *Drusilla*." I rub my temples as if it will make me less groggy and help me remember.

She's ignoring me and I'm frustrated because this isn't right. I've never even had a cold before, so me passing out doesn't seem believable. I try hard to remember what happened after coming home from school, but nothing rings a bell. In fact, I don't even remember dreaming about Sebastian. That's never happened before.

"I've spoken to the school board. Since all school-sanctioned events have been canceled until further notice, I've agreed to make your party a town event." She's giddy as she speaks. Lilith Fitzroy is never giddy. "I'm paying for everything. Patterson Mansion, catering, and security, so your masquerade ball will be the grandest event this town's ever seen."

"Gigi, when you were picking your herbs, did you happen to smoke any of them? Because you told me I would never have a birthday party, so why now? What's so special about seventeen?"

It's like I'm not even talking to her. She's talking to her new family and carrying on so much that I want to choke her.

"Bijou, let me introduce you to everyone. This is my younger sister, Tempest," Gigi announces, pointing to the redhead. "Her husband, Salif; his son, Niko; and my younger brother, Rowan."

The two men are quite unfriendly. At least Salif smiles slightly, but Rowan looks at me with eyes that say, *kill, kill, kill.*

"Come here, *jolie.* Let me have a look at you." Tempest examines me, compares me to a few flowers—which I think is supposed to be a compliment—and squeezes me tightly. Even though she's wearing loads of jewelry, I can't take my eyes off the emerald ring she's wearing. *Why does it look so familiar?*

I wait for an introduction to the petite girl but none is offered.

"What's your name?" I finally ask her.

She automatically looks to Tempest, still not raising her head.

"Sano," she answers quietly. Though her voice is low, it is obvious to me that, at full projection, her voice holds power. After she gives her name, she quickly retreats to Tempest's side.

She is trembling, but I don't think it's from being cold. I suddenly realize that since awakening, I haven't felt any of their emotions or been able to tell who's Typical or who's one of the Others.

I try being hospitable as long as I can, but it is driving me crazy. Breakfast is weird and watching Gigi is exhausting, carrying on like a silly school girl. Looking at the food is enough to fill my stomach, but I pig out. It is like a buffet, and the discussion about the elegant party Gigi is planning seems to have no end—everyone has ideas. Niko is sitting directly across from me and his staring is making me uncomfortable.

The first word that comes to mind upon looking at him is "majestic." His olive-toned face holds fine, delicate features, more sublime than a handsome man, yet statelier than a beautiful woman, slender in build, rather tall, and full of grace. His silver hair pulls away from his face, exposing narrow ears. From the corner of my eye, I could almost swear his ears are pointed. He is the personification of aristocracy.

* * *

After my shower, I can't shake the feeling that something isn't right. After throwing on denim dungarees and a white crop top, I tear my room apart in search of my satchel. *Why can't I remember anything?* I don't remember being sick. I barely remember coming home from school on Friday. How can I lose so much time, and why was I on the deck?

And then I hear it. Scratching coming from my balcony, like the other night. I open it to find the gray cat, perched on my satchel like she's been keeping it safe for me.

"I'm gonna have to name you, huh?" I ask, picking her up and collecting my bag. "Kitty Fantastico is too long, so how about Kit? Yeah, Kit. I like it."

I head over to my mini fridge and the best I can come up with is a tuna salad sandwich and milk, but she eats and drinks without hesitation.

"I'll read up on what kitties eat and buy you some food today, but you have to stay hidden or else Gigi will evict you."

* * *

"Bijou, could you come down here for a moment?" Everything about Gigi is annoying me right now, especially her voice, because everything that comes out of her mouth is a lie. I refuse to believe that I've been sick and sleeping since Friday. And this newly acquired family story is complete bull.

Wait, why am I being so antagonistic? Maybe she isn't hiding anything at all. I am being too hard on her.

"Coming, Gigi!"

She isn't in the kitchen when I get downstairs, and neither are her guests. I notice the garage door is open, but the lights are out.

I call her name, but she doesn't answer. Hitting the switch in the garage, my eyes are surprised to find Gigi seated behind the wheel of a brand new red Mini Cooper—my dream car. Everyone else is crowded around, watching.

"Gigi, you have to let me drive it to school. Please, please, please. I promise I'll be extra careful!" I can't hide my enthusiasm even if I want to.

"You better be careful because I don't see myself buying you another one anytime soon if you destroy this one." She climbs out of the car, looking at me instantaneously to catch my reaction.

"You mean—" I can't even finish the sentence.

"Yes, my jewel, it's all yours," she says with a warm smile that makes her timeless beauty shine through the lack of sleep.

I cup my mouth. I am speechless. Nothing I can say could show Gigi how appreciative I am for this gift—for everything. I jump on Gigi, hugging her tightly.

"Thank you so much, Gigi. I'm so sorry for giving you such a hard time. I just want to be normal, like everyone else—without the sympathy or special treatment from teachers—so, when you mentioned me staying home again, I kinda' freaked."

"That's just it, *chérie*; you're not like everyone else. You're—" She stops herself. "Just enjoy it. I want Niko to drive with you to school, so he can have the car while you're in class."

And just like that, my enthusiasm fades. She kisses each of my cheeks and I grab the keys from her. "You guys are going to get along so well, and he's so handsome."

Maybe my eyes are deceiving me, but as I make my way back into the house, Rowan's face contorts into what looks like an intricate Halloween mask from the Leprechaun films. When I blink, his face is normal again, and he looks like David the Gnome.

CHAPTER 14—REVELATIONS

Driving to school with Niko is odd to say the least. I'm driving, and whenever I look right, I get a glimpse of him staring at me. We arrive at a stop sign. I meet his glare, but he doesn't look away.

"Careful. You might turn to stone," I say with no humor, in an attempt to frighten him.

"Between you and I, Medusa was terrified of me." He says this with a straight face. As though Medusa is an actual person. A chill runs through my body as he begins to smile, slowly and deliberately. A half smile, to be exact, that accentuates his features, particularly his cleft chin.

My eyes return to the road, and I refuse to look at him anymore.

"So Lilith has finally stopped running." He breaks the uncomfortable silence.

"I'm afraid I don't know what you mean." *Does he know she's Anastasia Powers?*

"Come on, Bijou. Don't tell me you don't find it odd that you two move around more than the Romani?"

"Gigi gets stir crazy. That's all."

He laughs.

"She's crazy alright. Crazy enough to move you to the Ninth Circle of Hell."

Surprisingly, my own emotions are overwhelming and untainted by the emotions of others, and I am angry that he's speaking of my grandmother in this way.

"You must be just as crazy then, because you're in hell now, too," I say as we turn into the drop-off zone.

"Speaking of hell, are you familiar with the Eighth Circle—according to Dante, that is?" He asks in that annoying way teachers do when they think you aren't prepared for class.

I turn to look at his stuck up, smug face before I answer. He looks as though he's waiting to exhale.

"It's Fraud," I say with a smugness that could rival Sebastian's.

"At least you've read it. You'd be wise to remember, treachery follows fraud." This time, he doesn't smile. "Not all who smile at you have your best interest at heart."

"And on that note, I leave you in your inferno." I park the car, unbuckle my seatbelt, and grab my bag. "School is out at 2:35. Be here before three?"

I exit the car, only to see him follow. In seconds, horns are being blown and my classmates are staring. I'm already a spectacle here. Now I'm with a guy who's about our age and looks like Tolkien wrote him into existence.

He catches up to me, putting his arm around my shoulder with an amount of heat that makes me do a double take to make sure it's not Sebastian. It's somehow different, burning in the way Vicks Vapor Rub does, with a cooling effect.

"You don't like me very much, do you?" he asks, meeting the glares of onlookers intimidatingly, making most look away. Even though he's strikingly handsome, their eyes show fear, but I'm merely guessing. I can't feel their emotions.

"I like you about as much as I enjoy not being able to remember anything from the last week or so," I say with a smile as I remove his arm.

"Give me a chance to show you I'm not as bad as you think," he says as we come close to the school's entrance.

"Why do you care if I like you or not? You don't know me."

"First of all, you talk in your sleep, which is why I offered to watch over you while you were sleeping." I'm stunned into silence, afraid of what I may have said in my sleep.

"I know that you have a lot of questions, and Lilith isn't very forthcoming. I have some questions too, and I think we can help each other." His black eyes are surprisingly earnest. "Let me take you somewhere after school."

The bell rings and I see Sebastian and Amina on the other side of the door, looking on in horror.

"Okay. I'll go with you," I reply.

Niko kisses my cheek, catching me off guard, and walks away, his long hair trailing behind him in a neat herringbone braid. I stand there wondering if that qualifies as a first kiss and feeling as though I've somehow betrayed the Inconsistent Sebastian. Right then, he breaks eye contact, and Amina yanks open the door to begin her inquisition.

"We've been so worried about you. I went to your house and saw that your grandmother is back. Did you ask her about the scrapbook and the pictures?" Amina is bombarding me with questions I don't understand.

"I was sick. No big deal."

"No big deal? After what you showed us, and then you disappeared for four days. I'd say it's a colossal deal. Especially after the bookstore incident. We haven't even talked about any of it yet, and now the whole thing at the party with Aften." Amina is frantic. She isn't being playful or sarcastic like she usually is.

"I don't understand anything you're saying right now." I stop in the middle of the hallway, looking at Sebastian and Amina. "What party? What could I have possibly said to Aften?"

"You kissed me. Do you remember that?" Sebastian isn't playing around or smiling either. His eyes are serious and his body is rigid as he faces me.

"That's not possible. I couldn't kiss you. I mean not that I wouldn't. I just mean, me being the kissee would be more plausible." I'm babbling. "Why can't I remember anything?"

"Bastian, you kissed her? But dad said—"

"I don't really care what Dad thinks right now, Mina," Sebastian spits the name Aiden out like it's put a bad taste in his mouth. He runs his fingers through his hair. "Bijou, about four different people have bumped into you in the last minute and you aren't fidgeting or looking for your cards."

"It's no big deal," I shrug.

They look at each other. Amina's eyes are wide and telling, while Sebastian's forehead creases.

"We need to leave now," Sebastian declares, grabbing my arm and leading me towards the junior parking lot without awaiting my response.

"Get off me. I'm not going anywhere with you. We're already late for first period."

I start walking, not paying attention to where I'm going, only to bump into the last person on Earth I want to have contact with. Amanda DeVoe.

"Watch it, loser," she says, pushing me.

"I'm sorry, Mandy. Didn't see you."

Christa is with her, but Aften is noticeably missing.

"Careful Mandy. She might make you disappear next." Christa's voice is venomous.

"What do you mean *next*?" I ask.

"Jewels, let's go," Sebastian says, trying to pull me away, but I resist.

"Everyone heard and saw you threaten Aften at the bonfire, and she never went home that night. No one's heard from her since." Christa is being aggressive. So unlike what I've come to know of her.

"Aften's missing? Wait. When's her birthday?" I ask.

"Let's go, Christa. Stay away from her. It isn't safe." Mandy says, pulling Christa away from me like I'm about to attack them or something.

I'm so confused. Nothing makes sense and everyone is being so weird.

"Her birthday's June 21st. Why?" Christa asks, now at the other end of the hallway. Just as she's being pulled away, Sebastian and Amina are pulling me towards the parking lot.

"What the—?" I break free from *Heckle and Jeckle*. "I am not ditching school with you two. I have enough going on at home with my family reunion, my birthday party, and playing catch up at school."

"I can't do this anymore," Sebastian picks me up, in frustration, throws me over his shoulder, and carries me to his Charger. Of course, I'm shouting at him all the way.

"Bijou, being sick doesn't give you amnesia and take away your ability to be an empath. Where's the logic in that?" Sebastian shouts at me as he puts me down.

"I passed out, so maybe I bumped my head when I fell," I say, but as the words leave my mouth, I find that I need to convince myself as well.

Sebastian kicks his tire in frustration.

"Bastian, chill," Amina says. "We need to get out of here before someone sees us."

Sebastian is pacing like a mad person. "Bijou, we've come too far for you to just forget. You told me about how you can feel what some people are feeling and how they're the *Typicals,* and the ones who you can't feel are the *Others.*"

"I told you that ages ago in the library. And thanks for blabbing." I look at Amina, whose eyebrow is raised, maybe hurt by what I said. "No offense, Mina."

I turn to walk back into the building.

"Wait. When we kissed, I saw your dreams of the faceless boy," Sebastian says, causing me to stop. "I saw how you've dreamed of him every night and after moving here, the boy's face became mine."

I turn around to see the sincerity in Sebastian's face. His eyes are earnest. I have never told anyone about the faceless boy. Ever. He can't be lying.

Sebastian opens his backpack and pulls out the sketchpad I saw him with on the first day of school. The usually impertinent boy is now silent as he apprehensively hands it over to me. The first page makes me weak in my knees. It's a drawing of the building I lived in when we lived in France. He even has the number right on the building, 817. In the forefront is a faceless girl with a wild ponytail—bigger than her head—holding a balloon and the hand of a tall woman, who does have a face. Gigi. I look up at Sebastian, but I don't say a word. I turn page after page to find similar drawings—memories from my past. In each picture, the girl is a little older but always without a face. I turn the page, one more time to find a recent memory. It's us on the first day of school in Ms. Reaper's office, but this time, I have a face.

I drop his book, no longer wanting to run away.

"I dreamed of you every night before I ever met you, Jewels." He's facing me and holding my hands. "When we met, I knew it was you, and you felt something too."

It's like I'm dreaming. The only thing that breaks the trance is a tear falling down my face.

"Maybe this will help." Before I can ask Sebastian what he means, he kisses me. Not a peck or something soft and tame. It's fervent, as if it's all he needs to survive. I kiss him back, sucked into a vortex of familiar but distant images that seem more like a dream than any reality I've actually lived. The maze. The gray cat. The hooded man. Gigi.

I pull away from Sebastian.

"Let's go," I say.

* * *

"I remember," I finally announce as we drive down a winding, back road. "She did something to me."

"Who, Bij?" Amina asks as Sebastian takes his eyes off the road.

"My grandmother. I followed the cat through the maze, and then I heard voices and saw the hooded man. When I arrived at the center of the maze, there was a garden with a gazebo in its center. There was blood on the gazebo, and Gigi was there—dead. At least, I thought she was dead because her heart wasn't beating, but when I began to cry, she took a breath, whispered something strange, touched my face, and then everything went dark."

"Wait a minute. What maze?" Amina asks, turning around to look at me.

"You're telling me that there is a garden maze in your backyard that's large enough to fit a gazebo?" Sebastian asks.

"I didn't think it was that big, but when I went inside, the hedges seemed to grow taller and expand. I know it sounds crazy, but when I finally made it to the center, there was a fountain, a garden, and a gazebo. It just doesn't make sense."

The three of us ride in silence for a moment. I feel terribly uncomfortable, wanting someone to say something—anything!

"I know it sounds crazy," I laugh wryly, feeling stupid for telling him this.

"Do you remember the strange words she said?" Amina asks.

"I don't remember the whole thing, but the last words she said were Tabula Rasa." As I say the words aloud, I come to the painful realization that I've figured it all out on my own. "Tabula Rasa means blank slate in Latin. Gigi did this to me."

"The garden must be enchanted, and from what you tell me, you were put in a daze," he says.

"What do you mean a daze?"

"It's when a glamour is put on your sight, making you see what they want you to see, or in your case, to erase what you have seen. A daze can only work on someone who has human blood." Amina explains.

"What other type of blood would I have, if not human?"

Sebastian's jaw tightens, exposing a dimple for a second as he purses his lips—trying to find the right words.

Before I can make a comment, we are pulling into the driveway of a massive plantation house that looks like it's camouflaged, hiding behind monstrously large trees. There are no other houses near, just nature and a lake.

Sebastian and Amina are onto the porch before I can get out of the car. Amina pulls out a key, but before she has the chance to touch the door, it flings open and a little girl with raven-colored ringlets jumps into Sebastian's arms.

"Bastian, Bastian what took you so long? You said you would—" She stops mid-sentence, staring at me with wide eyes. Sebastian smiles at her wholeheartedly. I have never seen that look on his face before. She is so cute—like a doll come to life. She is dressed in an emerald-colored dress that matches her eyes. She has to be about six or seven.

"Is that her, Bastian? She's even prettier than you said. She looks like a princess. Can she stay?" It is all said in one breath. Her eyes go from glaring excitement to a doe-eyed, puppy dog pout in less than sixty seconds. She's good.

"Phoebe, stop bothering our guest." A soft-spoken woman about my height appears.

Her beauty is enthralling, with hair so long and dark, it's impossible to tell where it ends as it blends into her long black peasant dress. She's wearing a pendant of the All-Seeing Eye and her skin is a shade of amber I've only seen in jewels. She's magic personified. I'm drawn to her in a way that's almost as familiar as breathing.

"I-I know you." My voice shocks everyone, including myself. Her thick, un-arched brows raise as her eyes set on me. Her slender hand covers her mouth and she rushes toward me in a speed that would have been easily missed if I had blinked. She hugs me so tightly I feel I have no choice but to hug her in return. She's a complete stranger, but there's an overwhelming sense of familiarity.

She finally releases me, staring in my eyes with her slanted deep brown ones that are now filled with tears.

"You don't know how long we've waited for this moment." Her accent is thick, but far from Australian.

"Who are you?" My voice is no louder than a whisper as I realize I'm crying as well. Overcome by what's she's feeling.

"I'm Sebastian and Amina's mother, Sedia."

"It's very nice to meet you, ma'am."

A boy who looks like Phoebe—same face and size—emerges from the house, grabbing Sedia's hand and holding it tightly. Besides his size and the baby face, there isn't much else that seems childlike. He has dark, curly hair, similar to Phoebe's but shorter. He doesn't share the shining, emerald eyes. His eyes are an endless black that tell me he has seen things that someone so small should not have encountered. Both of them have skin like the amber-skinned woman, but not as dark. His eyes are probing me, but with no direct eye contact. Something about his gaze makes my blood run cold.

"Let's get you inside," she says in a strained voice. "There's much to discuss and not a lot of time."

What could a complete stranger possibly have to talk to me about? She takes my hand and leads me into their home.

The inside of their house is surprisingly warm and inviting—not as intimidating as the exterior. The two-story foyer gives a direct view past the chic banister and into the great room with a large, central fireplace. Across from the foyer is a bookshelf-lined study with books that look as though they are older than this house. The study stands adjacent to an elegant dining room that looks as if it has never been used. The house is breathtaking. It must have cost a fortune. They could give Gigi a run for her money. The thought of her being jealous of this house makes my lips curl into a smile. I have to stop myself before anyone else notices.

"Your home is gorgeous, Mrs. Sinjin," I finally remember to say.

She simply smiles.

"Before we get started, I'd like to welcome our guest, Bijou, to our home," says a fair-haired man. He is handsome, with delicate features, but still no comparison to Sebastian. He is a tall, slight man with skin as white as the full moon. He wears an exquisite, sky-blue, cable knit sweater that pales in comparison to his dazzling blue eyes. "Let's start with introductions."

Oh God, as if this wasn't bad enough on the first day of school.

"Of course you know Bastian, Mina, and Sedia. I'm Aiden, and this is Phoebe and Robin," he says, pointing to the two little kids. "And last, but not least, this is Moh." The boy he points to seems only a little older than I am. He's not unattractive, but looking at him makes me want to glance away quickly in intimidation. He has long, dreaded hair—so black it looks blue—and skin that glimmers as though it has been kissed by gold. He smiles brightly with perfect teeth, but he looks as if he is withholding something. He is about as tall as Sebastian but more muscular. His bone structure is as chiseled as Sebastian's, but there are no dimples to soften them.

Stop comparing every male to Sebastian.

Aiden motions us to follow him into the great room.

It is hard to tell that the sun is shining outside because of the dimness that devours the room. The blinds are closed, and no artificial lighting illuminates the room. There are a few candles lit here and there, but most of the light that makes my surroundings visible emanates from the faces of Amina and Sedia. I have never noticed how luminous their skin is until now.

It seems like everyone is in on some big secret and, as usual, I'm left out.

"Why don't you sit?" Aiden suggests.

"No, I'm fine standing." I cross my arms over my chest as everyone else sits, looking up at me. I feel quite awkward, but, since I have already refused, I stand my ground.

The tension in the room is so thick it could be cut with a knife. They all look at each other as if trying to decide who should start.

"Jewels' memory came back," Sebastian says.

"And what about her powers? Are they back as well?" Sedia asks anxiously.

I'm so embarrassed right now. It's like I'm standing on display and everything I've ever told Amina and Sebastian about in confidence is common knowledge in this house.

"What triggered it?" Aiden asks, studying Sebastian's face intently.

I look at Sebastian, then the floor, embarrassed by the answer.

"Something happened and it triggered a memory from the other night, at the party. All of her memories came back after that."

"And exactly what was this thing that happened?" Aiden stands as his soft features harden, his eyes narrowing on Sebastian.

"We kissed."

"I see. So this is a game to you, Sebastian? You and Amina are supposed to be protecting her, but instead you're playing love connection," Moh says. "She is not to be your friend or your girlfriend, and you know that."

Ouch. I feel awkward and hurt. Aiden's face was so kind just a second ago. Now, he doesn't want his children around me. Is that why I'm here?

"Protection from what?" I ask. "Why would it be their responsibility to protect me?"

Sebastian takes a chance to look at Aiden who nods, closing his eyes as if bracing himself for a blow. Everyone else in the room seems to be holding his or her breath as Sebastian stands and begins to approach me.

"No, I think it is better that I am the one to tell her," Sedia finally speaks.

Sebastian breathes heavily. A burden has been lifted off his shoulders. But he does not leave my side. They are scaring me with the number of precautions they're taking, and like the other night at the bookstore, I am in a room full of the Others, and can feel their emotions. Strangely I don't yearn for my cards. I finally decide to sit. Sebastian follows.

"Bijou, I want you to listen to what I have to say before interrupting, okay?" Sedia says.

It sounds more like an order, so I nod.

"Sebastian told us your teacher has been talking about djinn in your class." The way she says the word *djinn* makes me nervous.

"Yes?"

"Mr. Jennings only talked about the Otherworld and the two beings that were like Titania and Oberon, but he left out some pertinent details."

"You're saying it as if *A Midsummer Night's Dream* is historical fiction," I laugh awkwardly.

"Swap a few names and it is." Sedia's staring is making me uncomfortable.

I roll my eyes, but I don't interrupt.

"Do you remember the story Sebastian told in class?"

"Yes, I remember. His was the story about the Oracle's prophecy and the queen cheating on her husband with a disgusting djinn and getting pregnant."

She nods.

"That's the gist of it, but what if I told you those stories are true?"

I begin to laugh. It's not even because what she's saying is so preposterous. I'm laughing because, if I don't, I could possibly cry. I remember the day Sebastian told his story. He said he was unprepared, but he stood before the class and told that story like it was his family history, and he'd known it his entire life. He never stammered or looked unsure.

"Okay. It was nice meeting you all, but I'm crazy enough as is. I don't need to add alternate worlds to the mix." I stand, not wanting to listen anymore.

"Lilith is not your grandmother."

CHAPTER 15—PROPHECY GIRL

Sedia's outburst stops me dead in my tracks. I turn to look at her. Her face is angry but fragile. She's hurting and I can feel it, which is strange because she's definitely one of the *Others*.

"You're lying." My voice is trembling. "You're all liars."

Sebastian steps towards me. "So you believe Lilith is being honest with you? The same Lilith who poisoned you to make you forget?" He is raising his voice in frustration. "Sooner or later she'll reveal herself to you. Let's hope one of us is there to save you."

He has no right. No matter what he thinks he knows about my life.

"And why would you save me? You don't owe me anything!"

He lowers his eyes, refusing to look at me.

"Answer one question, Sebastian. Are you human?" My voice isn't demanding anymore. I am pleading with him.

Sebastian finally lifts his head again. His face pales almost to the color of the moon as he shakes his head slowly. "No, Jewels. I'm not. But I'm not that different from you."

"What are you?"

"You already know the answer to that question."

I think back to that night at Piney Run Park when I began whistling, and how quickly Sebastian was there.

He puts his hand over my heart. I try removing it, but it's as if it has been planted there.

"Do you feel that?" he asks, bringing my hand to his chest as well.

"Of course I can feel your heartbeat."

"Our hearts. They're in sync." He isn't lying. I can feel it. "Our hearts beat together as one and will do so for as long as you live," he explains, looking into my eyes. I don't get the feeling of doubt that always accompanies Gigi's words, but how can this even be possible?

"I reckon you should be here for this as well, Mina."

By the time I look in Amina's direction, she is already by my side.

He keeps his hand on my heart while Amina places my hand on hers.

The three heartbeats are in sync. I drop my hands slowly, looking at Amina's face and then Sebastian's.

"Amina and me—our sole purpose is to protect you."

He is serious as he speaks, so I don't interrupt. "When you were taken away from your mother, the whole scheme of things went out of whack, so instead of protecting you all these years, we've been searching for you instead."

"Sebastian, I was never taken from my mother. My mother died giving birth to me. She never even touched me."

I know they will be able to detect the horror I am feeling by looking at my face, so I avoid looking directly at any of them.

"We brought you here today to reaffirm what you already know, but doubt."

"How could I already know what you're telling me?" I interrupt.

"I'm not sure, but you seem to know certain things you shouldn't be aware of. For example, the story you told in class was not fiction. Jewels, the woman you spoke of in the story was your mother. I'm not sure how you even came to know it, but that is the story of how you were taken from her."

I want to choke him. "Stop it. Stop it. You're lying!" I shriek at the top of my lungs, sounding like a spoiled brat throwing a temper tantrum.

"What reason would I have for lying to you? We're probably the only people you'll ever meet who'll be completely honest with you." He pauses briefly. "Because I can't lie to you. I can find ways around the truth, but I can't flat out lie to you. I'm forbidden."

I stop interrupting him and let him continue. The harshness of his words and the tone of his voice prevent me from doing so.

"You're different. In fact, there's no one else in existence that's like you."

"So you're trying to tell me I'm the child of this prophecy?"

Sebastian is about to speak when Amina cuts him off.

"Look, Bijou, this is getting old really fast, and Sebastian being delicate doesn't seem to be helping, so let me try it my way. When the day lingers longer than it is intended to stay and before the earth has completely spun, a child will come forth, stealing powers meant for the sun. To one from here and one from there, it shall be born and shall be lost but impossible to stay hidden. For it is impossible to dim the light from the sun."

"Not this again. Didn't I already hear this?"

"The djinn were interpreting the prophecy all wrong. They were focusing on the wrong signs, forgetting about the other clues given in the prophecy. The first line about the day overstaying its welcome was a dead giveaway because that only happens on the longest day of the year—summer solstice. They all believed 'one from here and one from there' was in reference to two different elementals, but it turned out to mean 'one from their world and one from ours.'

"During normal times, every child born of both worlds was born with one djinn protector, who they were never meant to see. But you were different—born with two. Sedia always knew Sebastian and I were going to be your protectors—even before we were born. Our birth mother died in childbirth, so our father and Sedia raised us. For some reason, the universe decided you would have two djinn. Maybe because you are two elements—fire and water. We don't know for sure, but I can protect you in water where Sebastian isn't as strong. Sebastian can protect you in fire.

"We've been aware of our roles as your protectors our entire lives," she says with a wide smile.

"So, how old are you two exactly?" I ask, not sure I really want an answer.

"Djinn age differently. Time moves differently in the immortal world, so what feels like hours in that world has been years in the mortal world. Let me just put it like this: We were born way before your mother was even born, but what's odd in our situation is that we didn't start aging until you were born. That has never happened with any other djinn and their charge before. We will stop aging when you reach full maturity, unless..."

"What? Unless I die? Is that what you were going to say?" I ask.

"Yes, if you were to die before full maturity, we would immediately stop aging. We, on the other hand, will have no end. We will go on forever unless we are killed. If that's even possible."

"So, I take it that I am not immortal."

"We don't know," Sebastian answers as delicately as possible. "The only way to test your mortality is at the point of death. It's never the same. Sometimes these human-djinn hybrids take after the immortal parent, and other times they take after the mortal parent. With you, it's different because you're not necessarily a halfling, but you're not necessarily one of us either."

"I'm not human either. So where do I fit?"

"That's just it. You don't."

Once again, I am left thinking about how I would fill out an EEO survey because as of now, *other* just doesn't seem to cut it.

Moh leans forward in his chair and speaks. "Historically, the djinn hate these hybrid children, mainly because they have human blood which means they have the power to control djinn, if they know how.

Because of this, the djinn often play tricks on them to lead them to their deaths. Which is why it's so important for each and every one of them to have their own djinn, watching over them, protecting them. Unless the child has some remarkable power, the only way for a djinn to know for sure that a child is a hybrid is if their own djinn confirms it. There's this gravitational pull a djinn has to their charge. They know them when they see them, but before the Great Divide, the Oracle would simply tell the djinn who their charges were."

"If they hate hybrids so much, what's their fascination with human children? Why are there stories of changelings?" I ask, thinking of the Indian king's son in Shakespeare's play.

"The stories get one thing wrong. Changelings are almost always hybrid children. They are normally freakishly beautiful children or sometimes remarkably ugly. There's no in-between. And many times, there's trickery involved on the human side *and* the djinn side. An unfaithful wife, trying to pass an illegitimate child off as her husband's, and a djinn fooling a girl into falling in love and having a baby. Sometimes, the djinn truly loves the human, but at the end of the day, someone or something from the Otherworld will come to claim that child, unless they can stay hidden."

I think of Dodie Hemisphere and how no one believed her story, but I do. I believe it all.

"If it weren't for Aiden, none of us would be here," Sedia chimes in, coming to my side and sitting me down. "After I fought to save your mother, I was weakened, and—"

"Wait, you were the one that tried to save—" I can't continue.

"Yes, Bijou, I tried to save Femeni from—"

"It was my grandmother, wasn't it? She was the queen, and she took me away from my mother."

"Yes, Lilith was the queen, and Alieu was her king."

I probably should have been more surprised, but after seeing what I saw in her garden, it isn't all that shocking.

"But you were outnumbered. Why did you risk your life for her?"

Sedia finally releases the tears that she seemed to be withholding from the moment we met.

"I'm sorry. I didn't mean to make you cry," I say, rubbing her back, trying to comfort her even though I need comforting as well.

"A mother would do anything to save her child, and it was my prophecy that started this craziness." She convulses violently, sobs tearing through her chest as she speaks.

I can't even move. Had I heard correctly? Events from my life begin to replay in my mind. I now have answers to so many questions, but now that void has been replaced by pressure to be some type of savior to a world I never knew existed. Sedia composes herself.

"I'm still sort of lost. I thought the child would be born to the most powerful djinn, but my mother was human, right?"

"It was my vision that started it all. I was the Oracle who made the prophecy, but I didn't know that the vision I had seen was of my own grandchild. I just assumed—like everyone else—that Lilith would be the mother of this child because she was supposed to be the most powerful, but I underestimated myself. After I exposed Lilith's secret to Alieu, it started the Great Divide. The queen's followers against the king's. This is why there are so many subgroups. Faeries, Mami Wata, Gnomes, Weres, etc. We were no longer simply djinn. Lilith wanted me dead, so I had no choice but to leave the immortal world. When I had finally escaped, the first person I came in contact with was the town's young chief, Musa, a beautiful but lonely man. He was good to me. He understood the power I possessed because, although he was human, he was a descendant of a long line of West Africans with the gift of natural magics." I watch as Aiden shifts uncomfortably. He doesn't seem to like this portion of Sedia's story. "We soon married, and I became pregnant with his child. The night before I gave birth to the baby, I had a dream that Lilith found me, trying to hurt my child. I knew it wouldn't be safe for me to stay with them, so after I gave birth, I was forced to leave. This is entirely my fault. If I hadn't left, Femeni would have never married Alieu and—"

"And I would have never been born," I finish, feeling guilty for my existence.

Sebastian holds onto my hand tightly as Aiden rushes to Sedia's side.

"If changing anything would have cost me knowing you, then I would do it all again," she says to me in a comforting tone.

"What about the hooded man? Where does he fit into all of this?" I ask.

No one knows. Sedia shrugs and I can feel their confusion over it.

Sedia looks at me, touching the pendant on the necklace she wears.

"In our world, the summer solstice is a day of sacrifice. It's a regenerative day for the sun. Every seventeen years, the djinn relinquish their powers on that day, offering them to the sun. Those who partake in this ritual are said to be blessed with even more, once the day is over, but something went wrong on the day you were born. Before the sun could return the powers to the djinn, some force diverted the transference, forcing all of that power and energy into one source."

"Me?"

She only nods.

Sebastian seems to be miles away. His brows furrow as he says, "I think Bijou is some sort of supernatural amplifier."

Moh shakes his head. "But that's not saying much, Sebastian. You and Amina share a bond with Bijou, so being around her would obviously stir something within you." I still get the feeling he is withholding something.

"I agree with Bastian." Amina jumps up defensively, standing by her brother's side.

Sedia nods. "This is the All-Seeing Eye or the Eye of Providence. It is the symbol of the seer, those who have supernatural insight—the third eye." She holds up her pendant. "Would you mind showing me your mark?" she asks gently.

I almost question her meaning, but I'm pretty sure she is speaking about my birthmark, since Sebastian hasn't withheld anything from them so far.

I stand, lifting my hair to expose my *third eye.*

"Everyone wondered how I would know who the Chosen One was, but I just told them that I'd know when I saw it. What I never told them was that the child would be born with the symbol on its body. That's how I knew Lilith's baby wasn't the one." She stands, examining it. Touching it. My eyes darken and unfamiliar scenes begin to play in my mind that are so foreign to me, I'm certain they aren't mine. It's a different time. A different place. Maybe even a different world. The vision ends with scenes from my past, and it's obvious that I'm not controlling what's happening.

I begin shaking. My satchel falls to the ground, but I don't attempt to pick it up. They're all shaking too. No. The ground is shaking.

The Earth is moving, but it feels centralized. I'm doing this.

"She's seizing," I hear Aiden say, but my eyes can't seem to find him. Everything's blurry, so I squeeze my eyes shut and within moments, I'm engulfed in Sebastian's warmth and the scent of sandalwood.

He holds my hands, taking deep breaths. I focus on his breathing, mimicking as best as I can.

"الاستماع مع أذنيك وليس قلبك," he says three times.

"Listen with your ears and not your heart," I say. The tremors stop. "The last time you said those words, it was in English."

He smiles, looking at me with kind but sympathetic eyes, shaking his head.

"It was always in Arabic, Jewels. You just didn't realize it until now."

I want to deny it, but then I sound out the words once more, "Alaistimae mae 'adhinik walays qalbik. ...The-the bookstore. That lady said I spoke Mandingo." I turn to look at Sedia, whose eyes widen as if they are going to pop out of her head. She gasps for air as if she's been holding her breath the entire time.

Sedia staggers backward as if she's about to drop. Her head bends, and her hands clench into fists. Sebastian and Moh rush to her aid, but she holds up both hands in protest. When she finally raises her head, there is a spark that was absent only moments before.

"Sebastian and Amina are right," Sedia finally says. "Things are changing because of you. I just did something I haven't been able to do in nearly seventeen years. You allowed me to tap into your mind to see and feel what lay dormant or forgotten. I have some empathic powers, though not as strong as yours." Sedia grimaces as she curiously looks at me.

"You're not just an empath. You can distinguish the djinn from humans." Sedia is very different. No longer fragile. It's almost frightening.

"Oh. I just call them Typicals and Others. I used to only be able to feel human emotions, but it's changed since—well, today."

"What do you mean?" Sebastian asks.

"She can feel us now," Sedia answers.

Sebastian doesn't seem too pleased. He takes a subtle step back as if distance will hide his emotions.

I can feel everyone's embarrassment, but it isn't overwhelming. It's now more like background noise. Bearable.

"So hang on, is Bijou the reason Lilith has been able to stay hidden for so long?" Amina asks Sedia.

She nods. "Lilith has been able to use some magic because Bijou has been near. Using Bijou to grow her herbs and drugging Bijou to keep her weak."

I feel their sympathy and hell, I feel sorry for myself. All these years she's been using me, drugging me, and lying to me.

"But wouldn't Lilith have all of her powers, since she's been with Bijou all this time?" Amina asks.

"Bijou will come into her full power on her 17th birthday, so she's growing stronger by the day." Moh doesn't talk much, but he seems to know much more than the rest.

Sedia looks at Sebastian briefly. "Bijou, you had dreams of Sebastian before the two of you ever met."

It isn't a question.

I am so embarrassed. This would have been much easier had Sebastian not been a few inches away from me, but there is no use in lying. I pull away from her because every time she makes physical contact with me, she sees things about me I would never tell others.

"Well, every dream I've had since my childhood has had a faceless boy watching or warning me—my protector. But after I met Sebastian, the boy finally had a face, and it was his."

Sebastian tenses and they all exchange nervous glances.

"Excuse me," Sebastian says, going outside.

"I'll talk to him," Amina says, following him.

Silence comes over the large room.

"Bijou, before you leave here today, there are a few things that we must address."

"I have to go back?" I panic. How can I go back to my old life now that I know all of this?

"Yes, sweetie, you cannot let Lilith suspect that you know any of this. You have to go home and act dazed. Your last memory will be of school last Friday and nothing after. Don't overdo it."

"But why? If she's so evil, why do you want me to go back to her?"

"No, she can't go back." Sebastian reenters the room, his eyes smoldering. He looks tortured. "They're already here for her."

"Who are *they*?" Aiden asks.

"Lilith has called on some others to come and stay with them," he answers, grimacing in discontent as he speaks. "One of them brought her to school. He has silver hair."

Sedia, Aiden, and Moh are completely silent. They won't even look at each other. Sebastian and Amina look at me and I can feel how suspicious they are as well.

"Lilith says they're here to help plan my birthday party."

At the mention of the party, everyone in the room becomes volatile and anxious, though no one speaks. Sebastian shifts his weight from one foot to the other, showing an unreasonable amount of interest in his boots.

"Like I was saying before, Bijou, Lilith won't hurt you. If she wanted to, she would have done so already. In fact, from what I saw, I believe she cares a great deal for you. That's why she's been hidden for so long. She's been hiding you from the world to shield you from danger."

"That hardly sounds anything like the Lilith I remember," Aiden says.

"I know, but that's what I saw and felt from Bijou's mind."

"Maybe she's waiting for something—the party—that's why she hasn't hurt me yet."

"Perhaps. One thing you have to keep in mind is that, like humans, the djinn are beings of free will, so you can never be certain of their intentions," Aiden warns.

"So, how do I know who to trust?"

"You don't," he answers shortly. "You've seen what's been done to you. They are very tricky and capable of many things, enslaving some of their own kind, as well as mortals." I automatically think *Ali Baba and the Forty Thieves* and wonder how the djinn became bound to the lamp.

I should have been frightened by his answer, but strangely I'm not.

"I think it's time for us to head back to school," Sebastian says. "It's almost lunch time."

Sedia hugs me as if she never wants to let go. I take in her scent, just to be able to compare her to something when she isn't around. Jasmine. My grandmother smells of jasmine. I keep looking at her because for the first time ever, I see myself in someone else.

After all the goodbyes and warnings to stay away from the garden, to act dumb, and to trust no one, we leave the house. The mask that hides Sebastian's true self has been removed, and *my* Sebastian actually looks at me with the gray eyes that we occasionally share.

At first, his eyes are soft, but as he looks at me, they harden. He pushes me away, holding the car door open for me.

"Jewels, we can't. Ever," he says, point blank. "My sole purpose is to protect you, not to make you my girlfriend. You're meant for great things, and my role is to guard you so that you are able to accomplish them."

"What great things? You guys never told me the purpose of the Chosen One."

"To be the protector of the innocent." I don't think Sebastian realizes the irony of his words.

But Amina does.

"One girl in all the worlds, a chosen one. She alone will wield the strength and skill to fight and kill the djinn and the hooded man. She is Bijou."

"Louder Mina. I don't think they heard you in Baltimore," Sebastian quips as Amina goes on and on about my past Buffy references.

I sit in the back seat, my pride wounded. I can't bear looking at him. I need to stop thinking about Sebastian, but it is impossible.

I am doomed.

CHAPTER 16—INNOCENCE

I'm 16 years old and all of the world's magic lives within me, but it's still not enough to make the only boy I've ever loved love me back. Maybe the magic is the problem. Maybe if I were normal, he'd want me like he wants Mandy.

"I'm not hungry," I say to Amina for the first time since meeting her as we make our way back into the building just in time for lunch. The moment Sebastian sees Mandy, he ditches us for her, flirting and carrying on like everything is normal, and I don't exist.

"And then there were two," Amina says, with a touch of sadness in her voice. "I thought things would be different once we found you. I thought when the three of us met, we'd be powerful and inseparable, so we could have some normalcy. I thought maybe I'd get a boyfriend or a girlfriend. But things are complicated and Sebastian is getting weirder and weirder."

"What do you mean?"

"He's just distant, mate." It's rare, but when Amina uses Aussie slang, it always makes me giggle. "Oy, it isn't funny. It started after the bonfire. That night, I heard him talking in his room. I opened the door to see what was going on, but there was no one there. He wasn't even on the phone or anything. He nearly bit my head off."

"Maybe he was mad that you didn't knock." I shrug.

"Nah. That's never been our style. Bastian and I have always been two parts of a whole. No secrets. No boundaries. But now, he's distant and hiding stuff." Amina's voice is wavering and, for a moment, I think she's going to cry.

I expect to enter the cafeteria and be met by whispers and accusations, and of course, there are murmurs about Aften's disappearance. A group of girls see me and decide to carry on about how they're boycotting my party because I'm a witch. Just when I consider defending myself, I see a familiar face that is very unfamiliar to these surroundings. Sano.

She stands out beautifully in the crowd of normal teenagers, her eyes searching for something or someone safe or familiar to bring a modicum of relief. "Sano, what are you doing here?"

She looks relieved and tense all at once upon seeing me with Amina.

"Oh good, I'm here with the mistress and Master Phoenix, to fit your classmates for their masquerade masks." As Sano speaks, I realize for the first time that she speaks with an accent, but again, it is unidentifiable.

"Who?"

"Oh, I'm sorry. Your Aunt Tempest and Nikolai," she says bashfully.

Amina and I look at each other, exchanging curious looks.

"Don't be sorry. This is my friend, Amina. Amina, this is Sano."

Amina smiles warmly.

"Nikolai Phoenix. Now, that's a name," Amina quips, making Sano comfortable enough to carry on a conversation with her as we make our way down to where all the excitement is taking place.

Amina can't quite seem to tear her gaze away from the spectacle that is Tempest. Her emerald green maxi dress sparkles more radiantly than her eyes, making her stand out. The plunging neckline is intimidating as her boobs look like over-sized cantaloupes. If I didn't know any better, I would believe she's had a boob job, but knowing her true nature, they're probably real. I watch as the anxious students surround her and Niko with excitement in their eyes, trying to figure out which mask will be suitable for their ensembles. It is chaotic. Girls are falling over themselves at the charming Niko, who looks like he's stepped off the cover of Italian Vogue. The group of girls who were going to boycott are arguing over masks and fighting their way to the line for invitations. The female teachers, on the other hand, make the air thick with jealousy and distaste. Tempest's energy is volatile and abrasive. Her unmerciful eyes speak the truth of her wicked nature. Is everyone else blind to the fact that everything about her is evil?

I look to my left and see Mr. Jennings watching the chaos.

"Glad you're feeling better, Ms. Fitzroy. Even though you weren't well enough to make it to my class today." He isn't looking at me as he speaks. He's staring at Niko.

"I came in late sir, but thanks."

"They say we each have a doppelgänger, but the resemblance between those two is unreal."

"Who are you talking about?"

"Mr. Sinjin and the silver-haired gentleman. Look at how people are drawn to the both of them without any effort on their part, but see the way they handle all the attention." I look up to see Sebastian, a few feet away from Niko with Mandy, surrounded by a group of his own. As Mr. Jennings looks at the two boys, his forehead creases, and his brows furrow as if he is looking at pieces to a puzzle that just don't fit. He mumbles something else, but it's inaudible.

I stop to grasp the importance of what he is saying. They're both surrounded by a group of peers, yet they stand out. The difference is Sebastian interacts as an equal, even though they perceive him as superior, while Niko looks as though he is doing community service by addressing those beneath him.

Amina and I head over to Niko, who is distributing invitations to anxious hands, while Sano reluctantly joins Tempest, who's distributing masks. The invitations are in various hues. Some feature delicate lace filigree borders, while others dare to be bold with loud feathers, and some with pearls that look too believable to pass for costume jewelry.

If I were to get an invitation like this, resembling something that the Queen of England commissioned herself, I would think the person was trying too hard.

I'm at a point where fitting in is crucial, but this makes me stand out like *Jonathan* in "Superstar." I just want to be normal, but everything about me screams abnormal, even down to my name. Why couldn't I have been named Maggie or something?

"Can I have one?" I ask, sneaking up on Niko as he barely gives a second glance to the female population, who seem to be bending over backwards to get his attention.

"You should be handing these out."

"Just give me one, will you, Nikolai?"

He raises an eyebrow, then looks at Sano and nods.

Reading it makes me sick. It is written—not typed—by a stable hand in an elegant script that reads:

You are hereby cordially invited to the

Crystal Ball

The Birthday
Masquerade Ball of

Miss Bijou L. Fitzroy

on the 21st day of June
at Patterson Mansion
beginning promptly at 7 p.m.

Elegant Attire and Masks are a must.

Please RSVP by May 16th.

Monetary and/or wrapped gifts will be kindly accepted.

"What's L for?" Amina asks, looking at the invitation.

I give her a look that should say, duh?!

"One guess."

"No. Did she really name you after herself?"

I nod, shaking my head as Amina laughs at Gigi's narcissism. Thinking of her as Gigi just infuriates me. I can't help but see her as family. Stockholm Syndrome at its finest.

Amina and I head over to our table in an attempt to get away from the commotion.

"Well, what do you think about Niko?" I finally have to ask. She is taking too long to comment. "I mean, do you think he's cute?"

She's oddly quiet for a moment.

"Bij, Bastian and I think you should stay away from him."

"Well, that's going to be a little hard to do since they're staying at my house." I find myself becoming angry for some reason. "And besides, you guys want me to stay away from Sebastian. Well, this is me, staying away from Sebastian."

"Do you know how long they're going to be here?"

"I'm not sure, but they sure are making themselves awfully comfortable. And what do you think is up with Sano? Do you think I can trust her? She doesn't seem anything like the rest of them. She's terrified of them."

"Don't trust any of them. Weren't you listening today?" As Amina speaks, she is more serious than I have ever seen her before. This version of Amina is a lot like the hidden side of Sebastian. The usual presence of excitement that emanates from her has vanished. "From what you've told me, Sano sounds like some sort of prisoner, although you can never really tell."

Amina stops briefly, looking at me with dread in her eyes as a short woman approaches our table.

"Hi, Ms. Fitzroy. I know I haven't had a chance to formally introduce myself to you, but I'm Vice Principal Hartley." She walks and speaks with authority—as if this is her palace, and we are all her loyal subjects. She is as short as she is round, wearing blush that is so red it looks like her cheeks have been stung by bees. Her hair, wardrobe, and makeup seem to be following a theme. There is so much hairspray in her brown bee-hived hair that if she were hit in the head, she probably wouldn't feel a thing. And it's no surprise at all when I notice her outfit, a black silk blouse and a blindingly yellow pencil skirt that seems to be squeezing the life out of her.

"It's nice to meet you."

"Who's your little friend?" she asks, examining Amina with a raised eyebrow.

"Just leaving. I'll be in the library, Bij."

"She's pleasant," Hartley comments, watching as Amina flutters away. "I've been meaning to have a word with you. Do you mind if I sit?"

I actually do mind, but before I can part my lips to respond, she is already making her way to the chair across from mine. She has that look on her face that cops get when they're about to interrogate someone.

This is going to be interesting.

"Isn't it a shame about your missing classmates? That's every parent's worst nightmare."

I can see subtlety isn't her strong suit. I sit there emotionally detached, waiting for her to come out and say what is really on her mind.

"I've received many reports that you threatened Aften Noble on Friday night at a party held after the new curfew."

I can't believe it. The administration actually thinks I had something to do with Aften's disappearance based on rumors.

"I didn't threaten her. She pushed me, and I pushed her back. Then we exchanged words. And then Sebastian took me home."

"You mean Sebastian Sinjin?"

"Yes, he's right over—"

Before I can finish my sentence, Sebastian and Mandy head up the staircase, Sebastian's arm hangs laxly over Mandy's shoulder. They stop to talk to Mr. Jennings, following him in the direction of his classroom.

"Do you know that Aften is the sixth girl to go missing?" I nod. "Did you know Priya or any of the other girls?"

"No. You actually believe I had something to do with their disappearances just because I had an argument with one of them? First of all, I try to avoid Aften as much as possible. Secondly, I wasn't even a student here when these disappearances started. Lastly, I wonder what my grandmother would say if I were to tell her the school's vice principal approached me in a public setting to accuse me of a crime." I'm so angry, my hands are trembling.

"You misunderstood." She does a one-eighty, trying to apologize as I look around to see that all eyes are on us.

I gather my belongings to rush off in an attempt to catch up with Amina before lunch ends. Instead of finding her in the library, I find Amina on her tippy toes, spying through the window, leading to Mr. Jennings' classroom.

"What are you doing?" I whisper, startling her.

She puts her hand over her heart as if she's relieved it's only me.

"Quick! Bastian's in there with Mandy and someone else, but I can't see who it is."

I don't understand the big issue with this until I see Sebastian and Mandy are arguing viciously about something. Whatever they are saying isn't clear, but my name is mentioned quite a few times. She's holding something in her hand, but I can't see what it is, and Sebastian is trying to take it from her. Sebastian tries walking away, but then the third person comes into view and blocks his path. I gasp, seeing the hooded man. Sebastian tries pushing past him, only to be stopped by the sound of a foreign voice that escapes Mandy's lips.

Now she's saying some phrase repeatedly, only I can't really understand or hear clearly. Sebastian staggers, dropping to his knees, trembling, overwhelmed by waves of immense pain. I reach for the doorknob, but Amina grabs my hand, stopping me. I can feel her fear as if it's my own. Maybe it *is* mine. As he tries crawling away from them, he begins to cough uncontrollably. Blood stains the linoleum floor. When his eyes reopen, they are cold—void of emotion.

Amina pulls on my arm and we run away and into the library.

"What the hell was that?" I ask Amina as we enter the nearly empty library.

"Do you think they know?"

"That Sebastian is a—" I look around, more paranoid than I've ever been before. "Slayer."

Amina is annoyed, but it's the only word I could think of on short notice.

She nods.

"But how is that even possible? Mandy may be evil, but she's a just a—" I don't even know how to describe her because she isn't just a *normal* teenage girl because normal teenage girls don't make up lies about people that can lead to incarceration. Well, not usually.

"The sheila's a bogan, but there's nothing normal about her. She knows who the hooded man is, and I'm starting to think Mr. Jennings started all this djinn and Otherworld talk to see who would react. I know Mr. Jennings is involved somehow, too. I think I saw him leaving the classroom before I got there, but I can't be sure."

"Sebastian reacted in class when Jennings started the djinn discussion. He told that story about the prophecy in Jennings' class. I think he thought Mr. Jennings was one of the Others. Djinn."

"Is he?" Amina's eyes are frantic. She's one blink away from tears.

"No. There's something weird about him, but I don't mean weird like the dark-haired woman from the bookstore weird." I want to tell Amina that she's like the lady in the bookstore too, but it will raise questions I'm not even prepared to ask. "She's djinn, but I could feel her emotions, just not as much as regular humans. As for Jennings, I saw his face change after class on the day I told my story, but I thought I was hallucinating."

"Maybe you weren't." We're both completely silent until the bell rings and we part ways.

* * *

When the final bell rings, I bolt out of the library, trying to find Amina before she makes it outside. Since I'm in a rush, I'm not watching where I'm going and bump into Sebastian.

"I'm so sorry," I say, refusing to look up.

"It was an accident. Where are you off to in such a rush?" He looks like Sebastian. He sounds like Sebastian, so were we wrong about what we saw earlier?

"I'm actually looking for Amina," I say, visually probing him in search of anything weird.

"I'm glad I caught you before Amina."

"Oh?" I ask suspiciously.

"Yeah, it's about that guy from earlier. I saw you and Amina with him, and I really don't think it's safe for you to even stay at your house anymore. Maybe we should talk to Sedia about you staying with us."

"Like you said Sebastian, your job is to watch me from afar, so—"

I walk away from him, passing by Mandy as I turn the corridor.

"How did your little heart-to-heart with Ms. Hartley go?" Mandy asks in a devious tone. "She was quite pleased to receive that little tip about you and your threats."

"You know, Mandy, you're doing a very good job at disguising how distraught you are over your friend being missing—not like Christa, who can't quite seem to hold herself together. I mean, how dare she have the audacity to show compassion for a friend who may be in trouble?" As I speak sarcastically to her, her face starts to match the pink atrocity that is her car.

"You little witch," she tries to whisper so Sebastian can't hear, but he does. "I am going to make your life a living hell, and the next time I see you talking to Sebastian, I'll—"

"Am I interrupting something?" Sebastian and Amina both cut into my quality time with Mandy.

"So the next time you see me talking to Sebastian, you're going to do what now?" I ask innocently.

Mandy goes from pink to red in zero to sixty seconds. She smiles nervously.

"Come on Sebastian. Let's go," she says, pulling Sebastian along, who loyally follows like some mindless android. He looks conflicted.

"I guess we'll finish our discussion another time. I say. "Oh, and, Sebastian, I'll keep in mind what we discussed."

Mandy flinches as the words come out of my mouth. She is livid.

"Nicely done," Amina comments, back to her usual bubbly persona. "I've been wondering when you were going to let her have it."

"Yeah, well, once she admitted she told Ms. Hartley, I had something to do with the disappearances, I'd had enough."

"And it had nothing to do with her telling you to stay away from my brother, yeah?"

"No," I lie.

"Here, take this."

Amina shoves her cell phone into my hand.

"Why are you giving me your phone?"

"Don't worry. I have another. I need a secure way to get in contact with you, especially with everything that's going on now." She pauses briefly and then turns to look at me. "Keep the phone on vibrate, and don't let any of them know that you have it."

I thank her as Niko pulls up, but before I can make my way to the passenger side of my new Mini, I look up to see Sebastian and Mandy in a full-on lip-lock for everyone to see.

My heart explodes, and I'm not even sure I remember how to walk anymore. The only thing that brings movement to my legs is Amina yelling at Sebastian as Mandy tears out of the parking lot in her pink monstrosity with Sebastian in her passenger seat.

I run to Amina, and Niko follows. My heart may have exploded, but Amina is absolutely shattered. Maybe it's because she's so petite, but in this moment she looks so fragile and childlike. As innocent and frightened as Sebastian looked in that classroom today.

"He didn't even tell me we weren't riding together." Amina isn't looking at me as she speaks. She's still staring as if Sebastian will return any minute.

"Is your friend okay?" Niko asks in a shockingly sweet voice. "If he was your ride, we don't mind taking you home."

Amina turns towards him, but I'm not sure if she truly sees him.

She laughs, but there's no emotion behind it.

"Thank you, but I have a car." She begins her walk to the Charger. "Maybe you're a superhero, after all, Nikolai Phoenix."

CHAPTER 17—EMPTY PLACES

Niko never revisits our earlier conversation about wanting to tell me something, and I don't bother reminding him. There's too much going on in my mind to really care. The questions I have are endless. What is Gigi's plan for me? Who's the hooded man, and is he the one behind this missing girls? Why is there so much supernatural activity in a town so small it doesn't show up on most maps? And now this whole mess with Sebastian. He and Amina are supposed to be my protectors, but I'm starting to think I'm going to have to do the protecting.

Then again, that's what the prophecy says: I'm the protector of the innocent. But what good am I when everything I do, think, or say always comes back to him? I know I'm not supposed to love him or think about him in that way, but it can't be simply because he's my djinn. Amina is my djinn as well, but I never dreamed of her before meeting her and I don't have feelings for her, either. But Sebastian doesn't want me, and who can blame him? Everything is so complicated with me. With Mandy, I'm sure things are simple.

Maybe it would have been easy to ask Sebastian and Amina's family all of my questions unrelated to

Sebastian, but their emphasis on trusting no one has become my new personal mantra.

After Sano takes my measurements for a dress I will probably hate, I just want to eat in my room and be alone, but I'm being forced to come to the table. Dinner is exhausting, as I pretend to be oblivious Bijou for Gigi and her crew. Each time I look at Gigi, I see those cruel eyes that took me away from my mother. I sit there, holding my tongue as Salif discusses his archaic ideas on how women should dress and act. Gigi seems like she's holding her breath, terrified my lack of a filter will be put on display.

"You're one to talk." I finally break my silence, draining the small amount of color from Gigi's pale face. "Every gown design you've earmarked for your wife has a slit high enough to see her uterus, so what's wrong with other women being confident with their own sexuality?"

"You insolent little brat." He slaps the table in anger, probably wishing it was my face.

"You misogynistic little man. You think—"

"Bijou!" Gigi shouts, cutting me off. Her eyes are wide. Niko looks entertained. Tempest and Rowan, not so much. Sano is scared stiff. "Go to bed!"

"*Fais de beaux rêve.*" I am all too pleased to leave them to discuss how rude I am and *their* party plans.

I enter my room to find Moh standing at my window, watching the sun go down.

"Sheeit!" I gasp with my heart stuck in my throat. "You scared the crap out of me. What are you doing here?"

"I need to talk to you privately."

Normally, this is where I'd make a smart remark, but something about the soothing sound of his voice calms my panicked body.

"All I've ever wanted to do is to keep you safe."

I roll my eyes, annoyed by this constant need for everyone to protect me.

Moh looks at me and smiles warmly. It's strange, but this simple gesture disarms me and suddenly, I do feel safe.

"You're a lot like her, you know?" His voice trembles slightly, but his smile remains in place.

"Like who?"

"Your mother," he says simply, his gaze returning to the moon.

"You knew her?" I ask, more attentive now.

He laughs, but the smile doesn't reach his eyes. Instead, his eyes become glassy, and I'm almost certain that if he blinks, tears will disburse.

"I'm actually shocked you haven't come to find me since opening the book."

Before I can ask what he's talking about, Kit darts out from beneath my bed and hops into Moh's arms, almost giving me a heart attack.

"What the hell?" I say, jumping back. "The universe is trying to kill me today."

"I think she likes me." Moh caresses the cat, who seems to approve of the gesture.

"She randomly showed up one day, so I claimed her. Kit's a secret though." I say, taking her. She nuzzles my neck and I sit her down on the floor. "So talk," I prompt, wanting to get back to the matter at hand.

He looks around the room suspiciously then looks at his watch. "We can't talk here."

"So then why—"

"Please be quiet."

He looks at his watch once more then quickly grabs both of my hands. As we face each other, the color fades from his eyes, making them as white as his wardrobe. He steps backwards toward my curtains, pulling me along with him, and I don't protest. When we reach the curtains, I notice the sun is beginning to set, and a strange feeling comes over me. The room begins to warp, changing its form completely.

"What's going on here?" My voice is barely audible as I want to pull my hands away from him, but there's a strange urgency not to do so.

The walls disappear. The ceiling disappears. Even the floor disappears. Everything is replaced with nothingness. All that surrounds us is darkness, but oddly enough, I can see Moh clearly, as if a spotlight is pointing directly at us.

"Wh-where are we?"

"We're between worlds. A place only changelings can enter, if they know how or by chance. This is the In-between. Think of it as the transit station between worlds. Only people like us can remain conscious in this place."

I try to let go of his hands, but he won't release me; instead, he holds on tighter.

"Don't let go. If you do, you'll fall into the abyss. I'm the only thing keeping you afloat."

All of a sudden, I become terribly afraid to look down or around us, forcing me to look directly into his face.

"Why do you make it a point to look into my eyes when most people usually avoid it?"

He laughs again. "I was expecting an entirely different question like, 'How are you doing this.' It's because I want you to see what's inside. Even some that wish you no harm may not be able to do so because there are things within themselves they want to keep hidden. I'm sure there are tricks and a few ways around it, but that's generally the gist of it. You see, since you're an empath, you can sense things about people that they might not want made public, but your power goes much further than that. You're different than all other empaths because you can also see the things they are hiding just by holding eye contact."

"But how do people know I can sense those things? Because even the humans are afraid of my eyes."

"Instinct. All living beings sense—on some level or another—when something is off or maybe even a potential threat. And nature wasn't fair to you either by giving you eyes that change as frequently as the human temperament. They're afraid of you." His smile disappears, and his eyes widen as if he'd just inserted his foot into his mouth. "That didn't come out right. Your eyes are beautiful but threatening, so they intimidate people, making you seem unapproachable."

"How are you even capable of doing this?" I resist the burning urge to look around me, but from what I can see there is nothing. An empty place.

"It's one of my gifts, and yours, too. While I'm not officially your protector, I've been conducting my own private surveillance of you since the moment we all suspected that you were the one. Bijou, I have a special kinship with you because I was the djinn that crossed your father over to the human world."

"Wait, what do you mean 'crossed him over'? I thought there were only certain times that anyone could cross over."

He cocks a thick brow in surprise. "I see someone's been doing her homework. That used to be the case, but not anymore. The truth is, a Link was always needed in order to cross over." He already knows what my next question will be. "I know. What's a Link, right?"

I nod.

"A Link is born of a mortal and immortal union. The child's birth alone is spectacle, transporting the mother—along with anyone else within close proximity—between worlds uncontrollably, most times taking the life of the mother with the child's first breath."

He sighs and mumbles something I can't understand.

"What are you saying?"

"I'm trying to be very careful in what I say. I would love to tell you everything, but some things I'm not completely sure of and others I really just can't tell you," he replies with frustration in his voice. "If I do, it will disrupt an already unbalanced universe, so I can only tell you the basics, and hopefully you'll figure out the rest on your own."

"Wait. Why is the universe so unbalanced?"

"For once, I want you to just keep quiet and listen!"

I know deep within myself he isn't capable of hurting me, but his tone tells me that this is serious business, so I shut it. "Years ago in the Otherworld, when your father and Lilith still ruled, I was the apprentice to the Royal Link, Fahn. There was only one powerful Link in position at the Royal Court, and not just any Link, but a Link whose powers were strong enough to open the portals to the other side during every unstable time. Fahn could do that. In fact, he was so powerful that he could literally lift those veils in his sleep, but the one thing his powers could not withstand was death. This is why I do not believe in immortality. Yes, we live unnaturally long lives, but anything can be killed. You just have to figure out how. Anyway, when the Great Divide occurred, Fahn was ripped to shreds by Puck, Alieu's henchman."

"You mean the imp from A Midsummer Night's Dream?" I laugh, interrupting him once more.

"You've been told that fiction is deeply rooted in reality." I'm shocked by how patient he's being with me. "Many mortals have had encounters with Puck in his various guises. How do you think that play was written? How do you think Rowling came up with the idea of Platform 9 ¾ and the Gringott goblins?"

My mouth drops. I want to ask whether or not Harry Potter exists, but decide against it. Something else comes to mind.

"So was there really a changeling boy that Lilith and Alieu fought over?"

Moh looks away for a moment and when his eyes return to mine, they're sad, and he allows me to see his memories and feel his pain. I see Lilith even more dazed than I had been earlier as the Indian boy is taken to Alieu's court. As the boy's face becomes clear, I see that it's a baby-faced Moh, draped in gold. A pawn in Lilith and Alieu's war.

The vision ends. I open my mouth to speak, but he cuts me off, unwilling to discuss it.

"No matter the offense, Alieu kept Puck around because of the power he wielded and the fact that Puck was willing to do anything for him. He had the power to astral project himself and others into multiple places at once. Maybe it was his plan to take Fahn's place after killing him, but it wouldn't have worked because he's no Link. He can make a physical copy of a djinn appear, but he can't duplicate their power. When Puck destroyed Fahn, all of his powers were forced into me. I was too young for the responsibility, so I panicked and escaped the court with plans of leaving the Otherworld for good, but I ran into Alieu, who had very different plans for me."

He pauses briefly to read my reaction, but I don't know how to react because he is being so forthcoming with this information, and I have no idea why.

"Anyway, I became the most powerful Link alive, and of course Alieu wanted to use me to his advantage. He forced me to lift the veil for him, and I joined him as his—"

"Henchman? Were you doing his bidding or something?" I couldn't help myself, and from the look on his face, he is growing impatient.

"No, I was somewhat of his live-in Link, lifting the veil for him when and wherever he wanted, causing unsuspecting mortals to get lost in an unknown world full of turmoil. But to the outside world, I was his business assistant." I feel my heart slowly breaking with each pause. He laughs uncomfortably—almost like a stalling engine—trying hard to dodge my eyes now. "For all intents and purposes, I was his slave."

I don't want to cry, but his words paint such a vivid picture that nothing I attempt can stop the tears from falling. I can feel the torment he felt, but what shocks me is the brightness I feel within him. He exudes a positive energy that fills me with warmth, and in that moment, I somehow understand his ever-present smile.

"Hey, don't cry! I haven't gotten to the good part yet, but I must warn you, with the good comes the bad. When Alieu married Femeni—your mother—she was very kind to me, and in time, I became something of a confidant to her. She would always sing to her belly. There was one particular song she would sing that I couldn't help but fall in love with. Let me see if I remember..."

"*Ce billet doux est toi...mon bijou.*" We both sing it conjointly.

"How did you know?"

"The hooded man whistled it, and I somehow knew the words." The joy that fills my body is incomparable. I want to act nonchalant and tough, but my happiness overrules my pride, my smile spreading so wide that I'm sure my molars are exposed.

"Remarkable," he says, but he's worried about something. "As I'm sure you know, bijou is French for jewel, so it became a habit of everyone to refer to you as *the jewel*." His smile widens, competing with mine. "Your mother and I were the best of friends."

"Best friends, huh? Close enough for you to lift the veil for Lilith to steal her baby as well as her life?" I scold, but the anger that I want to evoke won't awaken.

"I did no such thing. I never did anything to hurt her. I—I loved her. Probably a little more than I should have, but it's the truth," he admits, almost sounding defeated. He bows his head in shame. "You did it. You lifted every veil that has ever existed when you began to make your way down the birth canal. And when you were finally born, you sealed every single one of those gates, leaving everyone and everything that crossed over that night stuck. Nothing could leave the Otherworld or enter it. No one could leave the human world or enter it from the Otherworld."

"Then how are we here?"

"We're in between. Like I told you before, we're neither here nor there."

We are both silent, and then some harsh realities begin to sink in as well as the burning, sinking sensation in my chest.

"Wait, if I lifted the veils, then it's my fault. I made it possible for Lilith and her flunkies to kill my mother."

I'm so shocked by the realization that I accidentally yank my hands back. I feel myself letting go.

"Bijou, what are you doing?"

Gravity sets in, and I begin to fall. Twisting and tumbling. Tumbling and tossing. Tossing and turning.

As I fall, I can hear Moh shouting. He's getting closer to me, and I can now see his bright light as he shoots toward me head first like a speeding bullet, his blue-black dreads trailing behind him beautifully.

"Bijou, I want you to try something. Think of your happiest memory and hold onto it." I can hear his voice clearly as if he is whispering into my ear now. His voice is calm, but as I stare at him—still too far to reach—I notice his lips never move.

"Why?"

"Just do it!"

I don't have to sift through my memories to determine the happiest...it's easy. My happiest memory is when I discovered that the boy from my dreams was Sebastian. Abruptly, my descent into nothingness ceases, and I can't help but smile at the thought of Sebastian—not just any thought but a vision of the first time we met. I think of how he made me smile inside, his eyes lingering on mine, looking past the surface and into the core of my being. And I remember, in that moment, that Sebastian did love me. Something's definitely not right with him now.

When my eyes reopen, I am now facing Moh again.

"I knew you'd be a fast learner."

"And how were you talking without even moving your lips? This is just too much."

I don't know if I am sad or afraid, but I feel tears sliding down my cheeks before I can even try and hold them in.

"Bijou, it's imperative you listen to what I have to say now with no interruptions." There's no smile with this warning. His face hardens without becoming cruel, but the seriousness of his tone is a warning to heed.

Now I nod, afraid of the next revelation that awaits me.

"Soon after Lilith was exposed and Alieu left her, there was a lot of speculation about the prophecy. Many thought Sedia was a fraud, while some thought she'd always known the union between Lilith and Alieu wouldn't produce the Chosen One. Along with the speculation came the outlandish rumors about Sedia being in love with Alieu and faking a prophecy in order to make a fool out of Lilith. An even smaller group believed Lilith did indeed bear the Chosen One, and Sedia lied to be spiteful. None of those speculations were true, but the rumors made Lilith hate Sedia more than she had before."

"Wait, why did Lilith hate Sedia before the whole prophecy debacle?"

"Jealousy. The thing is, Lilith always envied your grandmother. In fact, she hated her so much she had her enslaved in her court. Can you imagine the most powerful oracle the worlds had ever seen being a common handmaiden?" He wears a disgusted look, slightly shaking his head and hissing through his teeth. "Whether you can imagine it or not, that is exactly what Lilith did. Sedia was more powerful than Lilith, though she didn't know it. Lilith knew, and she couldn't stand it. Though she had everything, she was always looking for a way to one-up Sedia. When she finally found a way to gain power, Sedia had already escaped before Lilith could test her power on her."

I look at him with wide eyes, knowing exactly what he's going to say next. There is sympathy in his eyes that can't be hidden.

"It was blood, wasn't it? One of the characters from Gigi's novel, *The Old Ones*, drank blood during her pregnancy to become more powerful."

Moh nods. Then the full weight of my words catches up with him. "Wait. Lilith wrote a book about the Old Ones?" Moh's voice wavers between shock and fear.

I nod, sick to my stomach thinking about her ingesting blood. Why did she need to be so strong when she had everything already? Well, not everything because she didn't give birth to the Chosen One. But in the end, she got that as well.

"Bijou, you need to be prepared for what's to come. The book Hawah gave you was written by your grandmother, only she doesn't remember anything about it. The night before Lilith gave birth, something weird happened to Sedia. Her eyes sank in. And I don't mean that her pupils turned white. There was nothing there. Sedia began speaking a language that I have yet to identify and pacing irrationally. When her fingers began to shake, the only thing I could think to do was to conjure something she could write on. She wrote nonstop for what may have been a day and a half. No sleep. No food. No breaks." He stops speaking. I'm not sure if he can finish the story.

"I've read that book before and can recite it verbatim. It's not about anything you just said. It's about keepers of the elements." I lace my hands with his and look deeper into his teary eyes, traveling past them and into his memory. I don't know how I know what to do, but something inside me tells me that I know what I am doing.

The room is dark and depressing, made of gray stones, with no windows in sight. The only light emanates from the unnatural glow that exudes from the two Otherworldly beings in the room. In the corner sits a younger version of Moh, still dressed in white but draped with gold accents, giving him a look of regency with his dreads neatly coiffed in an intricate updo. A hasty scribbling sound draws my attention away from him to the other side of the room where Sedia sits on a cold wooden chair. I move in closer, seeing what Moh described. Her eye sockets are completely hollow...she has no eyes.

She looks rabid. She rocks back and forth as her quill pen moves faster than humanly possible on the pages of a large book. She's saying something, but it's weird...not in English or any other human language. Whatever it is, she's saying the same thing over and over. She is madly disturbed. I can't help but feel sorry for Moh, who sits in the corner terrified. When the heavy door opens, in comes a petite girl in a green dress made of silk. The dress is beautiful, but it's nothing compared to the shimmering reddish and green translucent wings that flutter frantically behind her.

"What's wrong with her?" she asks Moh, who just sits there rocking back and forth like he's having a nervous breakdown.

"Hawah," he says, addressing the winged girl. "She's been like this since last night. I found her on the staircase convulsing and speaking this gibberish, so I had to bring her here before someone saw her and told Lilith. She won't stop writing."

Hawah stares at him—confusion in her eyes—then slowly begins making her way over to where Sedia sits in her unsettling trance. Hawah's eyes widen in horror when they fall upon Sedia. She has to clasp both hands over her mouth to stop herself from screaming. There sits a still hollow-eyed Sedia who has written until her fingers bleed, seeming to have no intention of stopping.

"Sedia, listen to me; you have to stop this. You're hurting yourself," Hawah says. There's no response, just the constant scribbling sound that's sending poor Moh off the deep end. Hawah tries grabbing Sedia's hands to stop her from writing, but she won't even budge. Hawah looks at Sedia with pain in her eyes and slaps her so hard that it's obvious she has hurt herself as well.

Sedia turns slowly in the hard wooden chair. All the while, her hands are still writing profusely. "Born unto her, she will never be. Born unto he, she will be. My womb will swell, and it shall almost be. When Alieu sees Femeni, it then shall be." Sedia repeats this over and over until there are no more free pages in the book. When she finally closes the book, her head flings back, and she desperately gasps for air. Her eyes open wide and return to what nature had intended them to be.

She gets up from the chair too suddenly, almost losing her balance and falling back down. Moh and Hawah quickly rush to her aid, but she shrugs them off. She faces them, still weakened by her previous state. Even so, she beams with a beautiful pride and power that makes Lilith's reason for jealousy clear. Her dark hair hangs freely over tattered clothing and bruised, soot-stained skin, yet her beauty still shines brighter than Lilith's.

"Tonight, Lilith will give birth to twin boys, but I will take the one who is destined to protect the Chosen," she says. Hawah and Moh stand there in stunned silence, afraid to interrupt. "And they are not Alieu's children but Zina's."

"Bu-but aren't there supposed to be two protectors, so shouldn't you take them both?" Moh stutters.

"The Silver Prince has no part to play in this." Sedia doesn't elaborate.

"Out of all of the creatures to mate with, why Zina?" Hawah shakes her head in disgust. Then she looks at Sedia. "My sister will never allow you to take one of her children. It's already enough of a blow that her baby won't be the Chosen, but she will never let one be the protector of the child who took his place." Hawah seems deathly afraid of her own sister. How can Lilith be her sister? "You're going to need my help. I'll distract her while you get away with the baby. Lilith must think the baby is dead."

The room falls silent for a moment. Sedia and Hawah avoid eye contact while Moh frantically searches both of their faces for answers. "You said *your womb will swell, so will the Chosen be born to you and Alieu?"*

"No, she will be born to my daughter and Alieu." She looks worried, and the color is beginning to drain out of her face.

"Sedia, you've been my governess all of my life, and you barely leave the castle walls. You've taught me everything I know about magic and my sight, and yet you couldn't tell me that you have a child? When did you have time to have a child?" Hawah thinks hard, trying to figure out if it was possible that she might have missed something, but she comes up with nothing. She looks hurt by the thought of Sedia keeping something so pertinent from her.

"The child has yet to be born. Until now, I had never even thought it possible for me to have a child, let alone for that child to be the bearer of the Chosen One." She thinks about it for a second, and then her eyes finally fall on Hawah, a single tear falling. "But I can't let the two of you get involved. It's too dangerous."

"We want to help," the two young djinn speak at once.

"Sedia, you've always been like a mother to us, looking out for us and guiding us. No matter the cost. I will gladly help you." Moh speaks with a voice that holds conviction and passion, and in that moment, he makes the transition from the Changeling boy many often pitied to a djinn sure of the power he holds within.

"I'm willing to make the same sacrifice," Hawah says.

The door to the darkened room opens and in walks a tall girl with eyes that are as disturbing as the eyes of a cat. If beauty could be described as evil, she would be the textbook definition. Her skin shines like refined gold; her brows are evilly arched in the way villains are meant to look in cartoons. Her dress is almost as white as her teeth. The length of her straight, black hair is hard to determine because it's tightly wound in an elaborate bun. Her full lips look blood-stained due to the deep red lipstick that matches the highlights in her hair.

"It's time! My father's demon spawn has begun its journey into the world, and Lilith wants you." Her father? I thought I was Alieu's only child. Her voice matches her wicked outward appearance. Without another word, she pivots and makes her way out of the prison-like room.

As the door closes, Sedia begins to give orders—a task that seems almost foreign to her. "Hawah, I want you to charm me so that I may have no recollection of the book. Moh, I want you to keep it safe. The two of you are the protectors of this book, and it shall only be placed into the hands of the Chosen."

"But what's in the book?" Moh asks in a voice that's barely audible.

"It holds everything the Chosen will need to know about our world, including its secrets and the role she must play." She leaves it at that, making me wonder if she truly does trust them.

"But what if something happens to us and it should fall into the hands of..." Hawah can't finish her statement without getting choked up.

"It is enchanted. Only the Chosen child will be capable of reading it."

Hawah waves her small hands once over the book and once over Sedia's face. I want to see what will happen next, but I can slowly feel myself slipping away from the scene.

"We have company." I hear Moh's voice, but the vision ends and I'm no longer in the empty place. Moh is gone, and I'm back in my room. Amina emerges from my balcony, trembling with wide eyes.

"I guess we have one more thing in common," she says, void of emotion. "We've both been lied to our entire lives by the people we trust most."

CHAPTER 18—VILLAINS

There is an irrational feeling of physical shrinking people get when they realize a conversation has been overheard. I've read about it in countless books. I witnessed it when Buffy discovered that Xander had been spying on her and Angel and everyone learned of her betrayal in season three. And I'm experiencing it for myself right now.

"What are you doing here?" It's all I can manage to say.

"I followed Moh, but I didn't know this is where he was coming." She's actually crying.

I attempt to hug her, but she hugs herself instead.

"You've known I wasn't Sebastian's twin for some time. Haven't you?" Her voice is angry.

"I just knew that I could feel some of your emotions and I could never feel Sebastian's. Well, until today." I still don't understand what's happening. "But how could you have heard us?"

"I've been thinking a lot since we saw what happened to Sebastian. And a lot of stuff didn't add up. Sebastian and I are both your djinn, but his powers are growing more and more every day. He can make smokeless fire with his bare hands now. I can barely bend my element. And that night, we both heard you whistle, but he heard it first and it was louder and clearer for him." She roughly rubs her face, wiping her tears away. "So I started to think that maybe Sebastian and I are both changelings because that would explain why his powers are more potent than mine, but he's not a changeling. I am."

She starts crying again, but this time she lets me hug her.

"I still don't understand how you were able to follow us, Mina."

"I hitchhiked."

"Huh?"

"There are stories of djinn with the ability to latch onto their charges and following them without them seeing or feeling. But it shouldn't have worked for the In-between. I shouldn't have heard or remembered anything from there. Like Moh said, only changelings can remain conscious there."

She gets up and grabs my satchel, opening it with a look of intent on her face.

"Amina, what are you looking for?"

"What you should have been anxious to find the moment you left the In-between." She pulls out the book Hawah had given me over a week ago, ripping the misleading book skin that reads, *The Old Ones: An Anastasia Powers novel.*

I remove the heavy book from Amina's grasp. It is leather bound, with no writing on the cover. We sit on my bed in silence, waiting for something to happen. Nothing dramatic occurs, but there is an urgency prompting me to close my eyes and feel the book.

My mouth opens involuntarily and I say, "*Redi facere quod perierat.*" When I reopen my eyes, the title of the book is now in plain English, and it reads, *Book of the Concealed.*

Amina and I look at each other, but before we can verbalize what we're witnessing, the book begins to shake as if it will explode. I drop it, but it doesn't fall to the floor. Instead, it rises in the air and flies open, its pages turning furiously. It's like those words, "Go back to that which was lost," had somehow activated it.

Symbols begin to escape from the book, flying through my room like someone from space is pointing a projection of images down on us.

"Are you seeing this too?" I ask.

"Uh huh."

One of the symbols comes close enough for me to touch, and so I do. The lights begin to flicker, but it isn't only happening in my room. I can see them flickering outside as well.

"They're all over your body," Amina whispers, but when I turn to look at her, I see the symbols, embedding themselves into her body as well. There is no color to them. They're deep, moving until they've covered her completely.

My room door flies open and in comes Niko, but not as poised as he normally is. His mouth drops. As if they have been awaiting his arrival, half of the symbols devour him, while the rest escape through the French doors.

The book falls to the ground and closes. The lights come back on and the three of us are left standing there, speechless, no longer covered in symbols.

I'm looking for an excuse to give Niko about what just happened, but how can I explain something to him that I can't quite understand myself?

"Multimedia experiment?" Amina shrugs. "That's the best I've got, mate."

In a surprising twist of events, Niko starts laughing. Amina and I back away from him, holding hands.

"What did you do to us?" It's the only thing I can think to say in an attempt to deflect.

"And here I was worried about how to tell you about the legend." He continues to laugh, folding over with his hands on his knees. "It looks like the Chosen One really is as special as they say."

The bluntness of Niko's words catches us both off guard. He doesn't deflect. He doesn't pretend to not know what's happening. He's honest.

"What legend?" I ask, wanting him to say it.

"If I have to repeat what—I *know*—you already know, we won't get anywhere, and time is of the essence."

"We know all about the prophecy and it mentions nothing about symbols attacking people." Amina has now become fiercely protective, moving me behind her to be the one who faces Niko.

"While you all are playing checkers, I've been playing chess. No one has been asking the right questions." His laughing ceases. "After all the years of humans and djinn coexisting in the two worlds, what could be so critical that the universe felt the need for a protector of the innocent to be born?"

I step forward as if being in close proximity to Niko will make me privy to more information.

"A bigger threat than the djinn?" I guess.

He nods. "Are you ready for our field trip?"

"Gigi will never let us leave this late."

"Why do you think I waited until they left to come to your room?" He looks at Amina. "From what I just witnessed, you need to come along, too."

Amina and I don't argue or question him. We simply follow.

* * *

The road we're on is confusing. Niko makes so many turns that it would be impossible to retrace my steps if the need ever arose.

"You know about the prophecy, but do you know the Creation Story?" Niko begins.

"Yes!" Amina says anxiously from the seat behind Niko.

"Please don't tell me Adam and Eve were Djinn as well."

"No. Our world started with four. One to represent each element—Earth, Water, Wind, and Fire. They once protected the humans and their world—their presence always known even though they watched from afar— but the selfish, cruel, and ungrateful ways of the humans drove them away, planning never to look back. They lived for a long time without any interaction with the human world, until one day when the first human crossed over into the Otherworld."

"Solomon," Amina whispers.

"Yes. King Solomon." Niko confirms. "He was the first to lose his way. The Ancients were so intrigued by this fragile being who called himself a king, with his tales of humans and the world that existed beyond the veil. Solomon told them stories of humans and how they lived limitlessly, even though they knew the fragility of their lives. He told them of the stages of life and how, with no extraordinary powers, they build great cities and empires. In return for his stories, the djinn gave him great knowledge. They told him the stories of the way the human world used to be. The hidden places of old riches, and more. Solomon was given more knowledge of his own world than any other living human knew. Well. Earth, Wind, and Water told him what they knew. Fire had a long memory and remembered the cruel ways of the humans, and refused to trust Solomon, never uttering a word to him."

"The four wondered how the man had found his way to their strange world when they had forgotten so long ago. The man offered to show them the route on the condition they help him overcome his hardships and struggles in the human world and grant him a wish. Feeling generous, after the wondrous stories Solomon told them, Earth, Wind, and Water decided to grant him one wish each. Solomon promised to do even better than showing them the way. He promised to take them to his world. Fire still refused to trust the man, so Fire asked the three to each leave their blessings behind as they left their own world for the human one.

"When the three arrived in the human world, even Solomon was shocked at the sight before them. Years had passed, and the world Solomon knew was no more. But to the surprise of the three, this did not disappoint him. As promised, the three helped Solomon to overcome all hardships and obstacles.

"When the humans found that their old king from long ago had returned without aging a day, Solomon was revered even more than he was before. He was now more knowledgeable than any other human in their world. But the Solomon that the Ancients had grown so fond of revealed his true colors, and they weren't as bright as he had painted them to be. The human world exposed a new canvas, and the picture he painted was dark and bleak. He made two of his three wishes. As king, he already had power and authority over humans, so his first wish was for the three to create an entire race of djinn, beings from each element, so he could have power and control over them as well. For his second wish, he forced the djinn to build him the greatest temple ever created.

"It took years to construct the temple. The three Ancients created their own djinn and some of the new djinn began having children with humans. When the temple was nearly complete, Solomon fell ill, forcing the Ancients to grant his final wish. He wished to acquire the secrets of life and death. And they gave him just that.

"You mean they saved him?" I ask, horrified and angered by the actions of a man who had been given kindness, and angered further by their stupidity.

"He took advantage of their kindness. He enslaved them. You see, Solomon wished to know the secrets of life and death. He didn't ask to be made immortal. Anger consumed Solomon because, although he now had knowledge he sought, he could not save himself from death. Solomon soon died. The Djinn continued to build Solomon's temple.

"Upon completion of the temple, they tried to remember the way back home, but it was lost to them. One day, a boy, who was an offspring of Air and a human woman, found the power, strength, and the way to lift the veil to the Otherworld, leading their people home. Once they returned with the new race of djinn, they realized many of the halflings had been left behind. Fire assigned a personal djinn to each halfling child ever to be born into the human world—one from their element of origin. As time went on, the humans forgot about the djinn and how King Solomon's temple was built. Air, Earth, and Water grew tired of living, so when Fire offered to give them their blessings back, they refused them, deciding to grow old by relinquishing their immortality. Fire grew tired of existing without Earth, Air, and Water, so Fire relinquished his immortality as well. But before Fire did so, Fire created its own race of djinn to leave behind. They weren't as many as the others, but they were stronger and more powerful because they were created from pure, smokeless, ancient fire. Magic. Upon the deaths of the Four Ancients, each of their blessings were sent out to the In-between, waiting to be reborn. But you see, because of Fire's wisdom and because Fire held on to the others' blessings for so long, parts of their blessings attached themselves to Fire itself.

"Additionally, though no one has ever been sure of what the secrets of life were, the secrets of death meant that they told Solomon the only way to kill the djinn of three of the Four Ancients. The only one protected in all of this was Fire because Fire withheld its secrets.

"There are a few who believe Solomon had confidants, which he referred to as his Knights. They were said to have kept all of Solomon's secrets, recording all of the knowledge he had acquired from the djinn, including his personal notes. The Knights passed these secrets down from generation to generation. All the while, they kept them from the rest of the human world, allowing the humans to believe the tales of the djinn were nothing more than colorful fables."

"I don't understand how they died if they were meant to live forever," I say, realizing many parts of this story aren't so farfetched. The part about the offspring of Air and a human was clearly the first Link.

"There are old things that—according to legend— can kill djinn, but I've never seen any," Amina says.

"But Fahn was ripped to shreds by Puck, so they must exist," I add, making Niko take his eyes off the road long enough to almost send the car into a ditch.

Amina and I both scream, bringing his attention back to the road ahead.

"How on Earth do you know anything of Fahn?" Niko asks, unable to keep his usual composure.

"The same way you have people in your corner, we have people in ours as well," Amina says before I have an opportunity to start spilling my guts.

"Well, Bijou's right. They must exist, because the hooded man injected Lilith with something that almost killed her, and somehow Bijou brought her back," Niko says, finally pulling into a congested community. There are rows of townhomes. Not the modern ones that have become so trendy, but small, old ones that look like they have history.

"We're here," he says, exiting the car without giving us an opportunity to ask questions.

"We're still in Sykesville and it took you over 30 minutes to get here when we could have gotten here in 10." Amina is annoyed, following Niko down an unmarked path that takes us away from the community.

"Had to be sure no one was following us."

Amina and I hold hands as we follow Niko in the dark. There are no streetlights. Just trees and a chatty owl.

Under the cover of trees, a pale yellow house stands alone on stilts.

"What is this place?" I ask, knowing there must be a story behind it.

"In the old days, this community was where all the black people in Sykesville lived. There was no school, so two men from the community approached the school board with a proposal to open a schoolhouse for black children. This building was the school that opened in 1904. When the county voted to sell the building, I bought it for one hundred dollars. Today, this street is still called Schoolhouse Road."

Niko pulls out the key and opens the door to a dark house. He flips the switch, exposing a scarcely furnished living room with thick blue velvet blackout curtains that probably wouldn't let the sun in during the day.

"You can come out. It's only me."

A hidden compartment in the floor raises, startling us a little, and two heads emerge. Aften and another girl, who I haven't seen before, but who looks familiar.

"What are they doing here?" Aften's voice is defensive. "You said you were bringing someone who could help."

"No, what the hell are *you* doing here?" Amina protests. "Everyone is looking for you, and today, at school, Ms. Hartley had the audacity to accuse Bijou of being responsible for your disappearance."

I'm so confused right now. I need to sit. I find my way to a gray microfiber couch, trying to make sense of what I'm seeing. Then I remember where I've seen the other girl.

"Priya Kapoor."

"How do you know my name?" She takes a step back. As she does this and I really get a look at her, I realize she is certainly a Changeling. She's the kind of beauty you see in the Miss World pageant, but something tells me she's not the pageantry type. She looks wild. Untameable.

"Spooksville. Your site helped me so much when I moved to Sykesville." She relaxes noticeably and finally smiles. "I'm Bijou."

"Nice to meet you. But Niko, it's time for us to move." She's very assertive. "Someone was snooping around outside today."

"Did they try to get in?" His voice is leveled, but I can feel the tension within.

"No, but they made it as far as the porch," Aften says, standing next to Niko as if they're a team.

He swears under his breath.

"Bijou and Amina, I mentioned the Knights of Solomon, but what I didn't tell you is that they're here, and they're looking for the Chosen One. They believe that the Chosen One is Fire reborn, and if they can capture the Chosen, they can control all djinn."

"They thought we were the Chosen," Priya explains. "I was working late at the library one night, and when I got to the parking lot, I was grabbed by something wearing a hood. Next thing I know, I wake up in a hospital room hooked up to all these machines."

As Priya speaks, I see compassion in Aften—something I never thought possible for her.

She rushes over to Priya. "You mean the psych hospital?"

Priya nods, peeking out of the window.

"That's the same property where Patterson Mansion is." Amina looks to me in that exaggerated telenovela way of hers. Dramatic. I just nod, not wanting to say more than necessary in front of Aften and Priya.

"The nurse came into the room to check on me and I knocked her out," Priya continues. "She had a needle with some red substance in it, so I took it, along with the charts and anything else I could find. I found my way into a tunnel, and it seemed like I was lost for days. It was so disgusting, but Niko found me and brought me here."

"How'd you find her?" My eyes narrow on Niko.

"I'm Priya's djinn. I think that's why I've always been drawn to this town. The universe wanted me here for her. I've watched over her since the day she was born, but when she went missing, I kept seeing her image pop up all around me, even though she wasn't really there, and I found my way to the sewer, beneath Springfield."

"If it weren't for Niko, I'd be there as well," Aften says. "The night after the bonfire, my car broke down on 29. While waiting for AAA, this guy turned up. He chased me into the woods and gave me some wicked burns," Aften says, exposing her arms with the familiar red marks, and for the first time ever, I sympathize with her, showing her my own marks I acquired from him the other day. "But before he could do any real damage, Niko showed up and scared him away."

We all head over to the small kitchen area, sitting at the table.

"Whoever this hooded djinn is, helping the Knights, he has to know the Chosen is here now," Niko says, rubbing his temples in frustration. "They were the cause of this happening 17 years ago, and the last time, seven girls were taken, who all share a birthday of June 21st, because they got their information wrong. They thought the Chosen was turning 17 at that time. They didn't know that the baby would be born on that day."

"But how do they determine who the Chosen is?" Amina asks, helping herself to a banana.

"The Trials," Priya says matter of factly, following Amina's cue by grabbing a fruit off the table. "According to the charts I stole, they put the girls through trials of each element. They believe the girl that lives through each trial is the Chosen One. What makes it worse is that some of the girls they're taking are completely human."

"Like you, Aften," I say. Her eyes narrow on me, but she says nothing.

"A friend of mine is preparing another safe haven for them so I've been waiting to move them, because they're sitting ducks out here." Niko's brows furrow and motions for us to remain still as he slowly makes his way to the closest window, and Priya turns the light off. We all become silent around the table.

I'm supposed to be able to save them. I'm supposed to be able to save us all, but all I can really do is feel their emotions and differentiate humans from djinn. What good is that? How is this even my life? My obsession with *Buffy the Vampire Slayer* has followed me into my reality. Why couldn't I have obsessed over *Gilmore Girls*?

Everyone is afraid, but one person's fear is more volatile than the rest. Before I attempt to figure out who, Aften runs toward the space in the floor from which they had emerged earlier, making the floor creak.

Within a nanosecond, someone knocks on the front door. My heart is racing. The fear in the room is toxic, but there's something more that comes from Amina and Niko: a fierceness that feels like they're ready and willing to kill if they have to in order to make it out alive. The door bursts open and in comes a petite woman, wearing an old-fashioned white nurse's uniform, atrocious hat and all.

"You are trespassing on private property," Niko says this with a guttural growl, sending vicious waves of emotional energy through me. Paired with Amina, there is a power that radiates off them like the sun's rays, beaming on a hot summer's day. There's an otherworldly light they exude that gives a whole new meaning to the phrase 'inner light.' I see in Amina what she fails to see in herself—strength.

"These girls are very sick and Dr. Menelik has been searching for them to help before it's too late." One would expect the petite, redheaded, human woman to run out of the room with raised hands, screaming bloody murder at the sight of Niko and Amina, but this is not the case at all. Instead, she shuts the door behind her, turning back towards us with a knowing look in her eyes. She holds up her right hand, draped with two silver rings on different fingers, both with a different colored jewel at its center. One green, the other yellow.

Dr. Menelik? Why does that name sound so familiar?

I can feel the woman's smugness as she slowly but deliberately makes her approach. There is no fear. How can a fragile and easily broken human not be afraid? Who is she?

Niko looks at me and nods. "My thoughts exactly. Who is Dr. Menelik?" he asks.

"What the hell? I never said that out loud." Niko just read my mind, increasing his creep factor by a bajillion.

"That I cannot help. Mindreading is in my DNA, just as saving you is in Amina's." Niko and Amina join hands and the moment they connect, the moving symbols return, devouring their bodies.

"No need to search for a way out. You aren't going anywhere." The woman smiles a sinister grin. With her right hand still weirdly extended, she digs into her pocket with her left hand, pulling out a syringe filled with a peculiar red substance. "Let's do shots!"

"I really didn't intend on increasing my body count today, but I'll kill you without hesitation if you touch them," Niko says.

She approaches him and Amina with unwavering confidence. "I'm getting pretty good at this, so let's see which one you are." Her smile is foolishly menacing. "Aura."

When Niko does not respond, her confidence falters, but only a little.

Niko's eyes narrow on the unusual nurse, wiggling his fingers like a cowboy in the Wild West, preparing to reach for his gun. I realize he's wearing a silver ring, exactly like the woman's, but his stone is blue.

What is happening here?

"Okay, then you must be Orbis Terrarium." She shrieks, bending another ringed finger as though she's counting.

When Niko doesn't flinch, panic surges through her veins. For a moment, I think her heart will stop, but she closes her eyes as if praying, and when she reopens them, her confidence dissipates.

Wait, Aura, and Orbis Terrarium? She has been naming the elements in Latin. She called air, and earth, but what happened to fire and water?

The woman's eyes open in absolute horror. Her delayed fear finally decides to kick in and I wonder what kind of naïve faith could have driven her to believe that she ever had control over this situation.

While Niko and Amina still hold hands, he raises his free right hand, showing the woman his ring.

"Am Stram Gram..." he recites the less controversial French version of eenie meenie miny moe, mimicking the way she counted the elements on her finger. "If you had been prepared, I'm guessing I would be the gram of your clever little game, but seeing as you're wearing only two rings, you've played the wrong game. It seems to me like you were playing Russian Roulette without even knowing it. And guess what?" He laughs in a way that has everyone in the room afraid except for Amina. "You lose."

The woman takes a few steps backward until her back is against the door.

He stops his taunting momentarily, tilting his head to the side to look at me exaggeratingly. "Bijou, tell me how to say water in the chosen language. Latin, that is."

"Liquidum." I respond quickly as if a delayed response would cost me my head.

"I don't quite like that one too much. Give me another one. It *is* Latin. There should be about a million other alternatives."

"How 'bout adaquo?" I ask, feeling like I'm trying to impress a teacher or something.

"I don't know. I quite like liquidum." Amina chimes in, laughing malevolently. Amina and Niko move as though they're one. They're now so close to the woman that if she exhales, her chest will meet Amina's. "Tell us who you're working with."

The woman refuses to speak and in that moment, there is a loud humming sound from unknown origins. The ground shakes beneath us, causing us all to lose our balance, except for Amina and Niko, who are standing perfectly still.

"You were pretty ballsy, not knowing what kind of djinn you'd be up against," Niko's raspy voice echoes over all the commotion. "But you're dealing with pure and potent, unadulterated—"

"Water," Amina finishes as they raise their hands as if conducting an orchestra.

The pipes burst, soaking us all, but something different is happening to the woman. The water that touches her skin seems acidic, scalding her until she looks like she has been dumped in a pot of hot soup.

Niko and Amina drop their hands. The shaking stops, as does the water. The syringe she once threatened us with falls to the floor as I watch the most horrible sight I have ever seen.

Her arms become a deep shade of red. From red, the skin changes to purple, then to dark brown as it burns. She screams violently, but it is brief because, with a minuscule movement of Niko's ring-adorned hand, she is silenced.

I am horrified, seeing that Amina and Niko are capable of such a violent act. The immense pain she endures envelopes my body as well. It is debilitating. I may black out, but I fight it. I focus only on what I feel at this exact moment. I focus on the anger and disgust I feel, knowing I may be capable of this and much more.

"Stop it." My voice is so calm I surprise myself.

The room reeks of burned flesh and hair, and I'm starting to feel the heat as well.

I don't know where the strength is coming from. Maybe it is my desperate need to protect someone who is defenseless, or maybe I don't want the emotional scarring and guilt such a heinous act will leave, but without further warning, I raise my hands in the direction of the woman.

"*Tui gratia Iovis gratia sit cures.*" I don't even recognize my own voice. It sounds deadly, old, and almost lethal, but it is mine.

A colorless essence escapes my lips and enters the woman's nose.

The woman takes a gasping breath and begins trembling violently.

"What did you do to her?" Niko asks, his voice weaker and raspier than before.

"I don't know!" I mumble as I clumsily back away. "It just sort of happened."

Her skin improves and she is alive but unconscious. Her arms still bear a striking resemblance to chili after it's been ingested and regurgitated.

"Okay. You guys need to leave now. Whoever she is, I'm sure she isn't alone, and we can't risk them finding you and Amina here. I have to move the girls. They aren't safe here anymore."

Niko shoves the keys to the Mini in Amina's hands, since mine are shaking profusely. With trembling hands, I remove the two rings from the woman's now scarred fingers. We leave Niko and the girls behind without questioning Niko's instructions. We run out of the house and back to the car.

CHAPTER 19—THE WEIGHT OF THE WORLD

The next few weeks go by in a blur. Since that night, I refuse to touch the book again. My life consists of classes, exams, and party preparations. Sebastian is still distant, but in class he stares at me. Maybe I'm wrong, but it's almost as if he's silently pleading with me. Amina has been noticeably absent from school, so I spend all of my lunch periods in the library.

The truth is, I'm so terrified by what I saw and what is happening that it's nearly impossible to sleep at night. The closer the calendar gets to my birthday, the more frightened I become because, with all I've learned, it looks as if the solstice is—perhaps—doomsday. The entire town is talking about my party and these people—The Knights of Solomon—know its significance, so there's no telling what will happen. I haven't seen Niko since that night, and when I asked Gigi about him, she teased me about falling for him and how cute a couple we'd make.

Things have changed so much that I haven't been able to bring myself to binge on *Buffy the Vampire Slayer* in weeks. I've been watching *Felicity* and all it's done is make me miss New York.

June 20th, the day before my party, is one of the worst days of my life. I'm so on edge today that I tell Mandy I like her outfit. She proceeds to berate me, and I thank her. I'm a mess, and to top it all off, Sebastian and Amina are both absent today.

When I get home from school, I head straight up to my bedroom to retrieve the book from it's hiding place in my closet. Kit is sitting on top of it as if to say, "Enough of this avoidance BS."

I think about leaving it closed and remaining ignorant to the secrets that reside inside. I pick it up and run my finger along the pages of the closed text absentmindedly until a paper cut brings me back, forcing me to drop the book on the ground. An accident, right? But the way the book falls open when it hits the floor makes me feel that it somehow *wanted* to cut me. I sit on the ground beside it, but the pages are blank again. My index finger begins to burn, pulsating like it's about to explode. I want to suck on my finger, but have this overwhelming sense of what I'm supposed to do. I squeeze my finger, forcing a rose-colored drop to fall on a blank page of the book.

The blood sets off an immediate reaction; one drop is all it takes to bring the book to life. The pages turn swiftly of their own accord, creating a small wind in the room. I stare at the book as it suddenly stops on a page, and right before my eyes, the words begin to appear as if they have always been there, written in my blood. If I didn't believe what everyone's been telling me before, my blood awakening a once empty book is enough to confirm that I am chosen for something.

There's no need to turn a single page. The answers to the questions my consciousness had been asking are now right before my eyes. As I read, the long-delayed panic that I should have felt months ago begins to bubble below the surface.

Crap.

If I thought things were bad before, they just went from worse to ridiculous. This is more than enough proof that no good deed goes unpunished. Nothing is as it seems. According to this, everything Moh showed me is true. Sedia was present throughout Lilith's entire delivery. The midwife that delivered the baby was Hawah—the girl from the bookstore who gave me the book, who also happens to be Lilith's sister.

I know it's all too real to be a dream. Everything has definitely fallen into place, even though that place is down the toilet. The similarities are now beginning to make sense: the mannerisms, the heat, the gravitational pull they have on people, the androgyny of their features. Sebastian and Nikolai are the two princes born that night. *Lilith will bear two princes— one of silver and one of gold—not of Alieu's blood but of Zina's. The golden prince will lose his way; his existence I shall keep hidden from the world.* They are the twins, not Sebastian and Amina. Two babies were born that night. Sebastian was taken away by Sedia, his survival never known to anyone other than Sedia, Hawah, Moh, and one other. It doesn't say who.

I know Sedia took Sebastian because she thought she was doing the right thing, but that one decision to fake a child's death and steal him from his mother caused a chain reaction that has ruined so many lives.

The book says Lilith left Niko to be raised by Tempest in order to find the Chosen.

Poor Niko. No wonder Gigi lets him talk to her however he wants. She feels guilty. She is guilty. She abandoned him.

My hands tremble as I continue to read...

All the world will believe the Golden Prince died for the Silver Prince to live, but it will be a lie. A spell will be cast to change his full head of golden hair into raven black hair, making it easier to transport him without suspicion.

Fate has a way of giving people exactly what they deserve when they least expect it. If it wasn't for Sedia and her psycho prophecies, Lilith's baby would have never been stolen, and maybe Lilith would never have stolen me from my mother.

But with all that I now know, my heart still grieves for Sedia, who had been enslaved and ill-treated by Lilith for so long. Can I really blame her? Although her prophecies and visions started this whole uproar, she only did what was natural to her. I'm not saying that the lies and deceit are excusable, but if anything, they're justifiable. Sedia wrote it all out before it happened but has no recollection of it. But I wish that was all. The book was written in entries as if this information had been compiled over a long period of time, but I know differently. She wrote this all in one sitting with no light, hollowed-out eyes, and bleeding hands.

The book turns back to the beginning and reads:

In the beginning, there were four. Four, who gave birth to the elements. Four, who were tasked to be protectors of the human realm. Four, with the answers to the questions the Chosen will seek. Four started it all, and four will stop the end. The giver of life, the bringer of death, the creator of the everlasting, and the master of all. And then there were Four...

What was once forced into darkness will be touched by light, bringing all that's hidden to sight. Once all is exposed, chaos will ensue, and the hunter will become the hunted. For only one can stop the end. One who knows the secrets of death. One who lived to tell its secrets as well. The one who can awaken The Four.

Those words. Hawah said them to me, that night at the bookstore. It sounded like gibberish then, but she was talking about the creation myth.

The next page slowly reveals four figures dressed in robes. The images become clearer. The figures each wear a silver ring with a stone of a different color, their robes matching their rings. One green, one yellow, one red, and the other blue.

The creation story, my confusing dream about the four cloaked figures with the four babies, what happened on Schoolhouse Road—it all makes sense. The four figures were The Old Ones, each a representation of an element. They were the beginning of everything, our ancestors.

As I continue to turn the pages of the mysterious book, I find they are surprisingly full of information I am now eager to read. Eager to discover what was lost to an entire race. The djinn were left to believe that this story of The Old Ones was nothing more than a cautionary tale about the evil ways of man, but this is real, and if King Solomon did indeed learn the secrets of the djinn and kept records of their secrets, we are in big trouble.

My heart races as I view a depiction of a familiar scene. The figure, wearing the blood red cloak, takes on the symbols that once rested on the skin of the other cloaked figures. It's just like my dream. I turn another page and I'm greeted by a sight that triggers an immediate gag reflex. I push the book away from me as if it's on fire. My hands tremble as I cover my mouth in absolute shock. Slowly, I crawl back to the book as if my approach will change what had been there only moments before, but there is no such luck. There, on the page, is a depiction of the blue-cloaked figure, whose hood is now removed, exposing long silver hair. He stands beside the figure in the red cloak, whose hair is as dark as night. The odd part of it all is that this looks like a wedding ceremony. The woman is wearing a white dress beneath the blood red cloak, while the silver figure holds the hand of the woman as if presenting his bride to the world. But the worst of it all is that they have faces. It's me and Niko getting married, while the two other cloaked figures stand behind us. Sebastian, wearing the green cloak, Amina, wearing the yellow. It seems like they're *together* as well.

I turn the page roughly, hoping there is some other explanation on the pages that follow, but the moment I turn the page, it goes blank once again, erasing all of the information.

Tears sting my eyes, my heart aches wickedly, and I begin to sob. How can this be? It should be Sebastian, not Niko. If I were meant to be with Niko, I would have been dreaming of him all this time—not Sebastian.

How could the universe play such an evil prank, especially on Amina and Sebastian, who have spent their entire lives as siblings, not lovers? But this isn't just the universe. I blame Sedia for starting this, making us all vulnerable when we could have spent our lives knowing the truth, preparing for what's to come.

I have to confront her. I tiptoe downstairs in an effort to sneak out and realize I have walked in on a conversation I wasn't meant to hear. It's obvious nobody has any idea I'm home, so I get closer, praying they won't realize I'm listening—spying.

Gigi and her "family" are all seated around the dining room table. Additional chairs are brought in for the new members of the clan. I can't see everyone, but there are at least ten people there.

"It's vital that she joins us as soon as possible."

Niko squirms in his seat, fighting the urge to interrupt Gigi as she speaks, but it's beyond obvious he can no longer sit silently, despite the looks from Tempest and Rowan urging him to do so. "What do you expect me to do, cuff her and force her to join our cause?" he says. "You of all people should know it won't work. Besides, Bijou knows just about everything already. She just needs time."

Gigi locks eyes with him, on the verge of losing her cool, but something stops her from doing so. Maybe it's the defiance in his eyes that causes it, or maybe it's the guilt—I believe—she feels from not being there for him. Whatever the reason, Niko seems to take pleasure in being her weakness. "Okay, Nikolai darling, how do you propose we handle the situation?"

Momentarily, the entire room is still as Niko stands, looking at his mother, ignoring all others. "Well, as you can see, Lilith—"

I could say that Gigi ran across the room to Niko, but that would imply I actually saw her feet touch the ground. It was more like she flew, her movements as swift and aggressive as her tone. Her eyes grow black with anger. "You will show me at least a modicum of respect. I can't force you to address me as your mother, but you will not—I repeat, will not—call me by my first name."

Niko only laughs. "Whatever you say, Mother." The natural blackness of his eyes is still darker than the temporary darkness that is slowly vacating Lilith's eyes, giving way to their unnatural, icy blue.

"We need to give her an ultimatum. The Knights are planning something. There's no time to coddle the little brat," Salif says, probably still bitter from me putting him in his place.

"No, she's not ready yet." Gigi almost sounds as if she is about to cry, but she turns her back to them all. I can feel her heart breaking. She cries inwardly, her pride restricting the tears.

The tall woman I remember from the bookstore comes into view and speaks to Gigi with disgust in her voice. "When will she be ready? The solstice is tomorrow, and the prophecy said she will come into her full power. Lilith, you have hindered that child. The purpose of you taking her was to either prepare her or to kill her, yet you have done nothing but spoil her rotten. The point of your masquerade ball was to call all of our enemies out of hiding, but she's weak and powerless." She takes a sip from her wine glass and shakes her head at Gigi. "You have gotten soft. You aren't the queen I once served. Sedia would laugh if she could see you now."

In a manner similar to the one in which she came to Niko, Lilith flies over to the dark beauty, lunging for her throat. She growls, baring her teeth, and stretches fingers like claws, making her look feline. "Ramatu, I will kill you. If I had my full powers, you wouldn't dare speak to me in such a manner. Shouldn't you be more concerned about where your crazy daughter is? How long has it been since you've seen her?"

"You shouldn't be worried about where Mariam is. She's with Alieu, you know, her father. Therefore, she's safe."

My father's here? In Sykesville?

Ramatu seems to be rubbing in the fact that she is the mother of Alieu's child, something Lilith wasn't capable of. "But you *should* be worried about the fact that we would have all gotten our full powers back if you had killed that little twerp long ago. That child is nothing but a threat to us all."

"That child has a name. She's Bijou. My Bijou, and you will not lay a finger on her." Gigi is now collaring the cocky woman who wears a smirk to disguise the fear that's rapidly rising within.

Even though I can practically feel Ramatu's fear, she seems to be growing more and more defiant as Gigi's anger grows. She laughs darkly, almost forcing me to flee the safety of my hiding place.

"Oh and by the way, did you ever figure out who the bleached blonde girl was, the one with the hooded man, who attacked you? I mean, what teenager takes on the great and powerful Lilith and lives to tell the tale?"

The description fits only one person I can think of. Mandy. Gigi never revealed anything about the incident. She hasn't bothered coming up with an excuse because she thinks I don't remember anything about that day.

"Okay, enough of this." Tempest separates the two women before there's any bloodshed. "Let's put it to a vote, since we are incapable of agreeing. The fate of Bijou will now be decided. All in favor of eliminating Lilith's precious jewel before she becomes even more of a threat, raise your hand."

Lilith steps back, instinctively walking toward her son who—for someone who claims to be at odds with his mother—looks like he wants to attack Ramatu in Lilith's defense.

Ramatu straightens her black satin blouse, a devious smile tugging at the corners of her full lips. The air in the room is thick with angst and animosity. The first raised hand belongs to Ramatu, which is no surprise. The next hand is Rowan's, then too many raised hands to count. Gigi and Niko are the only ones whose hands remain down. Their anger is so potent, I tremble in fear.

"I won't allow it." Niko's voice commands the attention of the entire room. His regal bearing, normally aloof and cold, wavered when he revealed his passionate determination, and it seemed to frighten some of his elders. "Things may not be as they were in our world, but I am still your prince. Ramatu, you were no one in our world, and you are nothing in this world. Your only claim to fame is that you bore Alieu's first child. So what right do you have to decide what happens? Bijou is the only hope we have of surviving, so she lives!" The room becomes noticeably warmer as Niko's anger grows into a ferocious rage. His face contorts into a malicious snarl that's wondrously strange and frightening all at once. He doesn't mention anything about the Chosen being Fire reborn, and I am grateful for that. He looks like he is about to burst into flames, but how is that possible when he is Water reborn?

I can feel the fear from everyone in the room. This outburst even catches Gigi by surprise, although I wouldn't necessarily consider her emotional state as fearful. It feels more like pride.

"The great Silver Prince has spoken, so it is the gospel," Ramatu laughs. I remember what I felt from her on our first encounter. She isn't the same as the others. She's a changeling. "But once you hear what I've learned, I think you might want to change your vote."

Whispered speculation fills the room as Ramatu saunters off into the kitchen. Moments later, she returns, dragging a badly beaten Hawah behind her. I clamp both hands over my mouth to stop myself from screaming. Somehow Hawah's pleading emerald eyes find mine, and she mouths the words, "I'm sorry."

My heart plummets down to the pit of my stomach. I don't want to believe what is about to happen.

Gigi almost jumps out of her skin at the appearance of Hawah. "How dare you do this to my sister. I will kill you!" She's about to attack the dreadful woman when two hideous, Neanderthal-like goons prevent her from doing so. I can feel the vehemence in Gigi as she swears—using words I could have never imagined coming from her mouth.

"Don't act high and mighty, Lilith. In this world, we are all the same. You're no queen, and Hawah sure as hell isn't royalty. Just like Tempest left our world with Sano as a trinket, I decided to seize one of my own. She's very obedient. It's hard to believe the same blood runs through your veins. Brings back memories, huh, Lilith? This doesn't even come close to how you treated Sedia. You should be relieved."

"And this is supposed to change my mind? You're not going to blackmail me into changing my decision." Gigi speaks through clenched teeth as she shakes herself free from the grasps of Ramatu's goons.

"You should know that I think much bigger than blackmail. A little birdie told me that my little trinket has been keeping secrets from me. Secrets from us all." Ramatu grabs Hawah by the throat, forcing her to stand. Hawah's face is bloody, her mouth swollen, her clothes torn. Ramatu doesn't bother concealing her joy. I want to attack her. But before I can make what might've been the biggest mistake of my life, a hot hand restrains me, keeping me in the safety of my hiding place. I don't need to turn to know it's Sebastian. The fear and hatred that was building inside of me dissolves, filling me with a feeling of safety.

"Go on, Hawah. Tell your big sister what you told me," Ramatu orders.

Tears stream down Gigi's face as Hawah gives her a play by play of the events that led to my birth. Shock is one emotion I feel from everyone in the room, but the emotions coursing through Gigi, Niko, and Sebastian silence all others. The color drains from Niko's face, his heart rate accelerating, unsure if he wants to hold his mother or kill someone—anyone. Gigi drops to the floor, unable to shed another tear. She wants to rejoice that her son is alive, but I can also feel murderous impulses seeping through her skin.

When it comes to Sebastian, I can't quite tell what he's feeling. He's completely devoid of emotion, and for the first time ever, his skin feels cold. When Hawah stops speaking, the entire room becomes quiet and still. No one speaks. Ramatu is pleased with herself, and it's obvious where everyone else now stands on the subject of my fate.

"So, you chose to help Sedia over your own flesh and blood. You made me believe my son was dead while Sedia stole him to raise him as her own." Gigi's voice trembles, but there's nothing weak about it. I can feel her growing stronger. Rage pulls her up from the floor to walk toward her sister. She smiles an evil smile that contorts her appearance, giving her a look that fits the description of the Lilith from the stories I've heard. I can feel the coldness of her heart as she lifts her slender hand and controls Hawah like a puppet without ever physically touching her. "Something tells me that there's more to this story, so finish it. Where is this book now?"

"The book was given to Moh. I never had it in my possession, and I'm sure if he had it, Alieu must have found it by now," Hawah lies. I'm sure Niko knows the truth. He saw the book the night the moving symbols attacked us, but he says nothing.

Gigi twists her fingers ever so slightly, making Hawah yelp desperately. Sebastian holds me tightly as I hunch over, feeling Hawah's pain. It's like Gigi has reached into my insides, twisting my intestines into knots.

The djinn begin speaking amongst themselves, all wondering where Gigi's jolt of power has suddenly come from after remaining dormant for over sixteen years.

"Silence!" she commands with a force that puts fear into everyone. Even Ramatu fears her at this moment, sitting down, acknowledging that Gigi is now in control of the situation. "So then, her fate is sealed. Tomorrow night shall be the child's last."

The child?

I almost scream, but Sebastian's hand is solidly placed over my mouth. He picks me up, and in an inhumanly swift movement, we are standing just outside the front door. Sebastian whispers, "You will pretend as though you just arrived. You are tired, not hungry, and, most importantly, you are unaware of anything that just happened." Before I can argue or protest, he opens the door so he can slip out and so that I can pretend I'm just coming in.

I take a deep breath that isn't sturdy at all and shut the door, praying I can pull this off.

"I'm home!" I call as I casually make my way to the dining room. I have to clench my hands into fists to stop them from shaking, but it's no use, so I pull out my cards and the shuffling begins for the first time in weeks. It's the only way I can distract myself. "Hey, Gigi! So, I take it these are the rest of the clan, huh?" Ramatu, Hawah, and Niko are nowhere in sight.

She studies me for a moment as I study her. She is full of hatred, but she smiles all the same. "Yes, this is everyone. How were exams?" She doesn't bother introducing anyone which is fine with me. She looks at me, trying to figure out if I heard any of their conversation.

"They were fine, but I have a headache from all the cramming." I try keeping it as short as possible, afraid that if I talk too much she will see right through my charade.

"I thought you grew out of those wretched cards. What happened?" Skepticism is written all over her face, and the more she studies me, the faster I shuffle. Our spectators get lost in the swift movements of my hands.

I shrug. "If you need me, I'll be in my room."

I'm happy to have seemingly passed the test, but it hits me that the end is near. My party will basically be a celebration of my death. Somewhere—tucked away in the depths of my soul—I have always believed Gigi's love for me would shield me from the horrible things that were destined to happen to me, but the information that was revealed to her today has dashed that hope, along with the love she once had for me.

And what about Sebastian? The pain he must have felt, hearing that his entire life has been a lie and that Niko is his twin rather than Amina.

All of this is happening because of me.

My tears prohibit me from seeing clearly as I make my way upstairs. I can't help but grit my teeth in frustration, haunted by Gigi's face as she heard Hawah's secrets. Once I make it to the top of the stairs, I dive into my room, shutting the door on their ghostly whispers.

Upon my entrance, I find Sebastian sitting on my bed, his face buried in his hands. I know he is crying.

"Sebastian?" I whisper as I lock the door.

"Don't bother saying it. I'm not going home." His voice falters, but it's hard to tell if it's from anger or sadness. "I can't face them. I wasn't even sure I could face you."

I sit beside him, expecting rejection as I reach for his hand, but he doesn't stop me from touching him, torn between his anger and his need to be comforted.

"I'm so sorry, Sebastian. When Moh told me that Gigi is your mother..."

He sinks to the ground, still avoiding my eyes. I slide off the bed beside him, wanting to console him, but he pulls away. "You claim that you love me, yet you kept this from me?" His voice is hardly recognizable. "I would never keep something so big from you. Never!"

I feel the tension and pain in him begin to swell.

"So tell me, Bijou, what else are you hiding? Huh?"

I jump up, caught off guard by the animosity he has toward me. Before I can even blink, he is standing, walking toward me. I slowly back away from him. He looks at me with eyes much darker than usual. His eyes glaze over like he has no soul, like he isn't a person anymore. I don't even recognize his voice as he speaks to me. He's looking at my face but not my eyes.

The stress of the day and the news of my impending death pushes me beyond my ability to control myself and I lose it.

"You wanna talk about secrets? Let's talk about secrets. I only kept a secret from you for a few weeks, while you've been lying to me from the moment we met. You knew who I was the second you saw me but didn't see fit to tell me for months." I am the one in control now as I walk toward him, backing him into a wall. "You've played with my feelings, made me cry, and as of late, Amina and I don't even trust you. Who knows? You might even have something to do with the disappearances."

"I would never-"

"Maybe not before, but I'm not so sure of that anymore."

"I'm warning you, Bijou!"

"See what I mean? You never used to call me Bijou. In fact, you refused to. It was always Jewels. Why the sudden change, Sebastian?"

"Maybe because I have a girlfriend now, and flirting with you would be inappropriate!"

"Oh, let's talk about your girlfriend. She completely controls you! We saw you guys in Mr. Jennings' classroom. They did something to you, didn't they?"

"That's enough," he growls through clenched teeth, his face contorting as he squeezes his eyes shut in apparent pain.

"No, it's not enough! You're supposed to be my protector, Sebastian, and yet you've done nothing but hurt me." I am crying now, losing what control I had over the situation. Sebastian's eyes reopen, and I see something in them that I hadn't seen earlier, but what is it? "You're not you anymore. You're not the boy that I've been dreaming of my entire life. You're a pod person. The boy formerly known as Sebastian. What has she done to you?"

"No one understands what I'm going through."

"I'm sorry, Sebastian, but I do understand," I murmur.

"How can you understand? To find out everything you've been told about yourself is a lie..."

"You're right! How can I understand, when I've just learned that I'm only one-fourth human? I wouldn't understand, having been raised by the woman who stole me from my mother. No, Sebastian, I wouldn't understand at all." The sarcasm in my voice makes him cringe.

He looks down and shakes his head. "I'm sorry. I guess you're the only other person who can relate to what I'm feeling. But why does my reality have to be so ugly?" He finally looks at me, his eyes still smouldering with an unearthly red glow, but his beauty is not lost. "The difference between my reality and yours is that the one person I have spent an entire lifetime hating is the person who gave me life."

"Amina understands, too," I say. "She's going through the same pain."

His eyes look hurt. "She knows, too?"

I nod. I'm unable to translate my thoughts into actual words. Instead, I pull Sebastian into a warm embrace. A plethora of emotions explode inside him, and he loses control. As we hug, Sebastian gently kisses my forehead, sniffing my hair. "I knew this smell before I ever met you."

I stare at him, surprised. Sebastian was actually being open without being forced. "You did?"

He only nods, still brooding with anger.

"Bijou, there's so much I need to say, but I can't. It's impossible."

He turns, facing the window. I follow.

"Don't get me wrong, Sebastian. I love the company and all, but why are you here?"

I wait, hoping for him to say the impossible.

He takes a few steps toward me. "I don't know if this is going to work, but I want to try to show you the things I cannot say." His voice is soft and gentle as he speaks.

My heart rate speeds up as he stares down at me. "You know we have to touch in order for this to work," he whispers, pushing a stray strand of hair behind my ear.

For some strange reason, I am unable to speak and unable to take my eyes off him. It's almost like seeing him for the first time, without all the mixed, adolescent emotions. I place my right hand over his heart, expecting him to follow suit. Instead, Sebastian gently touches my face, cupping my chin in his hand until we are staring directly into each other's eyes. Before I can utter a word, he leans in, pressing his lips against mine.

He kisses me desperately, like this is goodbye. I breathe him in, not wanting to forget this moment, but before I can get too comfortable, I am sucked into a vortex of madness. Fragmented images and scenes swirl through my mind's eye. I see an image of

Sebastian amidst the crowd that usually surrounds him at school. He has his usual nonchalant air to him, only now I can differentiate his feelings from those around him. I can feel his loneliness and his yearning for something that's out of reach.

Then the image changes. I see myself in the administrative office on the first day of school and I can feel it. Sebastian loves me. And then it all changes. I hear a voice I have grown to hate—Amanda DeVoe. It's the scene in the classroom, but I didn't see this part before. Mr. Jennings is yelling at Mandy to develop a relationship with me and to forget about the nonsense the Knights of Solomon told her about the rings because they can't be trusted. Mr. Jennings leaves the room and the hooded man appears out of nowhere, telling her they can give the ring back to Dr. Menelik in exchange for a weapon to kill the Chosen. Sebastian is stiff and unable to move, and then the part Amina and I witnessed takes place. Mandy's voice becomes weird. I remember that part happening. Like someone else's voice was coming out of her mouth.

I have heard that voice before, in another time and place.

She calls to him, but it isn't his name. It's something else—a strange name, not Sebastian. That's when he drops to his knees. I open my eyes, realizing that Sebastian's lips are no longer pressed against mine. My eyes fill with tears when they find Sebastian once more.

"Did it work?" he asks apprehensively, staring down at me.

I can't quite find the words to express what I'm feeling, although what I saw was crystal clear. We were right about Mandy and Mr. Jennings, but who are they and why the vendetta? And who is the hooded man?

"At least you saw what I can't say. I hope it helps." His eyes focus on mine, filled with sorrow and relief. "Like I said before, I can't go home, so can I stay 'til morning?"

"Of course you can stay."

Although it was never said, it's obvious we both feel that this night together is a goodbye. After my shower, we don't talk much. Talking will only instill images and scenarios of the *ugly* into our minds, when our time together is so limited. He introduces me to his favorite TV series, *Doctor Who*, but only the Tenth Doctor because David Tennant was his favorite.

I lie in Sebastian's arms, afraid of falling asleep. Afraid of missing a moment of being with him. I take in everything, from the unnatural heat of his skin, to the scent of sandalwood that always seems to follow him.

I put my head on his chest to hear his heartbeat, smiling at the fact that it pulsates to the same rhythm as mine. But what will happen if mine stops? Would his go on uninterrupted, or would it at least skip a beat? And at that thought, I begin to cry silently.

It takes him no time to fall asleep. My body is tired, but my mind won't let me sleep. So much has happened that my mind can't settle on one thing.

One name comes to mind, blocking out tonight's events. Menelik. Menelik was the son of King Solomon and the Queen of Sheba.

No. He can't be the doctor Priya mentioned. I attempt to get up to get the book, but Sebastian holds me, stopping me.

"Go to sleep, Jewels. You have a long day ahead of you," he instructs as he plays with my hair.

I listen, hoping I'm simply making a mountain out of a molehill. I have more than enough to worry about.

I close my eyes, knowing that for one night, Sebastian is mine and mine only.

CHAPTER 20—THE GIFT

I wake up in a cold sweat. My head throbs and I tremble in fear. It's obviously a reaction to a dream, but I can't remember anything. I can feel something terrible coming, but no remnants of the dream remain to give me insight. Just as I begin to fret over my lost dream, Sebastian's arm pulls me closer to him, securing me in his safe, warm embrace. I look up to face him, this most exquisitely beautiful creature, and I easily fall asleep once more.

When I wake again, it's that time of morning when the sun hasn't risen yet, but it isn't quite dark anymore. I expect to be greeted by Sebastian's sun-kissed face. Instead I'm greeted by an empty bed. Sebastian is gone. There's a sinking feeling in my gut that makes me want to stay in bed all day, but that would be impossible.

"I was wondering when you'd wake up."

Startled by Gigi's voice, I quickly sit up, gritting my teeth together in hopes of stopping the hysteria from seeping out.

Calm down. If I panic, she'll suspect something.

"How long have you been here?" I ask, sitting up to find her seated in my rocking chair.

"About an hour. I figured you'd beat me to it—you know, being our tradition and all."

I clear my eyes of that disgusting morning crud to find myself surrounded by presents. They're everywhere, wrapped with expensive papers—no two exactly the same—and beautiful silk bows.

"What's all this? It's usually just one present when I wake up and others throughout the day."

"This is a special birthday for a very special girl. I just want you to know that you are truly loved, and nothing can ever change that. Happy birthday, *chérie!*" Her smile is genuine as she gets up to hug me. Seeing Gigi in such a manner almost makes me doubt the reality of what I witnessed yesterday. She's being loving.

I close my eyes, trying to tune into her emotions—a task that should have been extremely easy since we are touching—but I feel absolutely nothing. Not even a whisper of the emotions from the others that had invaded our house.

"Thank you, Gigi! It's too much, though. You're already doing enough, with the party and all." My enthusiasm is forced, since I'm still trying to read her, and I don't have to be an empath to notice the uncertainty on her face as she backs away. When she does, I realize she is draped in black from head to toe—no accessories, no makeup, with her hair pulled back in the familiar bun that has been missing as of late. "You're different somehow."

She doesn't even flinch at my analysis as she returns to the chair. "Why wouldn't I be different when I am as much of a stranger to you as you are to me?"

My heart drops, making it extremely hard to move. Was she choosing now to confront me with everything?

"What are you talking about, Gigi?" I try keeping my voice as even as possible as I struggle to my feet.

She studies me for a while, watching my every movement. "Well, aren't you going to open your presents?"

I force a smile and begin tearing through the gifts. It's a great distraction from all the scrutiny. There are expensive clothes, shoes, and jewelry. Even expensive luggage.

"They're all great, but Gigi, why so many gifts?"

"Things have been kind of strained between us lately, and I wanted to do something special for you." As she speaks, she squeezes her eyes shut as if they sting terribly.

"What are you talking about? What is so special about this particular birthday?" If she's going to kill me, I want her to face me for once in her life and tell me the truth.

"The number 17 is of great importance. It's known to symbolize the Star of the Magi. The 17th Tarot Card is the Star, which is a symbol of hope. Nicholas Flamel completed his 'Great Work' on Alchemy on January 17th. In all religions, including the religion of Magic, the number 17 is sacred. In the *Bible*, The Ten Commandments were given in 17 verses. Jewish law counts 17 blessings. In Muslim folklore, the number 17 appears especially in legends about the djinn and King Solomon."

Everything stops. Breathing. Sound. It all just stops.

Gigi is looking directly into my eyes and for the first time in 17 years, I am *seeing* Lilith.

Her face remains calm, but her eyes widen as she leans in to hug me.

"Bijou, you listen to me without saying a word." She starts her warning out in French. "You have to leave today," she ends in Italian. "I know you aren't as clueless as you would like me to think, and believe me, Bijou, I am fully aware of what you know." Her eyes are fierce, but she's hurting. "Niko told me what you know."

Incapacitated by fear, I struggle to form words, so I only nod. My Otherworldly senses are out of whack at the moment. I don't know why this keeps happening, but my intuition tells me this conversation is far from over.

Gigi holds my hands, still looking me in my eyes. "I know Niko has filled you in, but we now know that more djinni are working with the Knights of Solomon, so you have more enemies than you know."

"Do you know who the man in the hood is?" I don't even realize the words came out in Hindi until after they're spoken. Maybe my spirit is following Gigi's lead of using alternating languages to throw off possible eavesdroppers.

"Puck."

There are heaps of question I want to ask, but Gigi keeps looking at the door, her watch, and the window as if at any moment, someone or something will come through, guns blazing.

"Yes. That Puck. We don't have time to go through many specifics, but I can tell you this: the Knights have been watching you for some time. We've been running for 17 years, but we didn't exactly know the group we were running from were dangerous humans who know more about the djinn than the djinn themselves. Sometimes you'd give us away by unintentionally telling someone a dream you've had, and, next thing, that dream would come true."

As she switches from Yiddish to Arabic, she reminds me of the time I predicted the woman's pregnancy. "What you didn't know is that the woman had been told that she had endometriosis so severely that her tubes were completely blocked and she would never conceive naturally. When you hugged her, it changed something in her body and she felt it. So when she found out she was pregnant, she started telling anyone who would listen about her little guardian angel. One day a man came to our neighborhood, asking questions about little girls who lived in the area. That was the first time I saw one of the Knights of Solomon."

Things are beginning to make sense and I feel more conflicted than ever. She's still paranoid and begins to pack my new things in my new luggage as she speaks, switching to Mandarin. There is a slight tremble in her voice, but it never breaks.

"Niko has spent years trying to prove their existence, but not many djinn believed him. Honestly, in the beginning, I didn't even believe him until I saw a man, claiming to be a reporter, asking questions that only someone who knows about us would ask. That's when I started writing stories that mirror the creation story, changing my writing style in each book so it would point to other authors. I had no idea that Safe

Harbor is owned by the Knights of Solomon. That's why they sent us here."

I don't know why I'm crying, but the tears won't stop flowing. The black Sedan I met in the driveway the first time Gigi slapped me comes to mind.

"But Gigi, why would you keep the name 'Lilith' when so many people—so many djinn—know that name. Wasn't that a dead give away?"

"Names hold much power for djinn. The name has to be spoken regularly. Otherwise, anyone with human blood has the power to enslave the djinn if they discover their true name and say it three times. The enslaved djinn can't tell anyone what's happened, so they're basically trapped."

A wave of realization washes over me. *Sebastian.*

"If Sedia hadn't taken your son—" I hesitate briefly. "What would you have named him?"

Her jaw clenches and she tenses momentarily. "It doesn't work like that. Seers have the power to communicate with newborns, but if the seer doesn't do this in the first few hours of the baby's birth, the child will forever be at risk until the name is well known. The child will know the name when they hear it, but they will never be capable of saying it."

"I started this by enslaving Sedia," she says, closing her eyes as though she's in great pain, but she shakes it off and starts again. "There's another djinn whose true name has never been spoken before."

She stands, motioning me to get out of bed as she returns to the suitcases, rolling them toward the door.

"Who?"

"Puck," she growls, slightly baring her teeth in the way a wolf does in preparation for an attack. "He's cunning and devious, but he was abandoned in the woods after he was born, so there was no seer around after his birth. Alieu is the one who found him, lying to everyone about his true name being Robin Goodfellow, so Alieu knows about the power of names. And Mariam knows this all too well."

"What does my sister have to do with this?"

"Well, your sister is more like Puck's sister. Puck wasn't just Alieu's henchman. He was his first and only son. So wherever you find those two, I guarantee you, Alieu won't be far.

"Jou Jou, they all knew you could have been the Chosen when I registered you for school because that's when they confirmed your birthday and you found your djinn. Someone close to your djinn must know who you are. That is the only way they could know for certain that you're the one. It wasn't until Puck attacked me that I realized there are djinn working with them." She walks over to me. "Is there anyone in that family that doesn't fit? Someone who's a little too quiet?"

I shrug. It can't be Sebastian or Amina. It definitely can't be Moh. Sedia would never do something so heinous, especially since she sacrificed so much to keep all of this hidden. Aiden. Is he truly Amina's father or had he stolen her, like Sedia stole Sebastian, and Gigi stole me?

She hands me a pair of black joggers, a white T-shirt, and underwear. Everything is brand new. "None of them have seen any of the new clothes and things I have bought you. I have packed them in your new luggage and now, I want you to run, Bijou. You run like hell as far away from here as you can, and never look back. Change your hair and change your look, and don't ever look back. You hear me?"

"And go where Gigi?" Tears start to flow and I begin hyperventilating. I forget about speaking in code. My brain hurts from jumping from language to language, so I settle for English. "Why aren't you coming with me this time?"

If she's trying to save me, why isn't she coming with me?

"I cannot know where you are going. It's for your own good." As she speaks, tears begin streaming from her eyes. "Niko has organized a new identity for you, new passports, and you and the surviving girls will leave tonight. If you do not leave, I cannot be held accountable for my own actions." Her voice falters as the perfect Arabic leaves her lips.

My first instinct is to back away from her, but my legs are heavy. I can't move. She embraces me tightly as I remain rigid. The hug feels like goodbye, though she never says so.

She lets me go, making her way to the door. "By the way, leave the Mini behind. There's a 2017 black Rubicon with tinted windows parked in the driveway of the house with a For Sale Sign on Ryan Court. It's yours." She puts the keys in the palm of my hand, along with a piece of paper with an address. "Don't take any of your old things. Leave it all behind. Be sure to check the lining of your luggage, and meet Niko at that address. They're waiting for you."

I'm crying and shaking all through my minute long shower. I get dressed faster than I've ever been capable of, not bothering to touch my hair or look at a mirror. By the time the sun starts to rise, I'm tiptoeing downstairs as quietly as possible with my luggage and satchel. When I make it to the porch, I take one last look at the house and realize my home has never been a tangible place or location. It has always been with Gigi. My home was Gigi and I will never have that again.

I have spent my entire life questioning Gigi's love for me and spent the last few weeks hating her. And logically, I should hate her for enslaving my grandmother and taking me away from my mother, but she spent that time protecting me from every threat that came my way. So does the end justify the means?

* * *

As I drive to the Sinjin house in my new jeep, everything Gigi told me replays in my mind.

I remember something from the book; the prophecy said I will die, and their powers will be returned to them.

Right now, I have to decide if it's fight or flight. If I leave with the girls, they might live. But what happens to everyone else I leave behind? The djinn, who have waited so long for a protector. The families of the girls, who will be left behind, always wondering what happened to their daughters. Sebastian. He's supposed to be my protector, but he's become an innocent. I'm supposed to protect the innocent because that is the hand that fate dealt me. I cannot run and leave them all behind.

I choose to fight.

Pulling into their driveway, I don't know whether or not to remove my luggage from the jeep. I was never invited to stay with them, so bringing in my suitcases would be a little presumptuous.

Amina is waiting for me on the porch, pacing back and forth. I try feeling for her emotional state, but I get nothing. It isn't just those in my household I can't feel. I can't feel anyone anymore.

Why is this happening to me again?

Amina rushes to the jeep, wearing sweats that are a far cry from her usual music-festival fashion. "Bastian's gone and so is all of his stuff. Have you heard from him?"

Amina looks as though she hasn't slept all night. Her eyes are red and all that's missing beneath her eyes is Bloomingdale's signature, 'Big Brown Bag.'

"He spent the night at my house, Mina. And he knows everything. He heard Hawah telling Gigi about him being her son."

I thought she'd be in tears by now, but Amina's face shows no emotion.

Amina starts taking my luggage out of the car, so I follow suit. The house is surprisingly quiet. I'm not sure what I expected. Maybe for them to be huddled around in a strategy session to find ways to protect me. But no one's awake. I follow her up to her room. Minimalism is the theme. It's stark white with a few blue accents here and there. I'm afraid I'll mess something up by just breathing. I take my shoes off before entering the room to join her in her reading nook.

"Where is everyone?"

"Moh is keeping an eye on Lilith and her brood, while my parents look for Sebastian." There's hesitation in her voice when she says the word 'parents.'

"There's more." She tenses when I say those words. "I know who the hooded man is. It's Puck."

She looks at me with apprehensive eyes, and I'm afraid.

"I woke up this morning and Lilith was in my room. She told me everything."

"Yes, and I know that she's giving you a head start to run away with Niko. And I know she's Sebastian's mother and Niko is his twin brother." She stops briefly. "We should have seen it really. Mr. Jennings is the only one who called it."

My mouth opens, but no words come out. I remember that day in the cafeteria when he pointed out their similarities to us. The same day they took hold of Sebastian.

"How do you know all this?" I ask.

"When I woke up, I saw Lilith. I screamed when I saw her. I thought she had come to kill me, but then I looked around and realized it was your room, so I thought I must be dreaming. Only I wasn't. I was conscious, seeing and hearing things from your point of view."

I become nervous, because if she could see through my eyes, could she read my thoughts too?

"What else did you hear?"

"Bijou, do you really want me to give you a play by play of an entire conversation you were there for?" She rolls her eyes. "Sebastian's true name, blah, blah. Run away because if you stay, I will murder you."

"Point taken."

"I think it's starting again." Her voice trembles, but I'm not sure from what.

"What's starting?"

"Magic. Things are changing. Before you were born, djinn used to have sporadic flashes of their charges when they were in danger. But Bij, this wasn't a flash. I was there. It was like I was you. It's starting."

"If that's the case, then why aren't my powers working? I haven't felt anything since I woke up this morning."

"I'm not sure, but if I can see things through your eyes, it's probably happening for Sebastian too, and if that's the case, there's no point in running anyway, because he'll lead them right to us."

Us? Amina's words catch me off guard.

"Amina, you shouldn't have to be bound to me. I know they say it's your job to protect me, but what kind of protector of the innocent would I be if I put you at risk as well? This is my fight. I have to face whatever comes tonight."

"You're kidding me right?" She looks hurt. "We will face it together because that's what family does. They stick together. Now, how are we gonna help my brother?" She pauses, furrowing her brows. "What's with the face? "

I want to make a joke out of it, but that part of my brain doesn't seem to be functioning today, like everything else. "I think Aiden is the informant."

She gives me a side-eye glance that serves as a warning but says nothing.

"Think about it. Everyone here has a role to play in everything. Sedia was the Oracle. Moh was the Link. You and Sebastian are my Djinn. But Aiden, he's—"

She stands up and for a second, I think she may hit me.

"He's my father, so I'd think carefully about what comes out of your mouth next, if I were you."

"I'm just saying, he seems to be the only one who doesn't fit the equation."

She starts to make her way to the door.

"Love."

"Excuse me?"

"Love is what makes him a part of this equation. He isn't powerless, you know. Before all of this, he was the Griot. The storyteller of the Otherworld. It was his job to document history and he risked it all to protect Sedia and save Sebastian. Years later, Sedia told him his only child was to be the protector of the Chosen, so he gave up his whole life to join Sedia's cause."

"What *is* Sedia's cause?"

"Isn't it obvious?" She finally breaks and shows emotion as tears escape. "To find you. To protect you so that you can fulfill your destiny."

I feel horrible about my accusation, but saying I'm sorry just doesn't seem to be enough. So, I follow her downstairs, into the kitchen, where Amina does what she does best. Food.

For the first time in my life, I eat a meal from my country of origin. Liberia. She makes dry rice, fried tilapia, and fried plantain, sending me into a food coma.

* * *

I doze off in Amina's room. I wake up to the sound of commotion. Amina is arguing with someone downstairs, but before I can get down there, I'm struck by immense pain. The back of my neck feels like it's on fire. I rush into the bathroom to put a wet towel on it, but that does nothing. I head downstairs to find Phoebe and Robin sitting on the step. Eavesdropping.

I had completely forgotten about them because no one seems to talk about them. Ever.

"What are you two doing?" I try to put on a kid-friendly voice, but my attempt is futile as the pain is too much. I make an attempt to touch Phoebe's hand, but she jumps up, running downstairs.

"She's not going anywhere with you, Nickleby," Amina's voice is combative and aggressive. "And how do you know that Mariam is Mandy?"

"It's the only thing that makes sense. Mariam has spent her entire life hating this threat of a sibling her father loved without knowing, while she was right there, in the flesh. Bijou's a sitting duck here. If I can find you guys, how long will it take before the others do as well?" Niko's voice is panicked. "And for the last time, my name is Nikolai."

They're standing in the foyer, toe-to-toe as if they'll come to blows at any minute. Niko's hair is a mess. He looks disheveled, like he hasn't slept for days. My voice is what makes them back away from each other. "If Mariam is Mandy, then Mr. Jennings must be Alieu."

"Bijou, the girls are in the truck. We have to leave now."

"I'm staying!" I want to argue more, but the pain is becoming unbearable. The room begins to spin—or maybe it's all in my head—and my legs feel useless. I drop to my knees. The burning sensation travels from my birthmark down to my stomach, making it feel like I have an untreatable ulcer. By the time it makes its way back up to my esophagus, I know that if I don't somehow let out whatever this is, I will explode.

I am possessed by someone or something. It's as if I'm being used as a vessel, and I'm not in control of what's happening.

"The truth is never forgotten, only misplaced. Reveal to me what has been concealed." Although the words left my mouth, I have no idea where they came from. My voice is strong—unlike my usual whiny tone—anchored by vibrato. I begin to cough violently. There's something stuck in my throat. I can't breathe. Panic surges through my body as the taste of blood spreads throughout my mouth, and I cough up something disgusting that jumps out of my mouth, clearing my airway. I assume it's a blood clot, but something shimmers in the red mass that catches my eye.

I dig into the disgustingness before me, discovering what has been lost. It's Fire's silver ruby ring.

I hold it up and Niko is saying something, but I can't make it out. It's almost as if he and Amina are screaming, but it's muffled.

Before I can put the ring on my finger, I am struck from behind, sending the ring flying across the room. I look up to see Robin and Phoebe, looming over me like two vultures stalking their prey. If I weren't so confused, I'd laugh. I slide backward enough to really look at them and realize they aren't at all what they seem. I close my eyes and reopen them as the image of the two falters, becoming one, but when I reopen them, it looks like I'm being bullied by the Lollipop guild. Niko and Amina are completely still as though time has stopped for them.

I dash for the ring as Robin does the same. Phoebe jumps on my back to slow me down. We reach it at the same time, but my hand touches it first. When Robin's hand touches my hand that holds the ring, something bizarre happens. Amina and Niko begin to regain movement. Phoebe falls off my back, joining her brother, and when they touch, something that doesn't abide by the laws of physics begins to happen, something different and mystical. The two children merge together becoming one physical being. They become a man with a child's face, the legs of a goat, and horns. *A satyr.*

"Puck!" Niko growls.

"The Silver Prince." He laughs as if he's gotten away with the world's greatest con. Well, in a way, he has. "The ring for your girls and your Golden Prince."

"Never!" Niko yells.

"You have until midnight at Patterson Mansion to hand it over or the other two girls die and I let Mariam do as she pleases with the Golden Prince." With that, he jumps out of the window, shattering the glass into a million pieces.

Niko jumps through after him, only to return moments later.

"The truck and the girls are gone."

"I don't get how he's been able to pull this off when there's been no magic," Amina says. "Those kids are the reason we ended up in Maryland. We found them in Australia. They told us about how these men had taken them from their parents, and they had escaped. The only piece of information they had on them was a newspaper from the Sykesville Gazette. We figured this would be a good place to look for their parents, and then we saw an article about the missing girls, so we thought it was fate."

Niko nods. "The Knights of Solomon lured you here."

"They lured us all here," I say.

"Bijou, I don't believe you're ready to face them. You'll die if you do." Niko makes his way over to me, embraces me without hesitation, and simply holds me. It's hard to admit, but I feel safe in his arms.

I finally let go, backing away from him.

"Doesn't what happened here today prove what I'm capable of?" I wait for a response, but no one steps up to the plate. "I coughed up the ring of an Ancient who never actually left it behind. I don't know how or why it happened, but it proves I'm chosen and I don't think all this would be happening if I'm not ready for what's coming. You guys have to stop trying to shelter me." I remember something and run to Amina's room to get it out of my satchel. The yellow and green rings.

I run back downstairs, placing the yellow one on Amina's index finger, and I tell them what the book revealed to me.

We're all quiet for a while. They won't look at each other, or me.

"Okay Fire, what's the plan?" Niko finally speaks.

"I've been running my entire life, and for the first time ever, I know what's happening, and I actually have a purpose. We're going to that party, and we're gonna fight."

CHAPTER 21—CHOSEN

The sun is in hiding. On what should be the longest day of the year, the sun is noticeably absent. Setting the stage for my demise, as the djinn have all come to collect what was lost to them on this same night seventeen years ago. To them, there is no life without magic. They consider themselves dead without it. Tonight, it will all change. Tonight, I will die so that they can live once more.

I find Amina already dressed except for the terry cloth turban she wears on her head.

"Don't get me wrong, Mina. I know you guys get off on being different, but don't you think you're taking it a little too far now?"

"Don't be daft, Bij. I didn't come down in the last shower, you know. My hair will make its debut after I get you ready."

"You sound like him, you know."

There's a brief moment of silence as the thought of Sebastian lingers between us.

"I figure I should pay tribute to his devotion to the language of Oz in his absence. You know, just until he gets back." She becomes quiet for a moment. "I have a surprise for you." She runs out of the room, only to return with a garment bag twice her size. "Happy Birthday, Bij."

She holds it as I unzip the bag to reveal an off-the-shoulder, floor-length gown with a train made entirely of jewels. There isn't one stitch of detectable fabric. She holds a full-face, gold Venetian mask adorned with jewels and feathers that match the dress.

"Jewels for our jewel," she smiles the first real smile I've seen on her in weeks, revealing her dimples. "You like?"

"I love!" I say on the verge of tears, hugging her tightly.

"Sedia and I made it ourselves."

After getting dressed, Amina insists on doing my hair and makeup, so I oblige. She ends up straightening my hair, which takes forever, only to sweep it all up in an intricate updo. Little curly wisps of hair hang freely here and there, covering my birthmark. The makeup takes a lot of getting used to. My idea of wearing makeup is tinted lip gloss, but Amina goes all out. I feel like I'm wearing a mask, which is pointless since I'm going to be covering it all up with an actual mask anyway. I think about mentioning this fact, but I don't feel like hearing her whine about how necessary it is for a girl to wear concealer.

"So, what do you think?" Amina's question interrupts my appraisal of myself.

I turn to find a raven-haired Amina.

"You gotta be kidding me."

"Don't worry. I still believe blonds have more fun, but I look damn good."

I want to say something smart, but I'm still in awe at the bone straight, black hair that makes Amina look like an entirely different person. She's a beautiful vision in red, her hair trailing behind her, brushing against honey-coated skin, exposed by an off-the-shoulder gown.

"You look beautiful, Amina."

"As do you, hon," she says in a failed attempt at sounding like a Carroll County native.

We put on our masks and head out to meet Niko and our fate.

* * *

There's no need for a GPS because the fireworks light the path to Patterson Mansion. It's as though they don't want anyone to miss what is going to happen. Patterson Mansion stands out in contrast to the farmland that surrounds it. It is stately and beautiful, leaving me anxious to see what Gigi has done to the inside.

The ballroom is gorgeous, no question. Fairy lights drape the walls, giving off a soft white glow which radiates onto every person in the hall, causing all eyes to sparkle in amazement. The full room sways with the music, and a calming hum pulses from the stage and gives off a soothing atmosphere. It's nearly impossible to determine who is who because of the intricately designed masks they all wear.

The only moment I had been looking forward to on this night was the grand entrance I would make when I paused at the top of the staircase for everyone to acknowledge my presence. Yes, they all stop and stare as we enter, but no one knows it's us. We make our way through the crowded ballroom and I am grateful to not be able to feel the emotions.

They're expecting a lady in a red dress because Tempest had one made for me, but the one I'm wearing now isn't very inconspicuous either.

"I'll ease your pain and wipe your tears."

The words sound like they were perfectly extracted from another lifetime and have now been strategically placed into my reality. The raspy voice is one I know well.

I say nothing, but turn to find a man with a silver and black mask that covers his entire face, making it impossible to find any distinguishing feature. He holds out a white-gloved hand—an invitation to the dance floor. I'm almost certain it's Niko—rightfully dressed in a silver mask, signifying his place as the silver prince— but I'm afraid to speak for fear of establishing the fact that I am, indeed, the one they all seek.

He is not certain. The music plays loudly, making the absence of a conversation less awkward.

Keeping my guard up as we dance is harder than I expected, as I'm suddenly overpowered by an intense feeling of desire anchored by despair. I stop dancing briefly, examining the masked face, stunned by the fact that my powers are reawakening and the realization that it is Niko and he loves me.

With this realization, I want to escape his iron-clad grasp as I feel I have somehow betrayed Sebastian.

"It is you, Bijou," he whispers into my ear in an unsteady voice.

Is he crying or nervous?

I say nothing in response, knowing my voice would confirm his suspicions, only to realize my silence is incriminating as well.

"Run away with me, Bijou. It's how it's supposed to be. Me and you. Together. I can keep you safe." His tone is pleading. So different from the arrogant Nikolai Phoenix with all the answers. "Pl-please Bijou."

He feels my hesitation, and my body tenses up as he stumbles over his words.

The lights dim and somehow, Niko and I are separated as I get lost in the crowd. I don't see Amina anywhere. Confusion starts to take over as my senses are awakening and the overwhelming presence of djinn becomes apparent to me. The human emotions are potent, but they are nothing more than a hum compared to what's emanating from the djinn.

I almost panic before I see a figure in a familiar red dress.

Amina.

I begin making my way off the dance floor to follow her, only to see yellow curls and the back of the dress heading onto the terrace. I turn and step out to what I think is a terrace and am greeted by a sight I know to be utterly impossible. I am at the entrance of the maze from our backyard.

How did I get here?

I turn to look behind me and the building is still there, but this maze does not belong here. The hedges, the scents, it's exactly as I remember it. I am distracted by whimpering coming from somewhere within the maze. It's Amina's voice. I'm terrified, but I can't let anything happen to her. I run, pushing aside all fears. The only reassurance comes from the brightness of the moon that leads me through the twisted maze.

I know too much this time to get frustrated by the dead ends and the constant twists and turns. The whispers begin from within the dark corners of the maze. This time, they don't bother occasionally peeking through the hedges. This time, they are bold with no reason to hide. They know who I am, and they know why I'm here.

When Amina's crying gets louder, my heart rate accelerates. I can practically hear my blood pumping to my heart. When I get to the center of the maze, I find her lying face down on the ground. Her whimpering silences when she senses I am near.

Every logical fiber of my being screams it's a trap, and that Amina is being used to manipulate me, but I can't let that stop me. At this point in an Anastasia Powers novel, I would be having some sort of weird, out-of-body experience, watching myself walk into death's murderous trap. But even though this story was written by Anastasia Powers (aka Lilith Fitzroy, aka one of the other aliases she has used), there is no out-of-body experience, only a fear that makes me want to pee my pants.

Before I can get to Amina, I notice the body of a man laid face down on the gazebo, grotesquely spread-eagled, with a bloody wire hanger in one hand. A pool of crimson creeps out from under his still, large frame, staining the once white gazebo floor.

Blood. So much blood.

Every time I come here, there's blood on the gazebo.

"I think dad wore the suit much better than Mr. Jennings, don't you think?"

The disturbing voice reminds me that I'm not alone, but the voice I hear is not Amina's. Then it hits me. Amina's hair was dyed black tonight, so the person I saw in Amina's dress is Mandy.

My back faces her, but her emotions are loud enough to make me aware that she's behind me.

"When you say *suit*, you're not talking about a three piece, are you?"

"Very good, little sis. At least I don't have to tell you the exhausting story of the power the Knights have and how we possessed these two poor excuses for humans." She laughs. "Two broken people who've previously tried taking their own lives. Those are the easiest types to corrupt. Always wishing their lives were different. As fate would have it, we were around to make their wishes come true."

"You said *wore*, so if our father isn't in there anymore, where is he?" My stomach tightens, making me weak, but I fight my body's urge to faint. Mr. Jennings is dead, and she feels no remorse at all.

"We are at your birthday celebration, are we not? He's in there looking for his beloved princess." She looks as though she wants to spit on me. "He has this romantic notion that you'll take one look at dear old daddy and forsake all you know, simply to be daddy's little girl, but Puck and I've made a deal with the Knights. If we give them the ring, we can do with you as we see fit."

"So why did he have to kill Mr. Jennings? Couldn't he just leave Mr. Jennings' body without hurting him?" I begin to cry at the sight of my innocent teacher, murdered on the ground.

"Collateral damage." She shrugs with no remorse. "He wouldn't have survived, so I just put him out of his misery after dad was evicted."

I'm somewhat relieved that she's the murderer and not my father.

"Wait, if there's been no magic, how were you able to possess their bodies?"

"Earth's ring. Duh?" She laughs in such a sinister way that I hesitate before turning to see her face. "You're not so special after all. The rings have original magic. Real, unadulterated magic, more powerful than that watered down stuff running through your veins." She looks at me with pure disgust. "I just don't get what it is about you that makes you so special. I mean, besides the fact that you're a thief and just so damn annoying. You stole my dad from me before you were even born, you stole everyone's powers, and you tried to steal Sebastian from me, too."

"I didn't steal anything. I have no control over anyone's feelings."

"Now that's a lie. Word on the street is that you're an empath, baby girl. You can make people feel what you want them to feel, which is the only logical reason for why Sebastian ever loved you." She laughs, trying to exude confidence, but she has her doubts.

"I'm not desperate. I don't need to force anyone to love me. But then again, you wouldn't know anything about that because I can't see how anyone could ever love you." She hates me, and with every word I spit, her hatred grows. "Anyway, where's Amina, and how'd you get her dress?"

"What a loyal friend you are, Bijou." She slowly walks toward me, dusting off the dress she has no business wearing. "I mean, I'm sure you're aware of the fact that you're going to die tonight, and you still chose to come here. So, you're either dumber than I thought or just really noble. Either way, I'm going to kill you, and they're going to watch." She snaps her finger and Sebastian emerges from the shadows, appearing drained and pale, dragging a bound Amina who only has on undergarments due to Mariam hijacking her dress. Puck follows, dragging Aften and Priya.

The three girls tremble with fear which passes on to me. Sebastian is torn, his body acting against his mind and heart.

"Sebastian," I cry, quickly making my way toward them until Mariam stands in my way.

"Not so fast. I'm going to kill you. I'm going to—"

"Really, just stop talking. If you're going to do something, do it, and stop with the foreplay."

"Where would the fun be in that, little sis?" She laughs—a grotesque sound that erupts from her diaphragm.

"God, you're dramatic." And all this time I thought I hated Mandy, when it's really been my own sister I've hated with a passion. "I know who you are, and you definitely know who I am, so why don't you get out of Mandy's body so we can all see just how ugly you really are?"

Immense loathing projects from her toward me.

"Wait, you're jealous of me, aren't you?" I circle her, keeping my distance while projecting an artificial confidence. "This has all been a psycho case of sibling rivalry because I'm the daughter our dad always wanted. The daughter he neglected you for."

"Shut up!" she warns through clenched teeth.

"And then, the guy you're crazy about falls madly in love with me and never even acknowledges your presence." I laugh, shaking my head from side to side as I get close enough to whisper in her ear. "I mean, how desperate are you?"

I try moving after I realize her anger has finally reached its boiling point. But she blocks my path, and before I can blink, she strikes me across my face—hard. I back away, stunned that the physical violence has already begun.

"You were concocted. Our father listened to your half-wit grandmother's prophecy and extracted a formula that would create the so-called Chosen brat. What were you really chosen for—to start a war, to destroy our world, to steal all of our powers? All your existence has caused is destruction and chaos, but that all ends tonight."

She smiles widely as a look of realization comes to her evil face.

This can't be good.

"I won't kill you. I might rough you up a little bit, but I won't kill you, little sis. Sebastian will."

I shake my head violently, unable to say the words my mind wants my lips to speak.

She claps her hands in sinister delight, looking off into the night. "Picture it: the Chosen One, killed by

Alieu's ex-wife's illegitimate child." She's elated. "I swear, I scare myself with my brilliance sometimes. It's almost poetic, don't you think?"

"Yeah, a real soap opera from hell."

"Why are we wasting time? The sooner we kill her, the sooner we get our powers back." Puck is growing anxious. That, combined with the emotions of everyone else, is making me ill. I begin to shake uncontrollably, losing the ability to formulate words. I try thinking of something—anything—to calm me, but nothing works. The pain is devastating, urging me to fall to my knees, and it takes everything within me to remain standing.

As if on cue, thunder from above roars ferociously, and lightning strikes with blinding speed, booming with power. With every pang that surges through my body, another explosion goes off in the sky.

"Sebastian, I wish you would bring my sister to me," Mariam commands.

I back away from a shirtless Sebastian. "So, what now? You're going to do exactly as she says?"

Sebastian's face is pained, and his eyes are tortured, glistening and threatening to expel tears. "If she tells you to kill me, it's a command you have no choice but to follow?"

"I'm so sorry," he says through tears and clenched teeth as he's now so close to me that we are nearly touching.

"I wish you would make it hurt." Mariam is enjoying every moment of this as she becomes animated with an exuberance that dances all around her.

Sebastian's hand trembles as it comes toward me in slow motion. His eyes are wide—reminiscent of a character from a Hayao Miyazaki animated film—but very aware of the brutality he has been instructed to inflict upon me.

With my back against the hedges and Sebastian's brick-like figure blocking my way, there's absolutely no escaping.

"You have two options here: you can kill me right here and now with the knife in my front pocket, or you can remember my name, Bijou!" There's a sense of urgency in his words as he whispers to me.

"But I don't know it, Sebastian."

"Yes, you do. You gave it to Puck at the bonfire. Think hard, Bijou. I've been in every one of your dreams as I have dreamed of you since before you were born. So you have to go back to the beginning and remember."

With closed eyes, I think as far back as my memory goes, but nothing comes. I delve deeper, opening my eyes, connecting with Sebastian's. The harder I stare, the deeper I see. The grayness of his eyes melts away, along with the enemies that surround us. Darkness ensues and I'm taken back to every dream I've ever had. It's like the pages of my dream journal have been made into a montage, only it isn't exactly as I remember. In my dreams, he was never Sebastian Sinjin. He was never faceless. I've always known his face, but something forbade me from remembering it in my waking state. I have always known him to be...

"Arius Seraphim," I say. His name means "the burning immortal." I repeat it so that I've said it the required three times: "Arius Seraphim, Arius Seraphim." Then I lean close and whisper, "I wish to have *my* Sebastian back."

The utterance of the name and my wish breaks the robotic state that Mariam had sentenced him to. The moving symbols that once appeared on my skin, Amina's, and Niko's, now devour Sebastian. A devilish smile creeps across his face. He's back.

"Okay, now I'm in charge again, Jewels."

"When were you ever in charge?"

"Remind me to answer that question when this is all over, but for now, listen. You're going to put on an Academy Award-winning performance as I haul you over to Mandy/Mariam."

"And then what happens when we get there?"

"You use your weapon."

"What weapon?"

"You," he says.

I nod. "I'm gonna stall 'em, and you're going to get Amina and the girls out of here."

"I'm not leaving you with them. I won't do it."

"Just come back for me, and I promise it'll all be okay."

I look at him as if I have everything under control, but it's all a front. I don't have the heart to tell him that I won't make it out of here alive. I guess I'm a great actor after all.

"Ok, Jewels, ACTION!"

He rips the skirted portion of my beautiful dress, leaving only the top portion intact and my underwear exposed.

"Hey, what are you doing?"

He gives no answer, but I feel his internal laughter at my choice of undergarments as he throws me over his shoulder.

I fight, scratch, kick and scream, but Sebastian doesn't even flinch. He pretends to be the mindless drone that Mariam still believes him to be.

He drops me on my butt a couple of paces away from Mariam's feet.

"Just kill her so we can get our powers back. You're wasting too much time." Puck's venomous voice is anxious with the thought of a gruesome slaughter. "If your father gets here, she lives, and all of our sacrifice and hard work will go in vain."

She circles me like a tiger circling its prey. "Stand up!"

"You can't kill me now," I respond, still contemplating what my next move will be as I procrastinate on the ground.

"And why not?" she laughs menacingly.

"If you kill me, all your magic dies with me." Confusion breaks out amongst the murderous brother-sister duo. "And what good is living forever if there is nothing special about you? You will age like humans, only your pain and suffering will have no end."

The two move away from me—far enough so I can't hear what they're saying—and leave behind the weakened girls that Puck had dragged in behind him.

Sebastian doesn't take the opportunity for granted. One by one, I watch him carry away their weakened bodies.

"Okay, Bijou," Mariam returns as I stand there, wondering why I didn't run while I had the chance.

"Tell us how to get our powers back, and we'll let your friends go free."

"What about me?"

"You're supposed to be the brave savior, remember? They always die in the end." She's elated by her own words.

"Okay, I'll do it!"

She's surprised. "Just like that, you'll do it?"

"Just like that," I respond with a shrug.

She looks at me, suspicious, not sure of my motives.

"There's just one thing—you can't be in Mandy's body while I regift you with your powers. It won't work."

She's plagued with skepticism as she probes me with her eyes.

"Being in this *suit* is an insurance policy, so the answer is no!"

As they approach me, a figure quietly emerges from one of the corners of the maze. For a moment, I believe it to be Sebastian, but I quickly reconsider that conclusion when the moonlight hits Niko's silver hair. He smiles, lifting Amina off the ground and disappearing into the maze.

Before I have the opportunity to contemplate my next move, I'm pushed to the ground, and I'm kicked in the face by a size nine Louboutin stiletto, sending me sprawling backward.

I curse under my breath and spit while refusing to look down, confident I will find blood.

I stand back up again and Puck rushes toward me with a speed that makes it seem like he's flying. He grabs my right hand and rakes a small ornamental blade across my wrist. Shocked and unable to move, I weep because the finality and pain of death are becoming tangible.

I expect gash after gash, but he isn't out for the kill. He's after something else. There's a hunger in his eyes. He's desperate, craving for something. It isn't until my blood begins to spill that I realize what he craves. It's too late for me to run.

He grabs my hand, forcing my wrist to his lips and begins to drink my blood. I try to pull away, but he grips my neck and holds on tight. I don't have to look at Mariam to realize how disgusted and confused she is by Puck's actions.

"Hey!" a voice calls from somewhere behind Puck. I try looking to see who it is, but his grasp on my throat does not permit me. His hands stiffen, then he lets me go. I slip out of his grasp and realize it's Niko who is trying to get Puck's attention.

Puck ignores Niko. He looks down at his hands as if looking at them for the first time. As he examines himself, Niko rushes over and helps me up. I have never been so happy to see him before.

"I will take you directly to Sebastian and the others. Just promise me you won't look back. No matter what you hear." Niko's clothes and face are dirty. He helped Sebastian—his brother. He's willing to sacrifice it all—his allegiance to his mother and maybe his own life—for me. "Listen to what Sebastian tells you and don't argue. I love—"

I don't let him finish his sentence. I know what he's going to say. There is a strange urgency to kiss him, and even though this is neither the time nor the place, I lean in, place my hands on his face, and kiss him. As I do, something is being taken from me. This extraction makes me want to pull away from him, but when I try, his kiss intensifies and I feel myself weakening. I'm unable to stop him until I drop my hands. He staggers back a little, as if drunk, but when he raises his head, there's a renewed strength in his eyes. That wolfish smile returns, giving him a sinister yet ethereal beauty, and it's evident that the kiss was a transfer of power. But what is this power, and why do I feel like I should be afraid?

Before I have the time to contemplate anything else, Puck comes forward with the knife that he used on my wrist, but Nikolai dodges the swipe. Puck attempts again, and once again Niko dodges as if he's doing some sort of waltz. But then he turns, cracks his neck as a street fighter would do before a brawl, and raises his hands as if they are weapons. Mariam and Puck both stop moving. There is absolute terror perspiring from both of them, and I have no idea why until I look at Niko's skin. In what seems like a matter of seconds every visible part of his body seems to acquire an unnatural blue coloring as he takes slow but deliberate steps toward Puck.

"It's been seventeen years since I last did this, so give me a moment. I might be rusty." He raises his arm, and a blue flash of light comes hurling from the palm of his hand and into the ground, leaving a smoke-filled hole near where Puck stands. I'm not sure if he's just trying to scare him or if he keeps missing because, like he said, he's rusty. Puck takes off, disappearing into the maze with Niko hot on his trail.

Niko's intentions are good, but I'm now left with an even bigger threat than Puck. I am now alone with my unhinged sister.

My heart pounds so hard that my breaths come in ragged gasps as I attempt to calm myself. I will probably never see Sebastian again. The simple fact that Sebastian is no longer a zombie is the only comfort that puts me at ease as the fear nearly blinds me. Judging from the look in her eyes and her emotional angst, I only have moments to remain unbroken.

As teenagers, not much thought is put into how or when we'll die. Most of us just assume we'll die of old age. I never thought about the circumstances that would lead to my death before moving to Sykesville. All I ever thought about was being normal and fitting in. I certainly never imagined this.

Mariam walks toward me. "You said his name. You broke my hold over him, didn't you?" The look on my face answers her question, so she doesn't wait for my response. "You've stolen from me, and I promise my pain will not go unrequited."

After all that has just happened, she's back to talk of Sebastian. She glares at me, crouches, then charges toward me. I tumble to the ground as she jumps up and I quickly follow. Once again, she lunges at me, but this time she catches my left arm and sends me flying into one of the pillars of the gazebo. I'm winded for a moment but dodge when I see her balancing Puck's knife between her fingers, preparing for another attack. Puck must have dropped it when Niko chased after him.

"Ready to die?"

"Sebastian will save me, and he'll kill you instead," I say. My words only make Mariam charge for me with the knife once more. I try to dodge it as best as I can. I trip over my feet, and my head hits the ground with a sickening bang. Mariam gets on her knees over me and raises the knife.

I kick the knife out of her hand with one foot while kicking her in the chest with the other, knocking her down on her back.

"There, a nice fair fight now." I jump up.

"There's no such thing as a fair fight," she growls, jumping to her feet like someone in a Kung Fu movie. She springs forward. I gasp and leap aside. As if to prove her point, with a jaguar-like speed, she somehow sweeps down for the knife. But before I can dodge her attempt, she stabs me on the right side of my stomach. "Now, what advantages do you have?"

She cut me deep. I break character. I can no longer act like I'm in control. It hurts like hell and I can't keep my true feelings bottled up. So, I do what I feel.

I scream in horror, forcing thunder and lightning to ignite the sky. The pain is indescribable. I have never experienced such pain, not even when Puck cut me. This makes death feel more real. I have no snappy comeback this time. I'm afraid.

The pain is only intensified by the horrific enthusiasm my sister feels from watching me suffer. The stronger my pain becomes, the more thunder and lightning devours the sky.

"And after I kill you, I'll kill off everyone you love, one by one. Sebastian will be the last. I want him to watch everyone he loves die." How can I be related to someone so cruel?

Her words awaken something inside me that numbs the pain, urging me to fight. I feel like I'm on fire. There's fire flowing through my veins. Everything I see is red, and from the look on her face, she can see what's happening to me.

The intensity of the heat suddenly flushes down to my hands, and when I look down, there's fire hovering over each of my fingertips as if each finger has its own built-in lighter. She takes a tentative step back.

The numbness fades as I make my way toward her, my anger fueled by the immense pain. She's staring me dead in the eyes. She is paralyzed. I know that as long as I hold eye contact, she'll stay frozen. When I finally make it to her, I hit her with a force I didn't know I possessed. She flies back, breaking a pillar of the gazebo.

I follow her to where she landed, but the blow had broken the eye contact. She pounces on me, straddling me on the ground.

"I win," she says. Before the knife can reach my face, I grab her wrist. I struggle with her, pushing her face back with my other hand. The heat from my hands burns her, forcing her off me, but something else happens. I feel something strange after touching her face, but there's no time to dwell on it. I grab the knife. I'm still on the ground when Mariam charges for me, and we fall backwards. I feel a warm liquid on my hands. Only then do I notice that the knife is no longer in my possession. It's embedded in her chest, and her blood is on my hands.

She lies on her back, gasping for air. I kneel beside her as I realize she is moments away from death. I can't help but cry. Two people are dying—one completely innocent and the other my own flesh and blood.

She looks into my eyes, frantically attempting to speak, but the blood only makes her choke on the words. The harder I look, the clearer it becomes that I have done something terribly wrong. The person dying is not my sister. It's the real Amanda DeVoe. Somehow, Mariam no longer occupies the body of this girl.

"You have to wake up," I cry. I hold her hand as I watch her slip away, because of me. I'm no savior. I'm a murderer.

"You did it. You killed her." The familiar voice is barely audible. Sebastian's hand is soon touching my shoulder. "Jewels, she had to die. You did the right thing."

"No. You don't understand. That's not Mariam. It's the real Mandy."

A look of realization creeps onto Sebastian's face as he kneels on the other side of the body that has become motionless.

I stand, backing away from the scene in disbelief.

"Jewels, you're bleeding pretty badly. Let's say I take a look, eh?"

"No. I gotta go. I can't be here." My mind seems to stop working. I'm not even sure of what I'm saying.

Sebastian takes his eyes off me, paying an unusual amount of attention to Mandy's body. He puts his left hand down on her chest and pulls the knife out with the other.

"What are you—"

"A bit of shush." He grabs my hand and both our hands nervously hover over Mandy's body, watching. "Bijou, Amina said you gave her a ring and you have one for me."

"What's the point?"

"Now, Jewels!" he shouts at me.

I kneel beside him, pulling the ring out of my cleavage, snapping the thin chain that held it there, and sliding it onto his finger. As I do so, the rain starts to fall. It's as if the sky is in tune with my emotions. The longer our hands connect and hover, the weaker I become until I have to let go. I tremble, standing even though I'm weak and unsteady on my feet, but I have to get up because I can't be here anymore. The moment I turn my back on the horrifically bloody sight, the ground begins to shake and the once darkened stage is illuminated.

Sebastian holds his hands directly above the bloody spot on Mandy's chest.

Although I'm now far away from the scene, I feel what is going through him. I'm somehow linked to it. He lays his hands on the wound. Heat emerges from within him and travels toward Mandy's body. The angry rain stops, and the ground dries. The hedges of the maze begin to dry up as if the area had been suffering from a drought and Sebastian's hands glow with a blue light that devours him. It's just like Niko, only no heat came from him. The harder I look, the more Sebastian himself begins to change. The color of his hair leaves the deep shade of black behind as it transforms into an auburn color, landing on the golden shade he was meant to have.

As I look around, the field that once contained the maze is bare, and the djinn and a handful of humans are spread out across it. There are djinn that look like angels—so pure and beautiful that you feel obligated to bow in their presence. And then there are the others who are so terrifying and gruesome that the only place they could ever mingle freely is at a masquerade ball.

I couldn't run away even if I wanted to. The pain has reached its breaking point, but regardless, no one pays me any attention. All eyes are on the newly anointed Golden Prince.

Soon, the light fades and silence consumes the field. A cough comes from the bloody gazebo.

"She lives. The girl lives!" a voice shouts from the crowd. "The Golden Prince is a healer."

The crowd is going crazy. I turn to walk away, but my attempt is cut short by the echoing pain of the wound my sister inflicted on me. It takes me a second to realize this isn't the pain of the first wound. I've been stabbed again. As I look down, I see the same knife I had stabbed Mandy with now embedded in my original wound.

"I told you before. I win." I look up to see a face I had only seen in Moh's memory, a beautiful face that I once described as the textbook definition of evil. Mariam, in her true form. The delight radiating from her face and soul can't be hidden. The crowd scatters as I drop to the ground. Pain and shock prevent me from screaming.

I feel my chest rise and fall one last time. But I'm not afraid. The emotions of those around me multiplied by my own emotions make it all unbearable. Yet, there is one scream that silences all others—Sebastian's. I look up into his startled face.

He's going to blame himself. I know it. But it isn't his fault.

I would have loved to tell him this, but I only manage to open my mouth before everything spins out of control, and I'm falling.

If I didn't know any better, I would believe it's my soul leaving my body, but it's obvious what's happening. The magic they so greedily fought for is finally leaving my body and they will all get what they want.

It's finished. I am no more.

* * *

I have fallen into the inevitable vastness of nothingness. My mortality is proven. I am unlike the djinn.

I can no longer hear the voices. I love those I left behind, but that's why I have to stop fighting. They can go on to live normal lives, not having to worry about protecting me. They would never have admitted it, but I was a burden to them. They lived to find me, and when they found me, they had to protect me. What sort of life is that?

I'm falling into the abyss and I'm embracing it, but then I hear a voice that sounds so close it's almost as if it's whispering in my ear. It's a voice I have never heard before but I somehow know. It awakens something, touching a part of me I have never been able to reach.

The voice is so beautiful that if it were accompanied by any instrument, the instrument would detract from its beauty.

"*Ce billet doux est toi, mon bijou.*"

"Mommy?" It's my mother's voice. I know it's her. I don't know how to address her. Mom, mommy, mother? It's foreign to me. "Where are you? I don't have to see you. I just want to touch you. I just wanna'..." I can't speak anymore as I get choked up over emotions I have buried deep inside for years.

"I'm here, my jewel. I'm here with you now. I've been with you for a while. I may not be able to talk to you when you need me to, but I'm here and listening."

I don't even have to touch her or see her. I just want to be close enough to know her smell—something to identify her with.

"I only have a little bit of time, as do you," she says quickly. "It's not your time. You are not supposed to die."

"But I'm already dead. Please don't make me go back. It hurts too much." My heart is breaking.

"It is not your time. You have a destiny to fulfill. Your grandmother was right about what she saw in you. Baby, your work will have no end. You have to learn how to use your power. Just imagine, you've had all that magic tucked away inside you and never knew how to use it. No wonder you thought you were going crazy." She laughs, and it's like a child delighted by a simple joke. Even though I can't see her, there is an innocence about her that makes me sad as well. "Can't you hear him calling?"

"Who's calling?"

"You know who. And if you don't go back, who's going to protect the book?"

"I don't care about the book. I don't care about any of it. All I do is cause trouble for everyone I love."

"Bijou, that's not true. You saved them all. You were willing to sacrifice yourself for the sake of all others. You love Sebastian—you would never have endured everything he put you through if you didn't, but then there's Niko." She doesn't elaborate, but I know there could be something there too. As I listen to her speak, I realize she wasn't much of an adult when her life was stolen from her, yet she seems so wise. "And more importantly, because of you, the Four Ancients have been reborn. You have to go back to find out what that means."

"Wait, how do you know all of this if you're dead?"

"Oh, I'm not dead, just stuck."

"What do you mean *stuck*?"

"Bijou, there's no time for questions. If you don't answer his call, you'll never go back, and you'll never hear from me again."

"But—"

"Go! Answer him now!" She shouts. "I love you, my jewel. Remember, I'm always near."

She's gone.

"Jewels, please come back." Sebastian's voice is as clear as if he were right beside me, whispering in my ear.

Quick surges of electricity shock one millimeter of my body after another. Every time the darkness tries to overtake me, the tingling forbids it from happening. And then I remember where I'd experienced the familiar tingling. The first time I touched Sebastian's hand.

A violent shock rips through my entire body, causing my muscles to react. My eyes shoot open so fast and so wide that I think I'll break a vein. There's fire in my lungs as I inhale. The air feels like poison flowing down my throat with each breath.

Sebastian rocks me back and forth in his arms. I can feel his defeat.

"Sebastian." My voice is as raw as my throat.

He stops, unable to respond.

There's a dramatic shift in his mood, an emotion I can't even begin to put into words.

"You're alive." Tears fall from Sebastian's eyes, but he smiles through them.

I look at him, raising my hand to touch his hair. "Now you and Amina really do look like twins."

I try laughing but it hurts, so I settle for a smile. As I run my fingers through his hair, the gold begins to deteriorate, becoming black again. He is the Sebastian I know once more, though I'm sure he will always be the Golden Prince.

"Don't ever leave me again," he says, kissing my hair. "Promise me."

"I promise," I reply, tightening my grip on his hand.

He lifts me in his arms, facing the massive crowd. Soon my senses begin to kick in, and I have another great pang, but this pain is not physical. I look up to find Niko standing only an arm's length away from his brother. He looks so defeated, but even the look on his face can't compare to the hurt and anger he feels inside as he watches me. His eyes pierce mine and he doesn't look away. For the first time ever, I lower my eyes instead. Guilt and sorrow intensify my pain. He sacrificed so much for me as well.

I look around, but I can't seem to spot Mariam or Puck in the crowd which parts as we walk through. Amina and the rest of the Sinjin clan follow, but, strangely, we aren't the center of attention. There's another show on display amidst my "coming back from the dead" ordeal. When I turn to see what has them all enthralled, I see Lilith. Her hair flows vibrantly in the wind, her skin radiant under the night's full moon. She's different. I can feel her power. I can feel her emotional turmoil. Her anger and longing is undeniable. She's hurt. My attention is quickly stolen by the man who faces her, standing yards away. He is tall and regal, yet I can't see his face because it's completely covered by a white mask.

When we're about to enter the mansion, the masked man turns, staring directly at me. He's far away, but he holds his hand out as if reaching out for me, and in that moment I know it's my father.

ABOUT THE AUTHOR

Sang Kromah was born in Philly, raised in Sykesville, became confident as a writer in New York, but is Liberian at heart. She was a storyteller well before she could write, transforming her family's African folklore into evolved stories that her teachers would allow her to tell in class. As a communications specialist, her credits range from *Seventeen Magazine* to *UN Women* and the documentary *Half the Sky*. As a model, she's been featured in *Essence Magazine*, *Jet Magazine*, and more, but her greatest accomplishments are with Project READ, a female-run library initiative she started, and Project GirlSpire, an online global media platform she started where girls and women empower each other through digital storytelling. Sang can be found on Facebook, Twitter, Instagram, or Project GirlSpire.

Special Thanks

Special thanks to my parents for always pushing me to be authentic and the best version of myself. Thank you, Daddy, for introducing me to Femeni when I was two. If it weren't for your story, there would be no *Djinn*. Thank you, Mommy, for making me a reader and teaching me how important it is to always write and always tell MY story. Thank you for listening to my ideas and going over every single word of my story with me. Most of all, I have to thank my parents for giving me my best friend; Moh's the best gift I've ever received. Moh, you are my best friend and there's no me without you. You are my light, my inspiration, and I am grateful for you being there for me creatively, emotionally, and honestly.

A special thanks to Michelle Powers for helping in the early stages of the editorial process. You are awesome, and I truly appreciate you.

A huge thank you to Madeleine Hannah, Brionna Poppitz, and Ryan Swan. Your keen eye, brutal honesty, and editorial skills helped to polish Bijou's world, and I'm eternally grateful for how you slayed the editorial process.

Last, but most certainly not least, I'd like to thank Benjamin and Paige Gorman for seeing potential in this crazy world I created and taking a chance on me and Bijou.

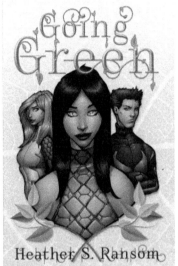

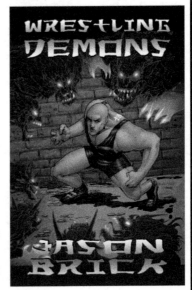

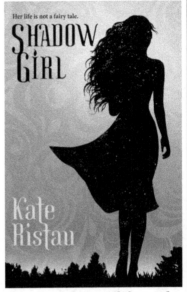

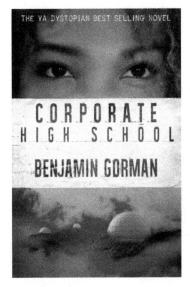

CPSIA information can be obtained
at www.ICGtesting.com
Printed in the USA
LVHW010943080720
660057LV00013B/261